ALL FALL DOWN

Richard Snodgrass

Book Three of the Furnass Towers Trilogy

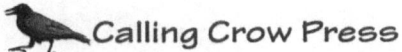Calling Crow Press

Pittsburgh

Also by Richard Snodgrass

Fiction

There's Something in the Back Yard

The Books of Furnass

All That Will Remain

Across the River

Holding On

Book of Days

The Pattern Maker

Furrow and Slice

The Building

Some Rise

All Fall Down

Redding Up

Books of Photographs and Text

An Uncommon Field: The Flight 93
Temporary Memorial

Kitchen Things: An Album of Vintage Utensils
and Farm-Kitchen Recipes

Memoir

The House with Round Windows

Published by Calling Crow Press
Pittsburgh, Pennsylvania

Book design by Book Design Templates, LLC
Cover design by Jack Ritchie

Printed in the United States of America
ISBN 978-0-9997249-8-9
Library of Congress catalog control number: 2018905827

This book is for Jack Ritchie
and, as with everything,
for Marty.

. . . in the late-night office, the figure in a black satin jacket, loose-fitting black satin workout pants and black cloth shoes, looks down at the body of Dickie Sutcliff lying on the floor. Blood oozes from the wound on the side of Dickie's head where he hit the corner of his desk as he fell, a dark stain growing in the carpet. The figure reaches down and feels Dickie's neck for a pulse but knows already he won't find one, gives a small regretful moan. But death doesn't surprise him, shock him. He's seen death before. An old acquaintance. He puts his hands together against his forehead in a blessing, then looks around, takes a handkerchief from his pocket and goes about the office wiping everything he might have touched since he was there. After one last look around, he uses the handkerchief to turn off the desk lamp, the fluorescents overhead, and leaves the office, making his way like a shadow along the corridor to the back door, the way he came in, and down the back stairs, in the soft shoes, the only sound the whisper of the satin cloth moving against itself, to the gravel parking lot behind the building and along the alley, as if he were never there. . . .

PART ONE

"May he rest in peace."

The Reverend Bryce Orr closed his Bible, looked around sympathetically at the group of fifty or so people under the marquee, standing before the casket placed on a temporary pedestal covered with Astroturf, and thought, Okay Lord, now what?

It turned out not to be an issue. Bryce no sooner gave his closing benediction than most of the people turned as a body and made for their cars. Not quite a stampede. But close.

Bryce didn't know what he was supposed to do next. It wasn't his service to conduct, it was the responsibility of the funeral home, and he wasn't sure what was expected of him at this point. It was all spur-of-the-moment, everything thrown together at the last minute. He wasn't even aware that Dickie Sutcliff had died until Julian Lyle called Sunday night asking him to officiate at the service this afternoon. Bryce still didn't understand why the big rush—apparently the incident happened late Friday evening, Dickie had a fall in his office while he was working late, and here they were burying him Monday afternoon. The service at the funeral home in Furnass lasted all of fifteen minutes—no viewing beforehand, no eulogies, no testimonials; the funeral director, J. Howard Griffith, gave a brief statement about Dickie's life, Bryce gave a short blessing, and they were off, out the door, on the way here to the cemetery. He recognized a number of the group assembled under the white canvas canopy but there was no one from his congregation in Drumlins, these were all Highland Hills and Seneca people, or local dignitaries, city and county officials, people who knew Dickie through his firm, Sutcliff Realty, in Furnass. Hardly anyone who would fit under the general classification of Friend of the Deceased. Other than Julian, he didn't see any of the old gang they had grown up with on Orchard Hill. Bryce wanted to do the right thing, but given the protocols of the situation—Did the grieving widow and daughter come forward for a final farewell? Did everyone file past and leave a flower on the casket? Did the pallbearers take off their gloves and leave them as a symbol of letting go? Or did they all just stand there while the casket was wheeled offstage to the actual grave site hidden discreetly from view?—he wasn't sure what the right thing was.

They're certainly not wasting any time getting away from here, are they? Bryce thought. Wonder what they know that I don't.

The open sides of the marquee formed a diorama of views between the support poles, a series of snapshots of the backs of the dark-clothed mourners as they headed down the slope, picking their way among the gravestones, a quiet hustle of bodies, to the line of cars along the gravel drive. Bryce came from behind the portable pulpit, hoping at least to offer his condolences to Tinker, Dickie's widow. But by the time Bryce stepped out from under the canvas, Tinker was halfway down the hill with the others. Even Julian wasn't sticking around, a leader of the pack, at the foot of the slope already getting into his car. Bryce noticed that Julian's friend Kim wasn't with him, strange to see them separated these days, Kim like Julian's shadow since the trial, or maybe it was the other way around. You'd think Kim would be here at least to pay respects to a fellow Furnass merchant, the town's nodding acquaintance with the third world, though I bet the Dickie-Bird owns his building, or did; probably no love lost there. For that matter I didn't see any of the black community here either, sour grapes toward the man who half the Lower End undoubtedly calls landlord, Mr. Sutcliff.

Bryce stood alone in the grass on the hilltop holding his Bible, a figure in a too-short raincoat over the black ministerial suit he wore only for funerals and weddings, his hands chapped with the cold. Behind him the wind ruffled the canvas of the marquee, a sound like beating wings. So what do you think, Lord? he said to himself. I guess they figure they did their duty and now off they go. Be passersby, said Thomas in his gospel, but this is ridiculous. Sorry, Dickie, I hope I didn't let you down.

As Bryce stood there, it occurred to him that he hadn't eaten since the morning, that he was ravenous. For a chocolate bar, of all things, something definitely sweet. He felt immediately guilty. Bordering on the sacrilegious.

It was midafternoon on the early December day, the pewtered sun already lowering close to the hilltops, though a streak of silver, as if someone had wiped a smear of polish across the tarnished sky, silhouetted the black trees. A crow dropped from a stand of distant maples, winged low over the stiff grassy fields beyond the lawns of the cemetery. Bryce turned back to the marquee.

Dickie's casket sat alone at the rear of the open canopy. This was the part he disliked about funerals these days. After the family and friends were gone, the casket was turned over to strangers to deal with. Workmen, contract workers most likely. The actual grave safely out of sight behind the marquee, a gaping hole with a pile of dirt beside it. As if it were somehow distasteful to see what became of it, Bryce thought. As if people are afraid to admit why we're here in the first place. Well, they're probably right, as far as that goes. Still, give me the good old days, the casket lowered into the ground with everyone standing around, the sound of dirt thudding on the lid. No pretending about that. Do I actually remember such things or is that only the way they're portrayed in movies, on television? What to believe? He wondered if he should wait at least until the gravediggers—Do they still call them that? he thought. Nowadays it's probably something like Grave Interment Specialists—took the casket away to the graveside behind the marquee.

I don't know why I should care. Certainly doesn't make any difference to Dickie. But then Dickie and I never got along that well anyway. Not friends really, just kids who grew up together.

Thrown together by happenstance, happened to live in the same part of town. Orchard Hill kids. Funny how the world puts people together. Really not funny at all. Though I guess I'm supposed to believe it's all God's will, everything for a purpose. Wish I could. Wish it was that easy. He paced along the edge of the marquee, not quite on the inside, not quite out, idly lining up his feet heel to toe in the grass, walking an imagined tightrope. The cold wind stung his eyes.

He was a squat stocky man approaching fifty with wispy brown hair, a nose that could still depress him for being too bulbous, and cheeks pockmarked as if he had been worked over at some time in the past with a meat mallet. After several moments when no one appeared, he walked down the slope a little ways to where his wife, Rachel, was talking to Griffith. Listened as she complimented the man on the service. That's like Rachel, he thought. Always a kind word for everyone. Hoped for a compliment himself.

When Griffith went to look for the Grave Interment Specialists, Bryce said to her, "So." Meaning, So, how'd I do? Was I okay?

"You just couldn't help yourself, could you?" she said, not looking at him, looking after Griffith and then at the cars pulling away. "You just couldn't resist taking one last swipe at Dickie."

"What?"

She was an attractive woman though not pretty, her face too broad and slightly oblique, her eyes too far apart, to be classified as a beauty. Bryce had decided long ago, as far back as when he first dated her in high school, that he could settle for character; besides, he knew he was no prize himself. He had intended to tell her how nice she looked today in her gray suit, her black fitted topcoat, but it was too late now.

"All things considered, I thought I was pretty generous. Considering it was Dickie." He had also decided, long ago, that if he couldn't get people to think nice things about him, he'd settle for outlandish.

She looked at him and shook her head and looked away again. Bryce shrugged, snuffled his sniffling nose.

All right, if he hadn't been exactly generous, at least he thought he had been amusing. In the course of his remarks, he had noted that people in Furnass had always known Dickie as "one of the Big People from up on the Hill," a reference to the Sutcliff family's big house on the bluff overlooking the town. "But if you had seen Dickie in the shower room like we did in high school, you would know he was just normal-sized." Seemed like an okay thing to say at the time, he thought now, if not appropriate, at least not inappropriate—always good to try to lighten up these services, enough bad feelings around, easy to get maudlin—but maybe Rachel was right. Too late now to do anything about it. Too bad for people if they couldn't take a joke.

A woman with thick black hair who had stayed behind in the marquee, keeping an eye on the casket, who had stayed at the periphery of the group during the service, passed them now on the way back to her car; she nodded in passing and Rachel gave her minister-wife's smile and mouthed hello. They watched as she continued down the slope, a lone figure in black, the wind playing with her hair about her shoulders, toward a midnight blue Corvette, sitting by itself now that the others had left, parked at the end of the drive, where it had brought up the rear of the procession.

"Do I know her?" Bryce ventured.

"Pamela DiCello."

"Does she belong to our congregation?"

Rachel turned and looked at him, her head at an angle, lips tight—impossible man.

"No, I mean I thought I'd seen her before."

"You wish. She was Dickie's girlfriend. They had a place together—or rather, Dickie had a place for her—out at that town-house complex he built at Seneca Towne Centre."

"But . . . what about Tinker. . . ?"

"Such things do go on in the world, Bryce."

"How do you know about such things?" Bryce said. Thinking, Why don't I know about such things?

"She's a nurse at the hospital. Though she mainly works nights—we all figured so she'd have the days free to play with Dickie. They've been at it for a couple of years. We're all wondering if now she'll switch back to days."

They watched as the woman got into the Corvette and tooled slowly down the lane, the mufflers throbbing, purring along the curving hills among the gravestones, heading back toward the main road, the car as it grew distant looking increasingly like a toy in the fading light. When it was out of sight, Rachel turned again to Bryce as if it was safe now to speak.

"Pamela thinks somebody murdered Dickie and that people are trying to cover it up. At least that's the talk around the hospital."

"How did you hear that?"

"Evelyn told me. When I called this morning to say I wouldn't be in."

"Hmm. Well, I guess it would explain why everyone was in such a rush with the funeral and all."

"You're joking, right?

I don't know," Bryce said. Pursing his lips as he thought out loud. "All Julian said on the phone last night was that Dickie fell and hit his head in the office. I wanted to ask for more details today but there wasn't time. And they certainly seemed in a hurry to get the Dickie-Bird in the ground. Dead late Friday, burial on Monday. . . ."

"That's a reasonable amount of time," Rachel said.

Bryce *Hmmed,* waggled his head once. "Seems to be pushing it a bit, if you ask me. I didn't see anything about the incident or the funeral in the Pittsburgh paper, maybe it was in the *Onagona Times.* And there was no viewing at the funeral home or anything, a closed casket—nothing like you'd expect for a person of Dickie's prominence in the community. Even if the community didn't like him. And they sure didn't like him. Yep, I'm afraid I have to agree with Pamela, it all sounds suspicious, like somebody's trying to cover something up."

"Oh Bryce," Rachel made a face, slapped him on the sleeve of his raincoat. "Be serious."

"I try to be serious and nobody appreciates it."

"That's because nobody recognizes it. 'Dickie was just a normal-sized guy' indeed." She looked at him disapprovingly, then couldn't help herself and smiled. At herself as much as at him. She placed the flat of her hand against his chest, then took his arm, the two of them supporting each other down the slope— So that's that, Bryce thought. Dickie Sutcliff's dead and I'm alive. The Dickie-Bird gone. How about that. This is my life, this is my wife. This is what I get. Thanks, Lord, I think. Fascinating rhythm. But it sure feels like I owe something to somebody— their footing uneven in the winter grass, toward their car. The sun low and striated with clouds, a bare glimmer above the trees sinking faster as they neared the flat of the road. Behind them, beyond the crest of the hill, came the sound of a backhoe starting up.

2

"And you had Bryce officiate at the cemetery?" Pappy said.

"As only Bryce could," Julian said. "He was able to work in a reference to the size of Dickie's penis."

His father laughed silently, shook his head. "That Bryce. Sit down, stay awhile."

Julian Lyle remained standing, aware that there was no place to sit among the clutter of the living room, and not feeling like going through the effort to get one of the straight chairs from the kitchen. For that matter, he figured his father kept it this way on purpose, to discourage longer visits. The old man sat in the tall wing-back chair, an afghan wrapped around his legs, his lapboard with stacks of official documents and genealogical charts across the chair arms as if he were strapped in for an amusement park ride, under the light of the single floor lamp, its shade the color of old parchment. The room, the entire downstairs of the house, was filled waist-high with boxes of things from the time the family lived in a grander house high on the slope of the valley, before they moved to this brick saltbox, before Julian was born, boxes of old papers and files from the family business, the Keystone Steam Works, before it went belly-up, the dusty oil paintings of Julian's grandfather and great-grandfather and great-great-grandfather, the company's founders and enablers and ennoblers down through the years, leaning in a corner, boxes and albums of family history, all brought from storage in garages and basements and attics by his father after his wife died so he could slowly and repeatedly sift through it all, looking for heaven knows what. At the moment, though, the old man was lost in his thoughts.

"Bryce never did care that much for those Sutcliff boys, either one of them. None of you boys did, sort of tolerated them as I recall. Came in handy of course, when you wanted something like a ride somewhere or a piece of sporting equipment none of the rest of you could afford. That Bryce, he was a strange one, all right. Last one you'd ever expect to go into the ministry, you know? All his love for those toy soldiers of his, you boys all playing army in the woods. Then later you boys going to those black jazz clubs up in the Hill District in Pittsburgh. Nope, not what I'd consider the ministerial type. Did I tell you he baked her?"

Julian sighed; his father's mind was veering off on another tangent. Julian was, as the saying went, cast from the same mold as his father, he was aware of that. Tall, rail thin, with facial features the Lyle family considered Lincolnesque though others might see simply as gaunt. The old man was no doubt eccentric, but the whole family was thought to be eccentric. The family itself, on the other hand, considered such a trait a badge of honor, an expression of their individuality, part of what made them special. It was a point of family pride that the Lyles weren't like everyone else.

"Baked her, sure as I'm sitting here in this chair. I can't ascertain from these newspaper accounts and old letters where they had been that day, maybe went into Pittsburgh shopping for provisions or something, but they were late getting back. It was during the time they were putting gas lines for streetlights in town and your great-grandfather, Malcolm Hayes Lyle, he insisted that his street be one of the first ones in town to have the new lamps— not even a street really, more like a road halfway up the hillside above the town. He had that kind of power in the town back in those days, the Lyles did. If Malcolm Hayes wanted it, Malcolm Hayes got it. Well, the street, road, whatever, in front of their house was all torn up, and his wife, Lydia Elizabeth, she was carrying the lantern, I don't know where she got it but I can imagine she insisted on carrying it herself, she was that kind of woman I get the impression. But when they crossed a makeshift bridge over one of the open trenches, she lost her balance and toppled in and the kerosene splashed all over her, all over the big dress with the bustle they wore in those days, and she caught on fire, went up like a torch lying there at the bottom of that trench. And what did ol' Malcolm Hayes do to try to save her? He grabbed a barrel off the back off the wagon, I guess he thought it was salt—at least I hope he thought it was salt—he grabbed a barrel and opened it and threw it on her, except it wasn't salt it was flour. Coated her with flour like a piece of chicken, and the flour didn't snuff out the fire like salt might have, the flour encased her in the flames and cooked her through and through. Baked her, he did. Doesn't matter whether he meant to or not, the results were the same as if he'd set out to fricassee her. The poor woman lived on for a couple days, but when they tried to take the remains of her clothes off her the skin came right off with them. Nothing they could do for her. Everybody thinks your great-grandfather was such a great man, Saint Malcolm Hayes, never did anything wrong. Well, tell that to his wife baking away there in that trench, see what she has to say about it."

"That's a terrible story."

"Isn't it, though," Pappy said, his eyes aglimmer. "I'm putting that in my book about the family for sure."

"Is that really the kind of thing you want to spread around. . . ?"

"Of course it is. That's what we're about, isn't it?"

His father's face shifted gears, focused on Julian as if the old man just realized someone else was in the room. "Why are you here, son?"

"I was wondering lately, where was the old Lyle house? I always heard it was up on the hill above the town somewhere, but I never knew exactly where."

"Up the hill there at the end of Fifteenth Street, after it crosses the railroad tracks. You can probably still see the remains of the foundation, if you look closely enough. The house burned down before the war, and what was left went up in smoke during the war when the shantytown up there on the hillside burned down, some folks say because of the KKK but I think that's an exaggeration, there were just some folks in town who didn't like the black element sprouting up there, that's all."

"Yes, that would certainly teach them a lesson if they're not going to live in decent housing like the rest of the good white citizens of Furnass."

Pappy squinted at him. "Like I said, why are you really here?"

"Why does there have to be a particular reason? Can't I stop by to see my father?"

"You can but you don't. The only time you do is when you've got something on your mind. What's bothering you? Bryce still a thorn in your side? You two always did—"

"No, no, it's nothing about Bryce. I just . . . I don't know . . . I was in the neighborhood and . . . ."

"Well, we both know that's not true. Even on the way back into town from the cemetery, you wouldn't stop in Orchard Hill unless you were looking for a dose of pain."

Julian had to smile. He cupped the top of his head, his close-cropped salt-and-pepper hair, scratched his cheek through his trim salt-and-pepper beard. "Actually, I did want to ask you about the location of the old house, and your story of Grandfather baking his wife reminded me. But you're right, as I was driving here I got to thinking about friends and the old neighborhood. About what it was like to grow up in this part of town. There were rich kids and kids whose fathers worked in the mills. And there was the college, it introduced a whole other element into the mix. Orchard Hill was a pretty special place, and I guess those of us who grew up here were a kind of closed society."

"Hah! So it is about Bryce after all."

"Not really, it was more about friends and friendship in general. When a friend does something . . . well, you know, questionable. . . ."

"You mean like Dicey-Brycey talking about Dickie's penis at the guy's funeral?" His father chomped down on his jaw as if he had just taken a bite of something.

"I guess I was thinking more about when friends let you down. . . ."

"Are you still mooning about that no one came to your rescue when your Furnass Towers got into trouble? Good Lord, son, get over it. Your friends are always going to disappoint you at some time or other. Just like you're going to disappoint your friends. It's part of being alive. The test is how you handle it after it happens. And none of that has anything to do with business. You have no friends in business, you only have other people doing business, whether they were friends before or not."

"Dickie at least started to come through at the end, but it sure wasn't from any feelings of altruism on his part, he had his own agenda like he always did. I'm hoping now he's dead—"

"And good riddance, I say. The Sutcliffs, Dickie's father Harry, and all the rest of 'em, they were always usurpers as far as I'm concerned. It was the Lyles who set the tone for this town, we made it what it was, back when the Sutcliffs were still hauling iron ore to feed the Lyle furnaces. The town always looked to the Lyles for guidance and direction, we were the visionaries who made things happen. That the town didn't follow what we told 'em only shows how foolish most people are."

"The point is, I guess, that they didn't listen."

"You can't fix stupid. But what do I know about anything? I was never good at making friends in this town, and even worse at keeping them. Fact is, the town never liked me all that much, and I wasn't all that crazy about the town either. For that matter, I probably wasn't all that fond of you or your mother and sister either, but that's a different matter."

"I think I'd better get going."

"Don't let the door hit you in the butt."

With that, the old man started rooting around again in the papers on his lapboard. As Julian turned and headed back through the piles of boxes and junk, his father muttered as if to no one in particular, "Say hello to Brycey for me. That boy. Talking about Dickie's penis at his funeral. Hah!"

Stepping out into the chill night air was almost a relief. Crazy old man, Julian thought, smiling with affection. Ol' Pappy, as Bryce would say, like it was all one word. Bryce called him that since we were kids, Father was always Pappy to the family but Bryce added the Ol' to it before he even was, Bryce's idea of a joke I guess. In the darkness on the open front porch, along with an old refrigerator, a broken table, more stacks of newspapers, were the remains—rusted gears and crawler assemblies, split boilers and broken gauges—of the quarter-scale models of steam tractors and well drillers the salesmen used to demonstrate the Keystone Steamers back in their day, a model of the Lylemobile— What was that?

Something dark moved in the shadows to his left, close to the house.

"Kim?" Julian said. When he didn't see anything further, he laughed uneasily at himself.

Visionaries? Or do Lyles just have a history of seeing things? Why would Kim be here, except to make sure I was okay? My protector, my kung fu guardian angel. It's a wonder Kim never went after Dickie, after all the crap I had to put up with . . . you don't suppose . . . but the report said that Dickie fell in his office . . . no. . . .

Julian put the thought that had been nipping around the edges of his consciousness for the last day or so out of his mind. Again. His thoughts turned instead to something his father said, Those Sutcliffs were always usurpers as far as I'm concerned, thinking of the difference between the Lyles and the Sutcliffs in relation to each other and to the town, thinking, Dickie's dead and I'm still alive, who would have ever thought it would play out like this, sorry, Dickie, but I guess it's my time now. . . .

All Fall Down

. . . and Julian crosses the patch of bare earth that serves as the front yard to his father's house, makes his way through the gate hanging off its hinges in the dilapidated picket fence and across the street to his ten-year-old rusted-out black Cherokee, and continues on his way back from the cemetery, drives along Third Avenue past the dark campus of Covenant College, the empty walks a series of lighted circles from the lampposts winding between the blacked-out buildings, then starts down Orchard Hill Avenue toward the main part of town, the lights of the town in early winter spread before him, maintaining their grid despite the curves of the black river, the lights rising up around him as he sinks down the hill into the town, absorbing him among the streetlights and bare trees and small narrow steep-roofed houses, thinking This is my town, this town is as much a part of me as I am part and parcel of this town, thinking again of what his father said back at the house, This town always looked to the Lyles for guidance, the Lyles set the tone for this town, we made it what it was . . . turns off at the bottom of the hill onto Ninth Avenue and travels through the back streets of the Upper End, to distinguish it of course from the Lower End, both the poorest of the working-class areas in town though the Upper End is considered slightly better because it doesn't have quite so many blacks, turns at Twenty-Fourth Street past Smitty's Service and the D&G and heads through the culvert under the railroad tracks and starts up the long grade of Downie Hill Road, lifting out of the dark streets of the town as a few moments earlier he sank into them, ascending above them as he chugs up the side of the valley, the engine of the old Cherokee pounding, the power train whining, thinking that it's up to him now to write the new chapter of the family's history, to bring his family's name back into prominence in the town, reinstate it back in its proper place (where he's certain it's been the whole time, the town just unable to recognize or appreciate it), a sacred trust that's befallen him, a quest that he readily

accepts, all too aware that his previous attempts to make an impact on the town have been unsuccessful, the ill-fated Alhambra Shoppers Bazaar and the multi-use high-rise Furnass Towers, turning left at the top of the hill onto Seneca Road toward Furnass Heights and home, buoyed now with renewed hope, the anticipation that with Dickie's death his fortunes are about to change, not that he's glad that Dickie's dead, at least not that he can admit to himself on any level of his mind, but it certainly solves a number of problems, opens up a number of possibilities for him, all the menial, meaningless work he did over the years for Dickie's wife Tinker finally about to pay off, for that matter all the menial, meaningless work he did for Dickie too—all the crap he took from Dickie over the years, all the . . . well, he didn't want to think about any of that now—thinking that Tinker will inherit Sutcliff Realty and all of Dickie's many properties and projects around town, including the massive multimillion-dollar Furnass Landing development at the former site of Buchanan Steel along the river, and that as Tinker's attorney he will be in the position to guide and advise her with her business dealings, a man of prominence and influence once again, there'll be enough work to keep him occupied and in retainers the rest of his life, he'll be able to pay off his debts, get back on his feet again, not only get on his feet but be able to fulfill the visions he's had to revitalize the town since the steel industry went away, maybe now he'll even be able to obtain new funding to complete the Towers project, already in his mind toying with the possibility of reclaiming and rebuilding the family's mansion on the valley's hillside, the main reason why he stopped to ask Pappy today where exactly it was located so he could scout it out, aware that he's jumping the gun thinking this way but unable to help himself, driving along Seneca Road, tracing the rim of the valley, his headlights picking out the windy road in front of him, a happy man, a man with prospects, content with his due in this life, thinking he's ready for what the future brings. . . .

3

The next day started off in ordinary fashion for Bryce. He woke at his usual time, a little before seven, staying in bed so he was out of Rachel's way while she got ready for work—from her long established directive, rather than from consideration on Bryce's part; not that he wouldn't have stayed in bed to be out of her way if he had thought of it, the point being that he never would have thought of it—then, when he heard her go downstairs, he shaved, showered, got dressed and shuffled down to the kitchen to join her for coffee and an English muffin while they caught up with the happenings of the world on *Today*. After seeing Rachel off to the hospital—he walked with her out to the garage and collected the *Post-Gazette* from the driveway (or today, from the rhododendron bush), waving a last good-bye as her taillights traveled down the short side street to Berry Highway and turned toward Furnass—he went back in the house and did up the breakfast dishes, took the sports section into the first-floor powder room for his daily and proverbial movement of the bowels—Bryce prided himself on being a regular guy—then, followed by Satan, their black-and-white tuxedo cat, named accordingly so that Bryce could say on such occasions, as he does this morning—"Get thee behind me, Satan"—shuffled to the far end of the house to the church office and his pastor's study, turning on his desk lamp and the light beside his reading chair, intoning into the shadows of the room, "God's Workshop is now open for business. Bring 'em on, Lord."

Some mornings he made his own trip into the hospital, to offer support to patients or family during a major illness or after an operation, or made house calls around Drumlins to a list of shut-ins—or shit-ins, as he thought of them. But this morning there was nothing on the calendar outside the parsonage. Not that there weren't a number of important church affairs clamoring for his attention. He needed to edit the items for this Sunday's bulletin; review the estimates from half a dozen local firms to replace the church's furnace; send out requests for proposals to fix the church's slate roof, along with trying to figure out how to pay for the work; as well as look over the latest recommendations from a splinter group of the Liturgy Committee regarding prohibiting bouquets of flowers on the altar until the Christmas Eve service. Oh good grief, he thought. The church could be without heat at any time, the first good rain or melting snow could see the roof leaking like a sieve, and these folks are worried about flowers on the altar. Pee on 'em, Lord, they know not what they do.

But Bryce was restless. Disconcerted. There were a number of things this morning that kept running through his head. Why did Satan throw up hairballs a couple times yesterday? Why, if Judas's betrayal of Christ was necessary and unavoidable—there was an early Coptic scripture that suggested that Jesus even told Judas to betray him—would Judas be condemned to eternal punishment? Why did Rachel always put the tube of toothpaste on the shelf in the bathroom with the cap facing toward the left, when, if you're holding it in your left hand to squeeze paste onto a toothbrush, it only made sense to put the tube on the shelf with the cap facing toward the right? But the main thing that kept popping up in his thoughts had to do with what Rachel said at the cemetery the day before about Dickie Sutcliff's girlfriend: Why did Pamela DiCello think that Dickie had been murdered?

The fact was he was feeling guilty about the Dickie-Bird. It bothered him that he and Dickie could both live in the area, only a few miles from each other as a crow flies, and not see each other to talk to for—oh, at least twenty years. Okay, so I never liked the Dickie-Bird all that much, he told himself, we never had anything to say to each other even back in high school, even back in grade school for that matter, but still. . . . It bothered him that he lived less than eight miles from Furnass and, except for his quick trips a couple times a week to visit Onagona Memorial Hospital, he had lost contact with his hometown and the few friends who still lived there. Well, maybe not friends. Guys he used to know, grew up with. He didn't even see Julian Lyle that much, only when something out of the ordinary came up. Thinking, What kind of person am I? Obviously one who doesn't think a whole lot about people from his past. Pity. No way to be. Not what I preach all the time. Do as I say not. Love thy neighbor, love thy old neighborhood. He heard gnawing. He looked down; Satan was chewing on the plastic roller of his desk chair. Good way to get a flat cat. He thought again about Dickie. Murder. Pamela DiCello walking down the long grassy slope alone, her thick black hair played with by the wind.

He thought of Dickie's widow, Tinker. Now, there was something he could do. He didn't have a chance to offer his condolences to her at the cemetery. It would seem natural enough if he went to see her. Maybe he could find out more about what happened to Dickie that way. Full of purpose, his spirits renewed, he hummed tunelessly to himself as he scribbled *OK* on the proof of Sunday's bulletin; picked one bid at random from the stack of estimates for the new furnace—Groovy. McCutchen's Plumbing and Heating. I knew Tyler McCutchen, must be the same family. Good basketball player in high school—and put it in his out-tray for Shirley, the church secretary; decided there was no money to pay for a new roof regardless; and crumpled the recommendation from the splinter group of the Liturgy Committee into a ball and made a three-pointer into the wastepaper basket beside his desk—Nothing but net. After reaching down and carefully moving the cat aside a few inches—"Get thee away from my desk chair, Satan"—he hustled back down the hall to the main part of the house to get ready for his outing.

In his yellow VW Rabbit diesel, the *God Runner* as he had christened the car when he first bought it—Rachel wouldn't set foot in the vehicle unless she had to because she said it smelled, meaning, unfortunately, that it smelled too much of half-eaten Big Macs and unfinished buckets of Colonel Sanders chicken, too much of damp wool and unbridled farts, too much of Bryce; Bryce with his plugged sinuses said he didn't know what she was talking about—Bryce took Berry Highway, then followed the twists and turns of the Yellow Belt—singing to himself in his monotone, "Follow the Yellow Belt Road, Follow the Yellow Belt Road"— from Drumlins, skirting Furnass completely, across the upper bridge over the Allehela near Indian Camp, past the new developments in Seneca and into Highland Hills.

Dickie's house in the expensive suburb was as well-known as the Sutcliff family's house in Furnass. From the private drive leading up to it the house seemed more like a compound, a villa in Tuscany—a sprawling Italianate structure that looked like many connected structures, of native sandstone with rounded towers and crenelated chimneys sticking up here and there and a columned entranceway. Bryce left his car in front of the six-car garage, beside a late-model black pickup truck, and followed the steps past reflecting pools and fountains drained for winter to the double front doors. He supposed he should have called first—for that matter, he had no reason to think Tinker would be home at this time of day, she could very well be at her flower shop in Furnass—but he liked to pop in on people, especially on his ministerial rounds, he wanted his visits to seem friendly, not formal; he also found it was easier to deal with people if they were caught off guard. Oh good heavens, it's the reverend! Quick, get some clothes on! At his touch, the doorbell sounded in the distance like the muffled chimes of Doom. When nothing happened, he leaned close to the intercom to see if he was missing something. He jumped a foot when one of the double doors suddenly opened. Dickie's daughter Jennifer looked at him curiously.

"Oh, hello! Jennifer. I'm Revered Orr. Maybe you remember me, I was a friend of Dickie's . . . er, your dad's."

"Yes, of course I remember you. I just saw you yesterday at the funeral."

Bryce made a little puttering sound, supposed to be a laugh. "Yes, well. Hmm." He dry-sniffled twice, his nose feeling like it was running even if it wasn't. "How are you? Well, I guess that's a superfluous question, isn't it, given what all has happened the last few days. Sorry I asked that, I hope you're holding up okay. Actually, I stopped by to see if your mother is home."

Jennifer watched him as he prattled on, like observing a strange life form. When he finally stopped for breath, she said, "I'm fine, thank you. And my mother isn't home. But you're welcome to come in, if you like."

She stood aside to reveal the interior of the house, closing the door behind him when he stepped inside. After a large circular entrance hall, the domed ceiling several stories tall, he followed her down a long cloister-like corridor with tall vaulted ceilings supported by stone columns, past a series of sitting rooms and a library and a formal dining room, toward an archway at the end filled with subdued sunlight. The corridor opened up into a large cavernous kitchen the size of a small diner, with sinks and stoves and a large central counter at one end and a sitting area at the other. He thought, I guess I don't rate the living room. Jennifer made for a grouping of furniture in front of a stone fireplace large enough to roast a pig; she stood in front of a leather sofa and motioned for him to sit across from her on a matching one.

"Can I take your coat?"

"That's okay," Bryce said, sloughing free of the sleeves. "I'll just keep it with me, in case I have to make a quick getaway."

He tossed the raincoat on the opposite end of the sofa and sat down. The soft leather cushions absorbed him; he adjusted a throw pillow beside him for ballast.

"Would you like something? Coffee?" she said, but sat down before he could respond.

"No, I'm fine, thanks." He looked around. "This is quite a house Dickie . . . your family has."

"It's a simple little place, but Mom and Dad called it home," Jennifer said, obviously being facetious, as she tucked her legs under her, sidesaddle, and folded herself into a corner of the sofa. She was in her mid-twenties, dressed in jeans and a Wellesley sweatshirt, sweat socks—they had passed a pair of cowboy boots standing empty in the front hall—her long auburn hair tied up under a blue bandana.

She's trying to be nice, Bryce thought, the gracious hostess, but it's not quite working. Understandable. Poor girl, the shock she's been through. Opportunity for me to be the good shepherd. Never quite sure how. This end of the large room was lit by a wall of windows open to the gray day, a cathedral ceiling with skylights open to the gray sky. Between him and Jennifer the glass-topped coffee table displayed its chromed framework and legs, the leafy pattern of the area rug beneath. Bryce sat forward rubbing his hands together as if in front of a fire, his elbows resting on his thighs, to try to engage her.

"I didn't get a chance to talk to your mother yesterday and thought I'd stop by to see if she needed anything. Your mom and I go back a long way too."

"So I've heard." The way she said it, Bryce wasn't sure how to take it. Jennifer went on. "I don't know when she'll be back. She's probably in town at her flower shop. Or raiding my father's office."

"Heh heh. I assume you're joking. . . ."

"Oh, it's true enough." She sighed, fixing him with gray-green eyes. "My mom's been trying to find out more about Dad's business for some time. Now he's not around to stop her. But she's not going to find anything. I know where all the important papers are, and they aren't just lying around his office where anyone could find them."

"How would you know where they are when your mother doesn't?"

"Because my dad told me where he kept them. She's also undoubtedly looking for his will, for obvious reasons. That, I don't know where it is. She won't find anything at Julian Lyle's either. That'll be her next stop, after she gives up on Sutcliff Realty."

"Julian was your father's attorney, right?"

"Julian liked to think so. Dad just let him do stuff occasionally because they knew each other growing up." She nodded his direction. "Another of your Orchard Hill friends."

The comparison, or the way she said it, linking him to Julian, made him uncomfortable. Beyond the picture windows were views of the surrounding hills, the landscape rolling away toward the distant cut that marked the river valley, the town of Furnass. Blue jays and finches flitted back and forth at a bird feeder, a flurry of activity without sound; a silent plane moved down the gray sky toward the horizon, Pittsburgh International Airport. He was feeling bulky in his sweater and sport coat, all folds and rolls of cloth. He hoped it didn't appear that he was actually this fat. It was worse when he tried to sit back so he leaned forward again.

"You and your dad must have been very close."

"We must have been." She thought a moment, picked at the seam on the leg of her jeans; apparently she realized that was facetious, even for her. "He trusted me with a lot. A few months ago he put me in charge of the Furnass Landing project."

"The industrial park that's going in where Buchanan Steel used to be." He said it as a question.

She nodded. "It's a multimillion-dollar project, the biggest development of its kind this side of Pittsburgh, maybe in the region. I couldn't help but know a lot of what else was going on in the company. My dad wanted me to know about all his dealings, we worked very closely." She looked at her hands, one holding the other, resting on her leg.

Bryce rubbed his own hands together self-consciously, looked around. The fireplace was smudged around the edges, the interior a black hole as if it were used often, though there was nothing on the hearth, the space devoid of logs or ashes or andirons. It was chilly in the room; he thought they could use a fire about now.

"That's impressive. A lot of responsibility. Dickie must have thought a lot of your abilities."

She looked at him as if to say, And your point is?

"What will happen to the project, now that your dad's. . . ."

"Oh, it will go forward. I'll see to that." She unfolded her legs and placed her stocking feet on the floor. All business. "Furnass Landing is his legacy. As for my mom, I have no idea how she thinks she's going to get involved now. Get a Realtor's license and take over the company? Not hardly. Besides, I wouldn't let it happen. I know the vision my dad had for the project, we talked endlessly about what we wanted it to be. I'm going to make sure it gets done the way he wanted it."

"Any thoughts of taking over the entire company yourself?"

Jennifer just looked at him. Noncommittal. Blank. Unknowable.

Bryce laughed a little. "Sounds like you and your mother don't see eye to eye on a lot of things."

"An understatement. That's why you caught me here at the house today. Most of the time I'm not around, I have my own place. I only came by today because I figured she'd be gone. And

I figured right. There are some things of mine, and Dad's, I want to rescue before she gets her hands on them. There's no telling what all she'll do, now that he's not around to keep things under control. Keep *her* under control."

Bryce looked around, stalling for time, trying to get his thoughts together. Thinking, If I don't ask her now I never will. "Do we know any more about how your father died?"

"What more is there to know?" Jennifer cocked her head as if to align him better in her sights.

"I mean, I heard that he fell in his office. I was wondering if we know anything more about how he fell. Or why."

"He hit his head on the edge of his desk, that's about all we know. The death certificate says he died from an epidural hematoma as a result of blunt-force trauma. I don't think there's much more to learn than that."

"I'm sorry to bring this up, the only reason I said anything is . . . somebody brought up the idea that there might have been foul play involved."

"Somebody?"

"Well, you know how people talk." He dry-snuffled, rubbed his hands together.

"Yes. People do." She looked away, out the windows at the yard, the empty swimming pool. Beyond an impeccably trimmed hedge was the statue of a horse's head mounted on a plinth.

"I'm sure the autopsy would have said something if there was any indication. . . ."

"I assume there was an autopsy but I don't know that for certain. The police said he died as the result of the fall, and I would think that would be good enough for all the somebodies who might have questions."

The way she said it left no doubt whom she considered included in the somebodies. She thinks I'm an idiot or a fool, Bryce thought. She's probably right. Before he could think of what else to say, she looked back at him, her head at an angle so that her hair caught highlights from the dull sunlight. She must dye it that color, I've never seen a red like that in nature. . . .

"Though there was certainly no shortage of people in this town who would want to see my dad dead. And be willing to have a hand in making it happen. The price of being who he was. What all he did. His position in town."

"I'm sure there are a lot of people who are very distressed that he's dead too. I know that I—"

Before he could finish she stood up abruptly, as if she'd heard enough, enough of him, no longer making an effort to smile. "You know, I really have to keep moving. I want to be gone before my mom gets back. It was really nice of you to stop by. . . ."

Bryce stood, gathered up his raincoat, and worked to put it on—the sleeves weren't cooperating; he flailed around like a man attacked by a coat—as he followed her back down the hallways toward the front door. Thinking, *I'm pretty sure this is what used to be known as the bum's rush. . . .*

4

Julian Lyle had planned to do a number of things in his office this morning. Continue making inquiries to find out if Dickie Sutcliff left a will, and if he did, where he left it; prepare for Kim Leong's custody hearing, which was coming up in a few days; look into a couple of business matters for Tinker Sutcliff. What he didn't figure on was a visit from Kim.

"Sheryl says Cory hasn't been home in three days," Kim said, walking unannounced into Julian's office, with Donna, Julian's secretary, trailing haplessly behind. "She doesn't know where Cory is and hasn't heard a thing from her. I asked her why she didn't report it to the police and she said she thought Cory would turn up on her own. Can you imagine that? I wouldn't have known a thing about it if I hadn't called over to the house."

As Kim uncoiled into one of the chairs in front of the desk, Julian motioned to Donna that it was okay and to close the door behind her. Then he looked at Kim over the top of his frameless glasses. "I told you not to call over there. For any reason."

"I know, but I hadn't heard from Cory for a couple of days and I wanted to find out what was going on. Now I'm glad I did. And Sheryl wonders why I'm claiming custody. There's your answer right there."

Julian had to admit, in regard to the custody battle, that Cory was missing was one of the best things that could happen. The custody hearing is coming up and the mother has no idea where the girl is; it might be the one thing that actually gave them a chance to sway the hearing in Kim's favor. Otherwise, Julian didn't hold much hope; courts in Pennsylvania traditionally favored the mother in custody disputes, no matter how bad a mother she was. And except for this instance, all indications were that Sheryl was a good mother. Julian thought it would be advantageous for Kim's case if the girl remained missing a little while longer—and immediately hated himself for thinking such a thing. He was as concerned as Kim that Cory might be in trouble somewhere, that something serious had happened to her. God forbid. He had to be careful how he handled the matter. Careful how he handled Kim.

Julian pressed his fingertips together in an open tent before his mouth and swiveled thirty-three degrees to the left in his old high-backed leather chair, swiveled sixty-six degrees to the right, before returning to where he started. He regarded Kim across the plane of his desktop, sitting in the shadows of his dark office beyond the circle of light from his green-shaded desk lamp.

"When was the last time anybody saw Cory?"

"Sheryl said Friday evening."

Julian saw an opening for something else that had been on his mind, a way to find out something that had been bothering him.

Even if it meant a bit of a lie. "That reminds me. I tried calling you Friday night."

"What about?"

"Nothing particular. Just checking in. I hadn't heard from you for a while, I was wondering how you were doing."

Kim looked at him curiously. "What time was that?"

"Oh, probably around ten or so."

"Why so late?"

"I don't know," Julian said, trying to be casual. "I just got to thinking, that's all. As I said, nothing special. I guess you weren't home. Or not answering the phone."

"I was probably over at the studio. . . ."

"I tried there too," Julian said. Pushing it. He shrugged to Kim, as if it were a mystery.

"You certainly sound interested to talk to me about nothing," Kim said, measuring him.

Julian smiled, swiveled thirty-three degrees to the left, sixty-six to the right and back again, shook his head as if it were not important. "So, do you have any idea where Cory might be?"

"I'm afraid she's with a guy named Stratton. I know Cory's been seen hanging around with him lately."

"If it's the Stratton I know, he's a good deal older than Cory. . . ."

"He's almost twice Cory's age, he's close to my age. That's why we got to go find her. I know he's dealing, a couple of my students told me. He could have taken her with him on one of his drug runs to New York or Florida. She could be strung out on drugs in a filthy crash pad somewhere, guys. . . ."

Kim was out of his seat and pacing in a tight orbit like an animal confronting bars. He was in his late thirties, a man of only medium height but whose body was lithe and muscular, his sleek long black hair below his shoulders. He was wearing the black satin workout pants he wore at his martial arts school, the black satin jacket he wore everywhere summer and winter. When he walked he made a whisperish sound like wind moving in leaves.

"Slow down," Julian said, swiveling to keep the younger man in his sights. "Get ahold of yourself."

Kim stopped pacing, ready to listen, though his hands began tracing patterns in front of himself, martial arts forms, his hands moving as slowly and gracefully as a Balinese dancer's. For a moment Julian was entranced watching Kim's hands, then snapped his head to bring himself back to present business.

"I want you to go back to the studio and stay there. I want you to forget about Cory, or at least try to, put her out of your mind for a while. I'll find out what I can about where she is, and if Stratton is involved. But it's critical for you to stay out of it."

Kim stopped working his hands. "You don't trust me?"

Julian thought, It never fails to amaze me. How this trained killer, a man who has killed other men, can turn into a hurt little boy from the least little thing.

Julian cupped the top of his head, flicked his hand across his bowl-shaped salt-and-pepper hair. "That has nothing to do with it. We can't afford to have you involved in any way with Cory until this matter is settled in the courts. Besides, I know what you'd do to Stratton if you found her with him."

Thinking, He's like a child. Since the trial for killing his father he'd be lost without me to look out for him. That old adage: Save another's life and you're responsible for him ever after. My privilege, really, knowing the way Kim considers most of the people in this town. Take that, good people of Furnass. And now that Dickie's dead and I'll be handling all the Sutcliff business with Tinker I'll have more influence in town, maybe I can do more for him. You know Julian Lyle, the attorney, he's my friend.

Julian got up and walked around his desk, put his arm around the other's shoulders, his hand momentarily getting tangled in

Kim's long hair as he guided him toward the door and the outer office.

"Look, Kim, I promise. The minute I find out anything about her, I'll call you and let you know. Maybe we can figure out some way for you to see her for a couple of minutes so you know she's all right. Donna here will be my witness."

The attractive middle-aged woman looked up from her type-writer and smiled. "I'll make sure he does what he says, Kim."

Kim looked at Julian, looked at his eyes, as if looking into his core. Julian thought, And more than a child too. Like something cornered. All eyes and teeth.

The younger man turned and left the office without saying anything more, moving like a whisper in his workout clothes and canvas shoes. Julian gave a sigh of relief.

"What did I just promise?" Donna asked Julian as he headed back into his office.

"I'll tell you later," Julian said and closed the door behind him.

5

Hmm. Can't say that went well. No sir. No siree. No siree bobtail. It's all very well to say that we should comfort the bereaved. But I got to tell you, Lord, some of these bereaved don't comfort worth a damn.

After Bryce left Jennifer at her parents' house, he was more determined than ever to offer his condolences to the family, whether they wanted them or not. Bryce was never one to let people's indifference, or outright disdain, stand in his way. Besides, driving into Furnass would satisfy his curiosity; all this talk about the town and his old gang of friends made him want to see the place again. See more of it than he did during his pastoral visits to the hospital. If he thought about it, he probably hadn't been in downtown Furnass, except to hurry through on his way someplace else, for ten years or so.

But driving along Seventh Avenue, the main drag of town, only reminded him why he didn't come here more often. It was depressing. Empty stores; boarded-up stores; stores with unfamiliar names—Dollar Mart, ABC Used Furniture, Not Quite New. Unhappy reminders of what used to be here when he grew up here. All the hallmarks, Bryce thought, to make it a typical Western Pennsylvania mill town in the 1980s, including a martial arts studio—What's that about? Seems like self-defense is the only growth industry in the area since the mills closed. But I guess if a bully came along and took away everything you had and worked for, you'd want to defend whatever you had left, or at least feel that you could—and a high-rise building, probably for senior citizen housing, sticking up out of nowhere, in this case Julian's abandoned Furnass Towers, its ten-story skeleton like a stack of see-through cubes against the winter sky. Down the steep side streets, the buildings of what had been the Allehela Works of Buchanan Steel sat abandoned along the river—those that weren't already leveled. Brownfields marked the former locations of the BOP Shop, Pickling Mill, the Sally Furnass. All gone.

Bryce parked near Eleventh Street, one of three cars on the block—he remembered when you had to circle the block for a parking space, especially on paydays at the mill. He tried at Tinker's Flowers, but Tinker wasn't there and no one seemed to know where she was. Or wanted to say. Back on the sidewalk again, he looked around, considering his options, weighing the possibilities. What do you think, Lord? Why not? He dug his hands deep into his pockets to pull his too-short raincoat tighter about himself—there was the feeling of snow in the air, if not later today then tonight, soon—and on the chance that Jennifer was right, set off along the sidewalk.

Sutcliff Realty was in a nondescript three-story building near Fifteenth Street, a narrow brick building squeezed in between the Pub on the corner and the Blue Room Pool Hall. When Dickie's father bought the building in the early 1950s, he modernized the front with double aluminum-frame doors and darkened glass, the name SUTCLIFF REALTY above the entrance in large aluminum letters attached directly to the brick; apparently Dickie had felt no need to further improve the facade, though eventually he took over the two floors above for more office and storage space. When Bryce asked the woman at the front counter if Mrs. Sutcliff happened to be there, the woman said, "She certainly is," rolled her eyes, and nodded toward an office door at the rear. "You can go on back." She didn't say so, but Bryce got the impression she meant If you dare.

As he ditty-bopped through the open work area—trying to spread the smile around, God's Own Messenger of Joy and Good Tidings—none of the dozen or so men and women at their desks looked at him. The atmosphere in the room seemed both restrained and frantic; those on the phones spoke in hushed voices; others stared at their typewriters or computer screens as if locked in place. Two men in shirtsleeves and a woman in what could pass for a party dress stood off to one side with their heads together like conspirators; they stopped talking until he passed. A copier spewing papers clacked rhythmically like someone beating time. Bryce was enchanted, a stranger in a strange land; it was all very different from his world of church affairs; parishioners talked to him about their jobs all the time but Bryce had no firsthand experience of life in the workplace, of the workaday world, only these occasional spelunkings into these unfamiliar caverns, whenever he could finagle an excuse to make a visit. Lord, they act like they're afraid of something. Are these places always like this? Fascinating. Captivating rhythm. He had spent his adult life concerned with larger issues, life and death, existence and spirit. The everyday was a mystery to him, but that only made visits to the world of routines all the more exotic. He was enthralled, loved it, thought it endlessly intriguing: people at work, going about their lives. Thinking, God love 'em. Somebody should.

The door to the office in the rear was open. Tinker stood behind the desk, its surface a pile of papers and folders, talking to a blowsy woman in a bulky knit sweater and open-toed mules.

"What do you mean you don't know where they are?" Tinker said, holding up a sheaf of folders. "These don't have anything in them at all." When Tinker noticed Bryce standing in the doorway, she said, "Yes, what do you want?"

"I guess this is a bad time," Bryce winced.

Across Tinker's face passed in rapid succession anger, resentment, curiosity, and finally, recognition. "Oh, Bryce. Of course. Come in, I was thinking of something else. We can talk about this later, Margaret."

Margaret was already pushing past Bryce, halfway out the door as Tinker said it. Tinker watched the woman go, shook her head, and dropped the empty file folders on the desk with the other papers. Bryce was prepared to give her a pastoral hug, but she kept the desk between them.

"What brings you to town? Oh dear, don't tell me Julian forgot to give you your honorarium or whatever it's called for the funeral."

"I didn't want anything for doing it, I told Julian that. Dickie was an old friend. I just thought I'd stop by and say hello and offer my condolences. We didn't have a chance to talk yesterday. . . ."

Tinker seemed indifferent, already thinking of something else. She brushed her fingertips idly over the piles of papers in front of her. "That's nice of you. As you can see, there's a lot to take care of. Now that Dickie's gone."

She was a wiry, angly woman, wearing a pink wool suit the color of impatiens that clashed with her short auburn hair. The room was thick with her cigarette smoke as if the world had gone fuzzy. Bryce was beginning to wonder if coming to see Tinker today was such a good idea after all. She certainly didn't seem like a woman in need of condolence.

"I stopped by your house and spoke with Jennifer. She's grown into quite a young woman."

"Hasn't she just. Dickie was very proud of her. They were very close."

"That's what she said. How is she taking Dickie's death?"

"All right, I suppose. As well as can be expected. With Jennifer you're never quite sure, about anything. She keeps a lot of things to herself. Also like her father."

Her attention drifted again. As she talked she went over to an open file drawer and walked her fingers back along the tabs of the folders, flipping through the names. It appeared that Jennifer was right to describe her mother's visit to the office as a raid. Papers were scattered everywhere; file and desk drawers were standing open; the room looked ransacked. As she searched, Tinker was working on two cigarettes at once. She took a long drag from the one left burning in an ashtray on top of the file cabinet; another in an ashtray on the desk trailed a thin plume into the air like incense. A tiny smoke signal.

"A sudden death like that is always hard for everyone," Bryce said. Thinking, That's really obvious. Could I be more inane? Just go ahead and ask her. . . . "Everything happened so quickly, Julian calling me at the last minute to do the funeral and all, I never heard the actual circumstances of how Dickie died."

"What did you hear?"

"That he fell in his office."

"Then you heard as much as anybody knows. He was here in the office late at night and evidently fell and hit his head on the corner of the desk." She pointed to the corner in front of Bryce. "There."

"There?"

"There."

At his feet was a stain on the carpet; Bryce juked back, realizing he was standing on the spot where Dickie must have died. He resisted the temptation to bend over and examine the corner of the furniture, but he could swear from where he stood there was blood on it, something else. Don't tell me, that can't be hair. Dickie's hair. Maybe it's dust.

"How did he fall? I mean, was he ill or something? Did the autopsy say anything?"

"Who were you talking to about autopsies?"

"Nobody. I just. . . ."

Tinker looked at him strangely before continuing. "The cleaning people found him a couple hours after it happened. That's about all I can tell you."

"That's awful. I'm sorry to bring it up, but I didn't know. It must be very painful for you to talk about."

She stubbed out the cigarette in the ashtray on the cabinet and came back over to the desk, standing behind it as if taking up a position.

"Yes, it was a shock. How it happened and all. But I'm not going to pretend, Bryce. It's no secret that there was no love between Dickie and me. We led separate lives for quite a long time now. That we still lived together was only a convenience. If you want to call it that. Actually, it wasn't convenient at all. A habit maybe. Not necessarily a good one."

"I didn't know. . . ."

"Why would you? And why would you care? I'm sorry that Dickie died the way he did, of course. I'm sorry he had to die at all, I didn't wish him ill. Or at least not like that. But I'm not going to pretend that my life won't be easier now with Dickie not here."

Bryce looked around the office at the mess she had made. "Jennifer said she thought you were interested in taking over the business."

"Oh, did she? 'Taking over' would be her words for it, I'm sure. But with Dickie gone it more or less falls into my lap. Or should. Julian's looking into the legalities right now."

"She said there was some question about locating the will. . . ."

"Little Miss Jennifer should learn to keep her mouth shut about family business."

"I didn't mean that Jennifer said anything that—"

"You don't have to defend her. I know she doesn't approve of me having anything to do with Sutcliff Realty. She doesn't think I'm capable enough. I heard it all before when I wanted to open my flower shop. Dickie said I'd never make a go of it, that the mills were closing and there were already two flower shops in town, that Furnass didn't need another flower shop. I told him it needed a *good* flower shop. And four years later, mine is the biggest flower shop in town and the others are struggling to stay alive." She stubbed out the cigarette burning on the desk. "I don't know why I'm telling you all this."

"Old friends," Bryce smiled.

"Not really. I wasn't from Orchard Hill, remember?"

Bryce clasped his hands over his stomach, then fluttered his hands away from each other, afraid he looked too ministerial. He remembered Tinker was this way when she was younger too, when he knew her in high school, direct to the point of wounding. It was why he had always been wary of her; she was right, they hadn't been friends, back then or ever. And time had only made her more abrasive, stronger. Dickie must have been a hell of a man, he thought, not only to go to bed with a woman like Tinker but to stand up against her afterward. Thank you, Lord, I never had to deal with anyone like that. Rachel, on the other hand. . . .

"I guess us Orchard Hill guys kept pretty much to ourselves back then."

"I don't know if you all thought you were better than everybody else, but you sure acted like it. In high school the only ones in your crowd who would have anything to do with anyone else in town were Dickie and Harry Todd. And that's because the Sutcliff boys took after their father: they wanted to screw every girl they could get their hands on. Excuse my French, Reverend."

Bryce waved it away. Why does everyone think ministers lead such sheltered lives? I guess because most of us do. . . . A lifetime of resentment and grudges seemed to be spilling out of her. He tried to change the subject.

"I didn't know Harry Todd was back in town until I saw him at the funeral. I didn't have a chance to speak with him either."

Tinker busied herself with more file folders. "Harry Todd doesn't speak to many people these days. He's become something of a recluse. Living with his mother before she died made him as dotty as she was. But he's still a bastard like every other Sutcliff male. He's one of the reasons I'm here going through all this. I want to make sure there's nothing Harry Todd can get his hands on. He's one person who certainly wished Dickie ill."

"I didn't think Harry Todd wanted anything to do with the business."

"He didn't for a long time. But after he came back from California, he seems to have changed his tune. Dickie figured the only reason his brother came back to town was to get what he thought was his share of the business. They even came to blows over it."

"A fight?"

Tinker cocked her head at him, looking up from under her eyebrows. "If you can call it that. Dickie pretty much cleaned Harry Todd's clock, from what I heard from Jennifer. And she heard it from Harry Todd himself, so I figure it must be true. I assume it was about the business. That and all the other bad blood between the two of them. There was no love between the brothers Sutcliff."

"It's beginning to sound like there wasn't much love between Dickie and anybody."

It was the wrong thing to say, he knew it as soon as he heard the words come out of his mouth. Tinker gave him a cold look. "Things aren't always so black-and-white as your theology might want them to be, Bryce. I shouldn't speak for Harry Todd, if you want to find out how he felt about his brother you should ask him. As for me, I think I've said too much already."

"I didn't mean to upset you. . . ."

"Upset me?" For the first time since they began talking, she smiled. But there was an edge to it. "What could you possibly say that would upset me? For that to happen, I'd have to care, wouldn't I? Why did you come to see me today, Bryce?"

He blushed. "I told you . . . I wanted to offer my condolences. . . ."

"Bullshit." She folded her arms and seemed to grow taller as she spoke. "None of you ever thought I was worth a hill of beans without Dickie. And except for my talents in bed, that included Dickie. Why are you here, Bryce? To find out how I'll manage now without him? To gloat? I know everybody in town thinks the only reason my flower shop is a success is because I was Dickie's wife, that he must have run my competition out of business by raising their rents or put pressure on the people who could, some such thing. Well, Dickie's not here now, and we'll see how well I get along without him. We'll just see. Now, you'll have to excuse me, I've got things to do."

6

Julian Lyle was aware that there were people in town who didn't think very much of him. Aware that, although they might not actively dislike him—though he knew there were some of those too—there were people, maybe a lot of people, who didn't take him seriously. Who might even consider him something of a joke. (Now, that one hurt.) He told himself it was understandable in a way. No one realized more than he did that he had never lived up to his potential, never lived up to his family name and accomplishments. If at times he had been the subject of the town's ridicule, he attributed it to that peculiar American fondness for putting someone on a pedestal, then taking great delight in trying to knock them off it again. It was the due, he supposed, of anyone whose birthright placed them above the huddled masses yearning to breathe free. What a relief to think, now that Dickie had . . . er, passed . . . and he would be handling all the Sutcliff Realty affairs with Tinker, that this air of failure—he preferred the term *unsuccessful*, if it had to be anything—would soon be cleared away.

Julian was mulling over such considerations as he left his office deep inside the old Alhambra Theater and walked through the remains of the mini-mall, the Alhambra Shoppers Bazaar, which he had tried to develop a few years earlier. People in town praised Dickie Sutcliff for his Furnass Landing project, even if they disapproved of the man himself, calling it the linchpin for the economic revitalization of the town after the mills closed. Julian felt sure his own Shoppers Bazaar could have accomplished much the same thing, or close to it, if people had given it half a chance. But they didn't, the town seemed to dismiss it out of hand—he tried not to think it was because he had something to do with it. Thinking, No, that wasn't it, you're just being paranoid. Furnass simply wasn't ready for such a thing, people are always reluctant to accept anything new, especially in this town. Most of these people are only one or two generations away from being serfs, peasants in Poland or Slovenia, it's a matter of education and exposure to better things. If I had had more time, and enough money for the right marketing, I could have made it work. He was the first to admit that, at the time, he didn't have Dickie's connections to make such a project work, or Dickie's talent for wheeling and dealing. As Julian made his way along the empty corridor, in the dim light from the few wall sconces that still worked, his shadow rose and fell across the plywood facades painted like stalls of an Arabian marketplace. He had to admit that in its present condition the Bazaar looked like the set for a Grade B movie. A bad Grade B movie. Well, he had learned a lot since then; people were going to be surprised at the regenerated Julian Lyle. He pushed through the padded theater doors and on through the outer lobby to the street.

The afternoon was getting colder; the gray sky lowering over the narrow main street held the threat of snow. Julian adjusted the scarf around his neck, pulled up the collar of his sport coat. The garland hanging over the main street, strung from lamppost to lamppost, wavered with the slight wind; the strings of multi-colored lights twisted among the fake pine boughs were mostly burnt-out or missing, the few bulbs that remained burning gamely in the graying afternoon light; the decorations on the lampposts, flat silver figures of angels blowing trumpets, were rusted and pockmarked. He could remember a time as a boy growing up here—not just at holiday time either—when the sidewalks would be crammed with people at any hour of the day, shoppers and men from the mill standing along the curbs waiting for their next shift, traffic bumper-to-bumper through the town. Now he was practically alone on the sidewalk, only a few cars traveled along the main street.

Above the two- and three-story brick farther up the street, he could see another reminder of his failed attempts to revitalize the town, the upper unfinished floors of the Furnass Towers Office and Apartment Building. He noticed a few days earlier that someone, probably art students from the high school, had painted a mural on the plywood barricade protecting the front of the abandoned construction site, crude figures of Charlie Brown and other *Peanuts* characters grouped around a small scraggily Christmas tree. Nice of them to ask me beforehand if they could do it. No matter, I guess. It's good that somebody is getting some use out of it. He glanced up at the building one more time, a smile on his face as if he knew a secret no one else knew, and kept going. On the other side of the street catty-corner from the Towers, in an art deco storefront that once housed Gelston Jewelers, was the Five Animals Kung Fu Studio. Julian thought of stopping by to see if Kim had returned there as he'd directed him, but decided it was something he didn't want to know—if Kim wasn't there, Julian would feel that he needed to find out where he was and he wasn't sure he wanted to know. Normally when Julian was out and about he would stop in the studio for a chat or the two of them would go for coffee at Augie's Kwik Dog, but today he was pressed for time. He needed to get back to the office as soon as possible, in case one of the feelers he had put out came back with information about Dickie's will. The sooner he verified Tinker's legal status, the better. The thought that his luck was about to change—it has to, it just has to—added a bounce to his step.

Mikey's All-Niter was at the end of the business district a few blocks from Julian's office, at the top of the hill to the Lower End of town. Sheryl was behind the counter, waiting while a lanky workman in a duck jacket dug in the pockets of his jeans for a few pennies to complete paying for his cigarettes. Sheryl looked at Julian over the man's shoulder but gave no sign of recognition. In the corner a teenager stood in rapt attention at a console, one designer sneaker resting on top of the other, playing a video game; the store was filled with the electronic sounds of aliens being zapped. On the shelf behind Sheryl, a radio garbled unintelligibly in her ear. The place smelled of chipped-chopped ham and disinfectant and spilt milk.

After the workman left, she said, "Hello Julian" without looking up from the cash register as she rang up the sale.

"You probably know why I'm here."

Sheryl sighed and cocked her hip as she regarded him. She was an attractive woman in her mid-thirties, a few years younger than Kim, with a broad mouth and an out-of-fashion curly perm. She was wearing a faded Furnass High letter jacket—there was a Stokers logo stitched on one breast and a basketball on the other—over her required apron against the cold air that rushed in the door every time a customer came or went. When Kim was arrested for killing his father, in what the *Onagona Times* referred to in a headline as "A Kung Fu Fight to the Death," it was Sheryl who picked Julian's name out of the phone book to represent him. It seemed strange now, in the custody fight for Cory, to be on the other side, against her.

"I told Kim when he called the house. Cory took off a couple of days ago. I guess it's been four days now, and I haven't seen her since. I thought at first she must be at one of her girlfriend's house, she's done that before without telling me, but never for this long. Now I'm starting to get worried."

Now? he thought. You're about three and a half days late. It was hard for him to remember that she wasn't his client; it was hard not to advise her about what she should and shouldn't do. The same as he had over the long months during Kim's trial and the years since, until she and Kim separated. Until she took Cory and moved out of the house.

"Did you and Cory have a fight about something?"

"No more than usual. You know Cory, she's no dream to get along with. She never was." As she spoke she moved down the counter, took a brick of cheese from the display case, and began running it through the slicer. "Kim thinks he'll make a difference in the girl's behavior. But he's got another think coming. She's too much like him. There's that wildness there. . . ."

"Kim has the idea that she might be with a guy named Stratton."

"Yes, that was a mistake, telling Kim about that."

"You're the one who told him about Stratton?"

"It kind of slipped out. I thought Kim was going to blow a gasket."

He was going to say Do you blame him? but a woman who had been in the back of the store came to the counter with a few items to be checked out. Julian moved off to the side, out of the way—thinking, Why would she say a thing like that to Kim? Is she trying to get somebody killed? Was she trying to set up Stratton? Or maybe set up Kim—looking at the covers of magazines on the newsstand until the customer left.

"Kim is justifiably concerned what Cory might get herself into with somebody like Stratton."

"Don't you think I've thought about that? Don't you think—doesn't Kim know I'm worried sick about her? That I've tried everything I can to keep her away from people like that? But the more I say to her, the more she'll go ahead and do it anyway. You know her, Julian."

He had to admit he did. Thinking, Cory's too much like her father. He grinned a little at the idea, but Sheryl's reproachful look sobered him again.

Following his suspicion again, the hunch, the idea that wouldn't let him let it go, he said, "Did you talk to Kim Friday night? Maybe around ten or so?"

"Why would I talk to Kim, Julian?"

"I don't know. I thought maybe you were starting to worry about Cory and called to see if she was with him." Julian tried to smile, disarm her. "Did he ever talk to you about Dickie Sutcliff? Anything to do with me. . . ?"

Sheryl looked at him as if she thought he might be crazy. "I don't talk to Kim unless I absolutely have to. About anything. And if I have to, I try to do it either through my attorney or through you. No, I didn't talk to him Friday night, and why would he talk to me about Dickie Sutcliff of all people?"

Julian hastily changed the subject. "What about Stratton? Do you know where he lives? How can I find him?"

Sheryl shook her head and went back to slicing cheese. "I only know he works at Sheetz Welding, or at least he did, down in the Lower End. And do you know how I know he works there? Cory made a point of telling me how she met him. She was down there one day with a couple of her girlfriends—I'm afraid to think what they were doing, they were supposed to be in school—and they walked by Sheetz's shop and Stratton was sitting in the doorway having his lunch and he called to them. Her girlfriends had enough sense to keep on going, or so she said, but Cory stayed and talked to him, and then met him after work. It's not a nice feeling, Julian, to think my beautiful baby girl, the girl I've done everything I could to protect, even from her own father, has turned into a slut."

Wait a minute. "What do you mean, protect her from her father?"

"You've got a blind spot when it comes to Kim. You think he's this great guy who's done all these wild and interesting things, who's gone all these places and had all these experiences that you've never had. But you don't know what he's really like, believe me. There's a whole other Kim that you don't know anything about. I know, I've lived with the man. A Kim you don't want to know. And that Kim scares Cory. Remember, the girl saw him kill his own father, right in front of her eyes."

"But he loves Cory. He was defending Cory."

Sheryl turned off the slicer and returned the now smaller brick of cheese to the display case, stacking the slices beside it. Her voice was muffled as she talked with her head inside the cabinet.

"I'm only saying that maybe Cory took off before the hearing because she was afraid her father might actually get custody of her. And I didn't make a bigger deal about where she is because she might be better off wherever she is, even with Stratton, than she would be with Kim. And that's all I'm going to say, about anything, until the hearing."

She looked up at him from inside the display case, her head cocked to one side to get a full view of him. As he watched, her pretty, determined face slowly disappeared into the mist as her breath fogged the glass.

7

When Bryce left Tinker at Sutcliff Realty, he knew little more about Dickie's death than when he started. Tinker confirmed that Dickie had hit his head on the desk in his office, but that still left a lot of questions up in the air. What caused him to hit his head? Did he fall, trip, skid, slide, slip, tumble, dive, carom? Was he sick? Drunk? On drugs? Or was there something else involved? Someone, perhaps? There had to be a reason why Dickie's girlfriend, Pamela—a nurse obviously familiar with accidental death—thought he was murdered. Fascinating stuff, Bryce thought. Mysterious are the ways of the Lord, huh Lord? All of it laid out just to confuse us, make us think. Up to us to find the thread. Otherwise what is there? Too scary. And there was the whole thing with Harry Todd. Bad blood between brothers. Two siblings fighting for control of the family business. Bryce was more intrigued than ever.

He went back to his car, circled the block, and headed up through the town. Noting the changes to the town like ticking off recriminations, cataloging regrets. Thinking, What the hell did they do to my hometown? At the upper end of the main street the junior high school had been leveled for a Kentucky Fried Chicken, which itself was now abandoned, the windows under the candy-striped awnings boarded up, the asphalt parking lot littered with dead leaves and crumpled papers. O'Brien's Hardware was a Church of the Redemption. Smitsky's Auto Parts looked bombed out. A skinny hunchbacked hound slunk along the sidewalk keeping close to the buildings, sniffing for anything it could find. The traffic islands beyond the business district, at one time park-like areas between the lanes, had fallen into neglect, the once manicured lawns now only scraggily clumps of grass among patches of bare earth, the forsythia and other shrubs gone wild. Bryce continued on, up the four-block grade of Orchard Avenue, past the Victorian spires of Old Main and ivy-covered buildings at Covenant College, to Orchard Hill.

Furnass was laid out in three geological steps along the river—Lower End, Business District including the Upper End, and Orchard Hill—each level considered a step up, or step down, the social ladder from the others, depending on which way you were headed. Bryce was more familiar with the changes here on Orchard Hill because of his regular trips to this part of town to visit parishioners at Onagona Memorial Hospital; but today the area depressed him more than the downtown. In the gray winter light, the once comfortable brick and frame homes seemed desolate, the lawns barren and unkempt. Houses of friends he grew up with—Sonny Rourke, the Binder brothers, Needle-Prick Brown the Insect Fucker, Stewie Hammerback—appeared empty, or worse, occupied by strangers. The sycamores along the sidewalks stood bare and lifeless, their black branches intertwined above the streets like fingers reaching.

He followed the street past the college, close to the edge of the bluff overlooking the river. A block beyond the edge of the campus was Julian Lyle's family house, an orange brick saltbox, one of the oldest houses in town. The front yard was a patch of dirt, the porch filled with broken furniture, an old washing machine, stacks of rotting cardboard boxes, machine parts. I thought Julian said Pappy still lived here, the house looks like it belongs in a slum. Why would Julian let it get like this? But I guess that's like Julian, it runs in the family. The Lyles always took pride in their messes, noblesse oblige or some such thing—no, noblesse do-whatever-you-feel-like, let everything pile up and go to hell and think it shows how grand you are, that you're above worrying about the small stuff. Tinker was probably right, we did act like we were better than everybody else, or at least some of us did. Sad. Next door, the house he grew up in was now an empty lot, opening up a view of the black hills on the other side of the valley, fog drifting among the bare trees. The gray sky was in layers, darkening toward the line of the hills. He made a U-turn and drove back through the quiet streets, following Fifth Avenue to where it became an oiled road and then a dead end.

The Sutcliff House, as everyone in town called it—the Big House on the Hill, the Big House with the Tower—sat on the edge of Orchard Hill overlooking Furnass. It was an orange brick Victorian, a collection of gables and peaked roofs and bay windows, a round corner tower like a castle keep. Below, the river made its S-curve through the valley, pushing the town up the slope of the hills, on its way to join the Ohio a half mile or so to the west. Bryce drove up the driveway beside the house and parked in front of the garages, following the walk to the front door. In the gray afternoon light, the rolling lawns where he had played as a boy with Dickie and Harry Todd spread disconsolately to the line of bare trees marking the woods on the hillside; around the side of the house the remains of a large bonfire, ashes and pieces of charred furniture, were scorched into the grass like the scar from some ritual burning. The veranda extending across the front and side of the house was filled with dozens of black plastic garbage bags. When he rang the doorbell it sounded remote and tinny, as if the house were hollow.

He cupped his hands against the etched-glass window panel to peer inside. After several minutes Harry Todd appeared out of the depths of the house, coming down the hallway like a ghost materializing out of the gloomy interior. Bryce laughed at himself for thinking such a thing, laughed with pleasure at seeing an old friend.

"I thought if I waited long enough, you'd go away," Harry Todd said as he opened the door.

"You can't get rid of me that easily."

"Never could. Come on in."

Harry Todd left the door for Bryce to close as he led the way through the dark entryway into the even darker downstairs rooms. He was a few years older than Bryce, wearing jeans and a tattered Berkeley sweatshirt. In the gloom Harry Todd's blond hair glowed dully like an off-white skullcap.

"How have you been, Dicey-Brycey?" he said over his shoulder.

"Dicey-Brycey. Been a long time since I heard that one. Can't say I exactly missed it." And you were Hairy Toes, Horny Toad, but probably shouldn't say anything if I want this to stay friendly. "I'm doing good. Yourself?"

Harry Todd shrugged as he led them into the living room. The old wood of the floors and framing creaked under their weight; their voices sounded increasingly hollow the deeper they moved into the house.

"As you can see, everything is pretty torn up. My mother seemed to have measured her life in terms of how much stuff she could collect. Find yourself a seat. Coffee? A beer?"

The room was a jumble of the black plastic garbage bags, piles of clothes, old toys, stacks of newspapers and magazines, more black plastic garbage bags. Harry Todd had taken down the drapes and blinds from the windows, the winter light washing in over the room. The exposed windows in the curve of the tower gave a panoramic view of the brown lawn, the line of black trees marking the edge of the bluff, the not-quite view of the town. Like living in a fishbowl, Bryce thought. A very murky fishbowl. But then that was always true of the Sutcliffs, wasn't it, they seemed to like it, look for it. . . . Bryce moved aside a stack of winter coats on hangers and perched on the arm of the sofa, unbuttoned his raincoat but kept it on. Harry Todd sat across from him on a kitchen stool.

"I didn't have the chance to speak with you at the funeral yesterday. I'm sure Dickie's death was quite a shock to you."

Harry Todd nodded, more like a shrug, acknowledging without comment.

"And I was sorry to hear about your mother last year. She hadn't been ill, had she?"

"No, it was very quick. Thank heavens. A heart attack there in the front room. I came down from upstairs and found her sitting in her rocking chair but she was already gone."

Bryce looked sympathetic. "Sometimes that's the best way. . . ."

"Oh yes. Mother wouldn't have made a good patient." Harry Todd thought of something. "We didn't call you for the funeral because. . . ."

Bryce waved away such concerns, pulled a face.

"You know how she felt about churches—no offense to you— and people in town in general, for that matter. We didn't even hold a service, one of the few things Dickie and I ever agreed on. We had her cremated and I scattered her ashes over the lawn."

Bryce thought about the burnt circle in the grass but decided it was inappropriate to make a joke. "I always liked your mom. She was always nice to me and the other kids when we were here with you and Dickie."

"She was an interesting old dolly, that's for sure," Harry Todd said, his hands resting on his thighs, his arms braced, surveying the clutter of the room. "I've been at this for months and you can hardly tell the difference."

The air in the house was musty; and there was a smell, of a cat or an old person. Or both. Bryce's and Harry Todd's presence in the room had stirred up the dust; slow-moving swirls of motes hung in the afternoon light as if in colloidal suspension. Bryce rubbed the tip of his nose like turning a small crank. From another room came the ping of a radiator, the old wood settling. "Do you plan to stay in the house?"

"That seems up for grabs at the moment," Harry Todd said, looking at the floor between his legs. "I'd like to, but I guess it depends if Dickie made any provisions for it in his will. We'll have to see what happens when the time comes."

"I heard they were having trouble locating the will."

"How'd you hear that?"

"I ran into Jennifer this morning, when I stopped by Dickie's house. And I saw Tinker . . . er, downtown."

"You're a busy guy."

"I wasn't their minister, but I thought I should reach out. . . ."

"I'm sure there's a will somewhere. My business-minded brother would never overlook a detail like that. It's just a matter of finding where he put it. I think it interesting that Julian Lyle considered himself Dickie's attorney, but evidently my brother didn't trust him enough to have him handle his will. But then Dickie had his own reasons for a lot of things."

"I would have thought this house belonged to your mother."

Harry Todd laughed, a puff of air. "You would think. But apparently somewhere along the line, my illustrious brother convinced my mother to put the house in his name. Why, I don't know. But I do know that after Mother died, Dickie threatened to sell the house out from under me. For no other reason apparently than to take away where I wanted to live."

"Why would he do that?"

"I think to show me that he could. He never explained why, but I got the idea he was holding it in case he needed it as leverage for some reason in the future. That would be like Dickie. I'm pretty sure he had no idea of selling it. Jennifer told me that Dickie couldn't stand the thought of anyone but family living here. So I don't know. As I said, Dickie had his own reasons for things, particularly when it came to me. Maybe he wanted to hold it over me in case I got too powerful within the company. Fat chance of that. He gave me a job with Sutcliff Realty, all right, then buried me in the back office out in Seneca with nothing to do. It's been good as far as getting a lot done cleaning out the house, but that's about all."

"Sibling rivalry can be a deadly thing. The story of Cain and Abel—"

"Spare me the sermon, Bryce. I remember when you were one of my little brother's playmates. It's hard to listen to you spout biblical platitudes when I can still see you running around the front lawn in a headdress joyfully scalping imaginary cowboys."

"Point taken." Thinking, And I can remember you as the football hero telling everybody how Donna Bruno would suck you off in the back seat of your father's Cadillac. . . . Bryce propellered the end of his nose again. In another part of the house the wood settled like someone walking about.

"So. Where did you see the Widow Sutcliff? At Sutcliff Realty?"

Bryce's face must have told the tale.

Harry Todd smiled to himself; he bracketed a thumb and forefinger over each thigh, rubbing his hands slowly up and down their length. "I didn't think she'd waste much time, moving in. She's had it in her mind to take over the business, or a fair share of it, for a while now."

"Funny, she said the same about you."

"Really." That seemed to please Harry Todd for a moment.

"I think it probably occurred to a number of people, that you had your eyes on the business. The fact that you moved back to town after all that time."

"You mean like Dickie? Yeah, it occurred to Dickie all right." Harry Todd thought a moment. "Though I wish I could say it was on account of something that grand."

"You mean the reason you came back?"

Harry Todd watched something faraway in the direction of the windows. "The only reason why I didn't go into the business in the first place is because my dad sent me away to college in California after Donna Bruno got pregnant. If I had been here, it would have been a very different story. Whatever else he thought about me, I don't think Dickie ever forgot that I was the one Dad originally wanted to take over the business, not him."

"But you could have come back to town after you graduated, couldn't you? I mean, there was nothing stopping you, was there? So your father, and Dickie, must have figured you didn't want it."

Harry Todd stood up. He wedged his hands in the pockets of his jeans and stood there a moment studying the floor in front of him. Against the leaden light of the curved windows he was a silhouette, a shadow without features.

"If it ever occurred to me to try to take over the company since I've been back, it certainly wasn't to run it, not in this day and age. I'm too far out of the local business scene to try anything like that. But that doesn't mean I might not want the business, or a part of it, so I could sell it. And now that Dickie's out of the picture, I don't see why I shouldn't have the whole thing. It was my father's business; I think I'm entitled to what it's worth. I think Father would have wanted the family to benefit from it, the immediate family, that is, not a questionable daughter-in-law. Though once I get it I might be willing to sell it to Tinker, if she's still interested. And if she could raise the money."

"Did Dickie know you were interested in taking it over, for whatever reason?"

"I'm sure he had a pretty good idea. As I said, I figure that's why he buried me out there in Seneca, and let me know my living in this house was by his good graces."

"Does Tinker know you're going after the business?"

Harry Todd shrugged, featureless in the backlight. "She might. But she has her own reasons for fighting for a share of it. Pride, if nothing else. She undoubtedly knew that Dickie was getting ready to leave her."

"For Pamela DiCello?"

"You are informed, aren't you?" Harry Todd said. "Did Tinker tell you that?"

The wood creaked in another part of the house. Both Harry Todd and Bryce looked that direction. Bryce thought, Is there somebody else here?

"I only heard about it recently—no, not from Tinker. But I had no idea it was to the stage that Dickie was thinking of leaving Tinker for her." Bryce thought a moment. Do I dare? Sure, why not? "Did you know that Pamela thinks somebody killed Dickie?"

"Really? Any particular reason why she'd think that?"

"I'm not sure."

Harry Todd looked at him warily. "Is somebody saying that I might have had something to do with it?"

"Why would they say something like that?"

"You never know in this town."

Fascinating. He's uneasy, Mr. Cool Harry Todd Sutcliff. Wonder what happens if I prod him a little. "I do know that Tinker said that you and Dickie weren't getting along, that there had been a fight. . . ."

"So Tinker is implying that I had something to do with Dickie's death?" He laughed, twisted back and forth, his hands still in his pants pockets like he was trying to corkscrew into the floor. "That's funny. If anyone had a reason to kill Dickie it was Tinker. If somebody killed him."

"Was there a police report? Because I think that would help clear up. . . ."

Harry Todd came closer to him and he could see his features now. They weren't friendly. "Why do you want to know about a police report? What are you poking around for?"

"Nothing. I just meant. . . ." For a split second Bryce was a little boy again, challenged by one of the older kids. He's going to hit me. Run.

Harry Todd looked at him a moment longer, as if sizing him up, then got a slow grin on his face. "You know, I really think I should be getting back to work here." He turned away, heading out of the room and back down the hall toward the front door, ushering him out. "Thanks for stopping by, Dicey-Brycey."

8

Sheetz Welding was tucked away on a back street in the Lower End among small manufacturing shops and warehouses, many of them closed now, abandoned, close to the river and the abutment for the highway viaduct that spanned the end of the valley. High above on the Ohio River Boulevard, headlights of early rush-hour traffic from Pittsburgh swept over the beginnings of the evening, tires singing across the grates, clattering over the expansion joints. The shop was in an old orange brick building, the brick smudged black from years of smoke and soot from the mills, triangularly shaped from the odd meeting of streets in the area. On the front of the building was the dim painting of a welder striking an arc, an advertisement from an earlier welding shop before Sheetz bought the place. The roll-up door was open, as it nearly always was; the dark street danced with flashes of pulsing white-hot light. Julian stepped inside cautiously, shielding his eyes with his hand.

Smoke drifted through the shop, reflecting the light of the acetylene torches and welders' arcs. A layer of soot and grime covered everything, machinery, floor. Toward the rear a grinder sent a comet tail of sparks up into the gloom, toward the exposed trusses of the roof. There was the smell of burnt leather from the men's protective clothing, the electric smell of the arcs, ozone. Julian ducked suddenly as a sheet of steel materialized overhead, floating through the shop from the hook of a small overhead crane; the operator, walking the crane with the dangling controls, grinned at Julian's timidity. Julian picked his way among the scrap metal and droppings of slag on the floor, being careful not to touch anything or let anything brush up against his tweed sport coat, to where Sheetz was changing the coil on an automatic welder. Sheetz squinted over his shoulder at him, watching Julian approach.

"Quite a place you have here, Don," Julian said approvingly, looking around. "I've never been down here before. Yes, quite a place."

Sheetz nodded; he wiped his hand on a grease rag but didn't offer to shake. Julian had met him, seen him a couple times, at Kim's studio when Sheetz stopped by briefly, but had never talked to him before; he was aware that there was some long-ago connection between Sheetz and Kim, but Julian didn't know what it was. Sheetz was the same age as Kim, in his late thirties, his African American face fleshy around deep-set eyes, his shaved head covered with a blue bandana. Sheetz continued to watch him, steady, giving him nothing. Julian tried smiling, thinking, He's looking at me like he wants to hit me. What did I do to him? All the class hatred in the world. Remember what Kim taught you. Trying to appear natural—it didn't quite work—as if he stood this way all the time, Julian assumed a casual variation of the horse stance—squared, balanced on the balls of his feet, hands folded in the area of his crotch, ready to fend off a fist or club—as he continued to gaze around.

"Yes sir, quite a place. I'm impressed. Looks like you can do it all here. If you ever need an attorney for anything, give me a call. My family was in the machining and tooling business, you know, the Keystone Steam Works, though maybe that was a little before your time." Julian gave a little laugh, more like a cough. "Yes sir, this all looks very familiar."

"I'll keep it in mind," Sheetz said, noncommittal. "What can I do you for, Lyle? You down here serving papers or something?"

"No, no, nothing like that," Julian smiled. "I wanted to talk to one of your employees. A guy named Stratton. I think his first name is Jim."

"Yeah, it's Jim. If you can find him, you're welcome to talk to him."

Is he making a joke? Is he trying to put me off? Julian looked around, trying to be good-natured. "Why? Is he hiding around here somewhere?"

"Stratton is a sometime employee. Sometimes he's here, sometimes he isn't." Sheetz went back to changing the coil on the welding machine, threading the silver wire through the feeder. "Right now, you're out of luck. I haven't seen him for several days. Maybe close to a week. Could be away somewhere."

"Any idea where he goes?"

"I don't know and I don't ask. When he comes around—if he comes around—and I've got the work, I'll give him a job. Otherwise. . . ."

"Do you know where he lives?"

Sheetz gave a shrug. "Not really."

"Don't you need that kind of information for his tax records?"

"Strictly cash."

"It sounds a bit irregular," Julian smiled.

Sheetz, bent over the machine, looked up at him unkindly. "You implying I'm doing something illegal?"

"No, no, not at all. I'm certainly not a tax attorney." Julian laugh-coughed again. "I mean, suppose you need to get ahold of him for something. . . ."

"Never happen. If he shows, fine. Otherwise, what he does is his business. What I don't know can't hurt me."

"I'm not sure that's true at all. Seems to me the things you don't know are the ones that end up biting you in the ass." He thought "ass" was a nice workingman's touch.

"Different folks, different strokes."

Sheetz tightened the fittings, goosed the manual switch until the wire was feeding smoothly. When the man didn't say anything more, Julian said, "And I suppose when Stratton disappears, you have no idea if anybody goes along with him."

"Like I said." Sheetz fit the cover back on the coil, wiped his hands again, then regarded Julian like a woodcutter evaluating a tree. "What is it you're really after, Lyle? Is it about what Stratton does in his spare time, or is it about who he does it with? Or some of both? Because if Stratton is mixed up with something illegal, I don't know a thing about it. I don't need that kind of trouble."

"I'm looking for a girl, a teenager. I heard she might be mixed up with Stratton."

Sheetz gave a little laugh without humor. "There are always young girls around Stratton. He seems to collect them like flies to sugar. Or dog shit. Don't ask me how."

"I've also heard it's often about drugs. Any truth to that, do you think?"

Sheetz shrugged, wouldn't comment.

"Doesn't that bother you?"

"Why should it?"

"Well, whatever he's doing with them, he can't be up to any good. . . ."

"What's 'good,' Lyle? You tell me. In Southeast Asia we turned the better part of a generation of young girls into whores by giving them a taste of our American way of life—that taste usually at the business end of a cock. Ten-year-old girls would do you if they thought it might get them a one-way ticket to our golden shores." Sheetz spit on the oil-soaked floor at the memory of something. "Those girls didn't know any better. Girls around here should. If they're foolish enough to get involved with a guy like Stratton, it's good enough for them."

"But if he's taking advantage of young girls, that's reprehensible. I don't know how you could stand to be around a man like that."

"I can stand to be around him because he's a beautiful welder. I'm lucky to get him, when I can get him. Maybe someday he'll turn his life around, who knows? And as long as he does his work while he's here, who am I to say anything about the way he chooses to live? What about you, Lyle? How would your life look if somebody took a real good look at it?"

Sheetz gave him a look from under his eyebrows and started to walk by him toward the stairs to his office. Julian put his hand on the other's arm to stop him. "Wait a minute. What does that mean?"

Under the gray work shirt, Sheetz's arm felt as solid as a thick wire cable. Julian removed his hand when he saw the look in the man's eye. When he spoke, Sheetz's voice was almost a whisper.

"I'd be real careful, Lyle, before I was so sure I was better than somebody else. At least a guy like Stratton makes no bones about who he is and what he's done."

"What are you talking about? What have I done?"

"I've heard all about the fancy little schemes you and Dickie Sutcliff were involved in, don't you worry."

Julian was both pleased to have his name linked as an equal with Dickie and concerned at the implication.

"Seems like I touched a nerve," Sheetz said, looking at him curiously, a wry smile on his face. Then he leaned closer to Julian. "But in the future, I'd be real careful about who and what you take hold of. You might grab on to more than you can handle."

Before Julian could say anything or react, Sheetz's hands moved in front of him, almost too fast to see, too fast to even juke away from, a series of cross-checks and open-handed strikes that brushed either side of Julian's face, barely touching him but enough to know that he had been touched, as fast and as gentle as puffs of air, Sheetz's face entirely without emotion, effortless, focused, deadly. When he relaxed again, he grinned and leaned closer to Julian, like a co-conspirator or confidant. "And do you really think that little horse stance of yours could protect you from someone like me?"

Julian was shaken. Sheetz leaned back and regarded him again—All the hatred in the world, what did I ever do to him?— then went on to his office.

9

It was late afternoon by the time Bryce got back to Drumlins, the day already turned to early evening. It was an older suburban community north of Pittsburgh, one of the first in the region to feel the effects of urban sprawl, a community that for the first half of the twentieth century was made up of small family farms and people who didn't want to live in the city but who still needed to be close enough for easy access to their livelihood, people who for whatever reason wanted to live away from the bustle and noise and smells of urban living, some houses surrounded by rolling fields of corn and wheat, others tucked back deep among trees, only to find after World War II that the city had come to them, or at least the northern suburbs of Pittsburgh, the fields and forests of Drumlins turned into car dealerships and strip malls and franchise restaurants, serviced by bigger highways and wider roads to accommodate the commuter traffic off Interstate 79, all of it, however, by this time, the late 1980s, because Drumlins was among the first of the growing suburbs, now looking worn and a bit seedy compared to the newer developments in Seneca and Cranberry and Wexford, the car dealerships too crammed for space to properly show off the stock, the restaurants badly in need of refurbishing and contemporary signage and color schemes, the strip malls with too many closed stores, the roads too narrow and full of potholes.

Graystone Church was a holdover from the days before the sprawl, an older congregation that every year lost more members than it gained, made up mostly of people who remembered when the church was a pillar of the community—when there was community enough to warrant pillars—and had the open space surrounding it to prove it. Now it sat at the end of a short side street off Berry Highway, most of its once proud lawns and parking lots taken over by the expansion of the Pets Aplenty Veterinary Clinic & Hospital on one side of the street and the back lot of Wild Bill Januzzi's Cycle World on the other. It was a squat, Romanesque structure of, as might be expected, gray stone— Bryce often wondered if he was the only one to question why it was called "Graystone," what else in heaven's name would it be called; for that matter, what other color would stone be, talk about belaboring the obvious—a single square tower like a battlement at one corner. The manse beside it, built of the same gray stone but the architecture from a later period, all high-peaked roofs and gables, surrounded by dark shrubs, looked homey, like the image on a greeting card, despite the parking lot of Pets Aplenty hard against one side. Bryce pulled into the garage and entered the house through the door to the church office, stopping in his study to hang up his raincoat and sport coat and check the few messages on the answering machine. Groovy! he thought. I got away with playing hooky, nobody died without me, nobody needed me to bail out their soul. Thanks, Lord, I needed that. He chugged down the hall, happy with himself and with his day, a bundle of energy, on his way to see his darling, arms moving like pistons, chanting in a low monotone to himself, "Watchin' o'er the flock, watchin' o'er the flock. . . ."

Rachel was in the kitchen, standing on the opposite side of the central island, peeling garlic. She looked up at him from under the row of pots and pans hanging from the iron framework above the workspace.

"I thought you'd probably show up if I started dinner. I'm starved."

"Hello, dear." He walked around the island to give her a kiss. She offered her cheek to him and continued peeling the cloves. She was still in her nurse's uniform from the hospital; her white shoes squeaked on the tile floor as she moved about.

"What a day, what a day," Bryce said, shaking his head, going to the sink to wash his hands. He dodged out of her way as she dumped some garlic husks down the disposal. Even with garlic in the air she smelled clean and antiseptic, as she always did after work.

"I was going to do ham and egg sandwiches," she said, taking the fixings from the refrigerator. "I thought that would be quick."

"That's fine, fine." He leaned the small of his back against the counter as he dried his hands. "Wait till you hear where I was today. I went into—"

"Did you see there were some messages on the machine?"

"Yes, I listened to them. Nothing important. Today I went into Furnass—"

"When I came in the phone was ringing, it was Bert Jarvis. He said the Maintenance Committee wants to know if you reviewed the bids for the new boiler."

"Bert Jarvis is a busybody who likes to get everybody stirred up about little things so he can offer his opinions."

"That's not very charitable. I always thought Bert Jarvis was a nice person."

Bert Jarvis can go to hell, well, at least go jump in the lake. "Let me tell you what I did today."

"Go ahead, I'm listening." She finished mincing the garlic and dumped it with olive oil into a skillet.

She's got enough garlic in there to kill a gaggle of vampires. I won't be able to talk to anyone up close for a week. . . . "As I started to say, I went into Furnass today. Down into town, along the main street, I'll bet I haven't been there for five years. You should see it—it looks like a war zone."

"I see it all the time. I go down to the Blue Boar with a bunch of the nurses every week or so, it's our treat at lunchtime."

"Well, I haven't been down there for—"

"Why did you go downtown? There are hardly any stores to speak of these days."

"I didn't start out to. First I went over to see Tinker at the house."

"How is she doing?"

"She wasn't there. But Jennifer was and I talked to her for a while."

"Is she okay?"

"She seems to be. She's developed into quite the young woman. But here's the interesting part. Jennifer wasn't sure there was an autopsy on Dickie, at least if there was she never heard anything about it."

"Why would you talk to her about a thing like an autopsy on her father?"

"It just sort of came out. I started thinking about what you said Dickie's girlfriend said about Dickie being murdered. . . ."

"You didn't tell her I said that, did you?"

"No, I—"

"Because I just repeated what I heard. For all I know Pamela never even said it."

"Let me tell you, will you?" Thinking, She always does this.

"I'm listening." Rachel worked her wooden spoon through the mixture of garlic and olive oil, then added slabs of ham. The skillet popped and sizzled.

"Jennifer didn't know anything about an autopsy. And she said she thought her mom was at Sutcliff Realty raiding Dickie's office. It seems they can't find Dickie's will and—"

"So you went down to Dickie's office to see Tinker? Why are you so fussed up whether Dickie had an autopsy or not?"

"It just seems strange that the guy would fall in his office and nobody would do an autopsy to find out the reason why."

"They didn't do an autopsy—that you know of."

"All right, yes. That I know of. I meant to ask Harry Todd about it, but we sort of got off on another topic—"

"You went to see Harry Todd too? Oh, before I forget, there's a letter from Mary. It's in on the table. She got a new apartment and I think she has a new roommate."

"Boy or girl? And are they sleeping together, boy or girl?"

"Bryce, your own daughter."

"It's a legitimate question. But let me tell you what I found out about Dickie's death."

"I just wanted to make sure you knew about Mary's letter. And it sounds like you didn't find out anything about Dickie's death. And you can start the toast."

She always does this. She never lets me tell her. Bryce found the bread in the freezer, broke off four slices, and dutifully put them in the toaster.

"Isn't that four-hole toaster wonderful?" Rachel said. "It was expensive but I think it was certainly worth it."

She never lets me tell her. It's like she doesn't want me to finish, doesn't want me to tell her things. Bryce sighed and turned to look out the kitchen window, at the empty Pets Aplenty parking lot; in the darkness was the murky image of himself looking at himself, Rachel working at the stove behind him. If you saw us from outside, somebody taking their cat to be neutered or declawed or their dog to be put down, I wonder how we would look. What would we look like? A happily married couple talking things over at the end of the day? Or a man who can't get a word in edgewise? I'm going to tell her whether she wants to hear it or not. . . .

"So yes, I went to see Harry Todd after I talked to Tinker. And yes, I didn't find out very much about Dickie's death. But that's the thing. Nobody I've talked to so far knows very much about it either. And nobody seems all that concerned to find out."

"Why does there always have to be a why? You always have to know the why about everything."

"I don't have to know the why about everything. But people just don't fall in their office late at night without a reason."

"I don't see why not. We get cases at the hospital all the time, people falling for one reason or another—"

"Not like this, they don't. And not with this many people who are happy to see Dickie out of the way. Tinker thinks Harry Todd wanted Dickie gone because he wants to lay claim to his share of the business, which in fact he does. And Harry Todd thinks Tinker wanted Dickie gone because Dickie was going to leave her for Pamela and she wanted to make sure she got the business for herself. There's two people with a motive right there. It's fascinating stuff—"

"Excuse me," Rachel said, moving him aside as she got the eggs from behind him on the counter. She cracked two on the edge of a small dish and slid the eggs into the skillet beside the ham.

"Isn't that fascinating stuff? I mean—"

"I think you're letting your imagination get the better of you. Besides, it's no surprise that Dickie had a lot of enemies. But his own wife or brother? That's pretty far-fetched." The toast popped from the toaster. Rachel nodded to them. "You need to hurry, these eggs won't take long. I like a lot of mayonnaise and just a little mustard, and you like mostly mustard and just a little mayonnaise. And you need to get the silverware."

Bryce sighed again.

"What was that for?"

"What?"

"The big sigh."

"Nothing."

"It must be for something."

"Well, I waited all afternoon to tell you about my trip into town, and all you do is interrupt me."

"I'm fixing dinner, Bryce," she said, turning to him. "Can't you see that? You want me to stop everything and let the eggs overcook so you can tell me your story? What do you want me to do?"

"It's just that—"

"Oh great, the eggs are overcooked already and next you'll complain about that too. I'll have to get two more, let me get in the refrigerator. . . ."

He moved aside while she opened the refrigerator door and removed two eggs. She scooped out the eggs from the skillet, dropped them down the disposal, broke the two fresh eggs into a bowl. "And now the ham is overcooked and the garlic is starting to burn."

Bryce finished spreading the toast with mayonnaise and mustard, and mustard and mayonnaise, dug the silverware from the drawer and headed into the dining room. Thinking, And now she's mad at me, I'm the one who ruined dinner, I'm the bad guy again. You can't win, Lord, no use even trying, hell, you should know that better than anybody, born to be hung out to dry on a cross. . . .

. . . and after a dinner that is spent mostly silent, watching the evening news on television, with only polite interchanges—"Did you get enough to eat?" "Do you want any help with the dishes?"—Bryce leaves Rachel as she redds the table and heads back down the hall to his pastoral study, and in just his shirt-sleeves and loosened tie, without bothering to get his raincoat or sport coat from the closet, a rashness he regrets the moment he steps out the office door into the cold night air, though he doesn't for a second consider going back inside to get one or the other or both, hunches his shoulders almost up to his ears and hustles down the walk between the manse and the hulking gray stone battlements of the church, the small spotlights sunk in the ground beside the walk to light the way creating shadow patterns among the thick bushes along the wall of the church, up the walls of the tower—for a brief second he sees someone standing in the dark bushes beside him, a figure that when Bryce wheels to confront

disappears again and becomes just another shadow and Bryce laughs to himself, Heh heh, uneasily, thinks Take it easy there, Brycey, like Rachel says, don't let your imagination get the better of you—as he hurries on, down the few steps and into the side door to the basement of the church, standing for a moment in the darkness until his eyes get used to it, then continues through a Sunday school room and up a stone spiral stairway and into the spaciousness of the nave of the church, moving in the dark along the communion rail past the elevated pulpit to the altar and up the central aisle through the curved waves of the pews—for a moment he thinks he hears something, someone moving in the shadows behind him near the altar but decides he's hearing things, there is nothing here, no one—continues through the dark church and out the double doors at the rear into the foyer and across to the stone stairway at the base of the tower and climbs to the second-floor choir loft, glancing down at the altar and pulpit, still wondering if he heard something there earlier—Spooks, right Lord? Some shiftless archangel with too much time on its hands, or maybe creepy ol' Death hanging around with his scythe, two red-rimmed beady eyes staring out from an empty hood, sorry, Old Timer, shake dem bones someplace else—unlocks a door that looks like just another wall panel that reveals another, narrower, steeper spiral stairwell, flicks on the light switch for a bare bulb halfway up, and continues up into the tower, the air definitely colder here with the unfinished walls, the interior face of the stone cold to the touch, ducking around the wood cross bracing, using the metal handrail at the top to help pull himself up into a sudden blaze of lights, the room at the top of the tower where at one time the bell ringers stood to pull the ropes dangling down for the rack of bells on the open floor above, the room his private refuge since he discovered it the first week he was assigned to the church a dozen years earlier, no one coming up here now since the bells had been replaced by an automated PA system, Bryce outfitting the room with an old area rug and an easy chair, a couple tables and bookcases, a stereo and his collection of jazz records—Art Blakey, Charlie Parker, Clifford Brown, nothing since Miles turned electric in the late sixties—the light of the brightly lit area from two poles of spotlights trained on the large ten-foot-diameter rose window that is the trademark of the church though when Bryce discovered the room he found the window completely blackened with soot and grime to the point of being totally colorless, a restoration project he took upon himself, spending evenings up here for the next year and a half scrubbing the stained glass with fingernail brushes and a mixture of baking soda and vinegar until the window was its true colorful self again, rigging up the light poles himself so at night the window shines now out of the bulk of the church sitting at the end of the dark street above the lights of Pets Aplenty and Wild Bill Januzzi's Cycle World and the other businesses along Berry Highway, a beacon to wandering souls to Bryce's way of thinking but then he knows he's prejudiced, turns on his space heater now and takes his old holey (and holy in its way, again to Bryce's way of thinking) cable knit cardigan from his armchair and sits down, in the reflected parti-colored glow of the window, at peace, the only time he is during his day, his time to reflect back over the happenings of his day, thinking Why does she do that, Lord, why does she interrupt me like that, I know she doesn't do it out of maliciousness, she's probably not even aware she's doing it, she's just anxious to tell me everything that pops into her head, but it certainly is effective in taking the air out of anything that interests me, that I want to tell her about, thinks Damn it, she's probably right, I do want to find the why about things, but what's so wrong about that, Lord, that's my job, isn't it, to ask the whys and get the answers too, thinking there are only two who mean anything to him in this entire world, God and Rachel, and neither one pays a whit of attention to him . . . while in her apartment one block above the main street of

Furnass, directly behind the abandoned construction site for the Furnass Towers project, the apartment her father gave her a few months before he died at the time he made her construction manager for the Furnass Landing project, Jennifer sits at the kitchen table, sitting on her leg folded under her as she's always done since she was a little girl, finishing off her beer from dinner, looking over the plans for Furnass Landing spread out in front of her, thinking about what she is going to do next on the project now that her father isn't around to subtly guide her in the direction he was thinking of in the first place, thinks about the visit she had at her mother's house today with Reverend Orr, the conversation they had about her father and the number of people in town who might want to see him dead, looks up from the plans and out the window beside the table, at the dark exposed framework, floors and columns and bracings, of the unfinished building across the alley and realizes, or rather lets herself accept what she knew before but never really wanted to think about before, that the reason her father gave her this apartment wasn't because he knew with her promotion at the project she was going to be putting in longer hours and would want to be closer to her job, or wasn't necessary because of that, it was as much or more that the apartment had become available because her father had moved his girlfriend, Pamela DiCello, to a new apartment out in Seneca in preparation for the time that he would leave his wife and set up housekeeping with Pamela, probably marry Pamela if his wife and Jennifer's mother would grant him a divorce and if not would move in with Pamela permanently regardless, unfolds her leg from beneath her and gets up and takes her empty glass to the sink, washes it and puts it on the drainboard with her other dinner dishes as she gets ready to leave the apartment, the thoughts of her father bringing tears to her eyes, not because the gift of the apartment is any less but in some way even more, it being in its way an expression or at least the result of the love that he *undoubtedly felt for Pamela, a love that seems irreparably sad to Jennifer because it was cut short, was never allowed to blossom and flower and in any way bring forth fruit, and thinks Oh Dad, I'm so sorry, I wanted you so much to be happy no matter what anybody thought of you, thinks The world and time cut him down before he had the thing he wanted most, love, thinks I wonder what it is that I want most . . . in the house in the suburb known as Highland Hills, in the house that, since the time it was built a dozen years earlier, is known as the Dickie Sutcliff House but now is hers alone, Tinker wanders through the showcase rooms, wondering if now or soon the house will become known as the Tinker Sutcliff House or will she always have to live under her husband's name even now when she no longer has a husband, as she makes a mental inventory of the things Jennifer must have taken today while she was gone, thinking that after all she can't be too upset with the girl, appreciating the irony that while Jennifer was making her foray into her parents' home Tinker was making her own foray into her husband's business, noting the missing items—the photograph on the mantel over the fireplace of Jennifer in her softball uniform standing with her father after her school won the regional championship; the collection of old forty-five rpm records that Dickie kept from the time when he was in a high school doowop group called the Exceptionals; the books missing from the shelves that Dickie used to keep close even if he didn't read them anymore, Tinker in noting their absence marveling all over again that Dickie had ever read them in the first place—*Ethics *by Spinoza, *Moby Dick, The Stranger—thinks that she should probably start putting up the decorations for Christmas, smiles to herself as she realizes she can put up the tree in the corner of the living room where she always wanted it rather than in the entrance hall where Dickie always wanted it and got his way, as he got his way with everything else, but the smile is short-lived as she realizes the victory is short-lived, thinks that the victory over Dickie is* *meaningless if Dickie isn't there to share it with or at least throw in his face, thinks for the first time since she received the phone call that night that Dickie had fallen in his office and that she should get to the hospital right away how much she's going to miss the bastard, of all things, thinks that the first thing tomorrow she better have the locks changed to keep Jennifer from coming back and making off with more of her own meager store of memories . . . in the other house in the area known as the Sutcliff House, this the big house with the tower on the edge of Orchard Hill that overlooks the town of Furnass, Harry Todd stands in the darkness of the room on the second floor that used to be his father and mother's bedroom, and then just his mother's bedroom, the tower room on this floor of the house, though the room is devoid of most of its furniture now, Harry Todd having already dismantled the bed and removed the nightstand and chairs and drapes and wooden blinds and knickknacks from the mantelpiece and shelves and anything else he could wrangle down the stairs and out into the yard to burn in the spot he's designated as the final resting place for all things Sutcliff, or at least all things Sutcliff that he can drag out there to erase from the world once and for all, leaving only the dresser and the built-in closet to go through, looks across the room at the bare black tower windows, only a sprinkling of lights visible from where he's standing of the town below sloping to the river, and thinks at one time the room would have been alive at this time of night with orange and yellow light, shadows dancing on the walls, from the furnaces at the mill, the night skies beyond the windows alive with smoke and steam reflecting back the orange-and-yellow glow, the explosion of light when the Bessemer Converters rolled in their berths, but that was then, this is now, turns on the two shadeless floor lamps he's brought from downstairs and floods the room with harsh light, the blackness outside in the tower windows replaced with multiple reflected images of himself, the variations determined only by the various angles of the inset windows in the curve of the tower, repeated images of a stocky, fifty-plus blond-haired man in an old T-shirt, like studies of an aging California surfer boy gone to seed though in his twenty-five years of living in California he never once surfed, confronts these multiple images of himself as he thinks about Bryce Orr's visit today and why he was asking all those questions about Dickie and wills and autopsies, thinking I wonder if he found out something talking to Tinker, I wonder how much the nosy bastard really knows, and he said he talked to Jennifer too, she could certainly give him an earful about her uncle if she was so inclined, why did I ever come back here, what did I think I would find or accomplish here, but I guess I know the answer to that one too, is pulled from his thoughts by what sounds like the old wood of the house settling but could just as easily be taken for someone moving in another part of the house, the all too familiar sounds like a dead sister making her way through these memory-sodden rooms, and Harry Todd thinks No, I'm not going to go there, I've got enough pain in my life, thinks of Dickie, remembers what he told Bryce and didn't tell Bryce about his brother's disdain for him and his abilities and wonders if his son-of-a-bitch brother was right about that too, that Harry Todd isn't much good at anything, thinks Help me, help me know what to do, to no one in particular . . . in his studio on the main street of Furnass, now that his last student has left for the evening, the kids and teenagers who have seen too many martial arts movies and want to be able to pound something or rather someone into oblivion and the middle-aged men, the overweight salesmen and unemployed millworkers and out-of-shape office workers who have glimpsed that they're eventually going to die and are frantic for something to help them feel less afraid of the world and the housewives who want to be able to protect themselves from the molesters and rapists of their dreams, Kim stands before the wall of mirrors, a figure all in black, his long black hair tied up into a knot, regarding himself at rest as a ballet dancer might before the start of solo exercises except that he is poised in the horse stance, feet spread in line with his shoulders and pointed straight ahead, his weight perfectly balanced on the balls of his feet, his knees slightly flexed and his hands overlapped in front of his groin so that he resembles a rider mounted on the back of an animal, then begins slowly, very slowly, to work his way through the deadly forms of his art, as if, after watching his students earlier this evening mutilate these centuries-old forms, he must perform them now correctly to reaffirm their sacredness and beauty and deadliness, performing them with exquisite and infinite grace, at times barely moving at all, fluid, then after completing all the linked postures of the form, performing them again with lightning speed, his hands and feet moving at times faster than the eye can see, than judges in competitions can keep track of—at the last tournament where he appeared several years ago, when an opponent, at the direction of the sensei of a rival dojo, tried with a kick to explode Kim's knee, Kim released a barrage of blows that had the young man's head snapping back and forth on his neck like a punching bag, which put the young man in the hospital with brain damage and got Kim barred from competitions forever; each month now Kim of his own volition and sense of justice sends a check to the young man's parents to help with the medical bills; a month after the incident, also from his sense of justice, when he had learned all he needed to know about why it had happened, Kim appeared at the rival dojo in Youngstown one evening when he knew the man's best students would be present and in front of the school proceeded to defeat the sensei in less than a minute and a half, permanently crippling him by executing correctly the strike to the knee that the man had directed his student to do to Kim; each month now Kim pointedly does not send a check to help with the sensei's ongoing rehabilitation and resists the temptation to send him an invoice not only for his time to teach his students a lesson but for the mileage to drive there, figuring undoubtedly correctly that the guy wouldn't get the humor though in fact the man's best students now travel every week from Youngstown to Kim's studio for special classes—a majestic dance to death, then draws himself up at the completion of the set of forms and is calm again, at total peace with himself and with his world, bows to his image in the mirror and touches his prayerful hands to his forehead, releases his long black hair from the knot at the back of his head before turning out the lights and crossing the empty studio in total darkness and without bothering with anything more despite the fact that it is below freezing outside puts on the black satin jacket he always wears over his black sleeveless T-shirt and leaves by the back door of the building, padding softly, cat-like in his black cloth shoes down the fire escape, the building on the downslope side of the street so that the first floor at the front of the building becomes the second floor when viewed from the rear, and makes his way along the dark alley, on a mission, a shadow among shadows . . . and in his home in Furnass Heights, the middle- and upper-middle-class residential district that stretches along the crest of the valley's hills above Furnass—not on the slope or even close to the edge where the inhabitants might enjoy dramatic views of the valley below, the peculiar predilection of well-to-do or at least better-off people in the area to avoid view properties along the crest that in other parts of the country would be prime real estate, leaving them instead to the working classes building from the bottom up—Julian stands in his bedroom before his wife's full-length mirror, himself performing some of the martial arts forms Kim has taught him, thinking What did Don Sheetz mean, my little horse stance, I'm doing it correctly, I could protect myself if I had to but with none of the grace or care or beauty of his teacher, Julian lacking the inherent physical ability necessary to ever perform the movements at anything more than a rudimentary level, though he nonetheless appreciates the precision of the art and the deadly mastery of the younger man he proudly calls his friend, tries to do a particularly demanding combination to turn aside an opponent's blow followed by his own elbow strike but loses his balance and nearly topples over and gives up, laughing at himself as he goes into the bathroom to brush his teeth, thinking about the phone call he made to Kim earlier this evening when he told him the result of his talks with Sheryl and Sheetz, told Kim about Sheetz's reluctance to tell him where Stratton lives and wonders as he stands over the sink brushing his teeth—fifteen, sixteen, seventeen—if he did the right thing telling Kim about that, aware as always of the danger associated with Kim and his capacity for violence, particularly when it comes to anything that might threaten those Kim feels protective of, thinking also about when Sheetz said, "At least a guy like Stratton makes no bones about what he's done, I've heard all about the fancy little schemes you and Dickie Sutcliff were involved in, don't you worry," and Julian's first concern was that he was referring to something Kim told Sheetz about Julian's relationship to Dickie and his mortgages—thirty-one, thirty-two, thirty-three—the time Julian told Kim that Dickie owned him, a choice of words he regrets now because they made the relationship between Julian and Dickie seem worse than it was, bad enough perhaps to send Kim off to kill Dickie if Kim thought Julian was threatened, because from what he's learned of Kim and the way Kim thinks in the time Julian has known him Kim is certainly capable of doing such a thing to protect Julian in Kim's code of honor and respect and payback for someone who represented him in court and kept him out of jail, and Julian looks in the mirror above the sink at the stringy, gray-haired, gray-bearded, rather unimposing fellow in his pajamas brushing his teeth across from him—forty-eight, forty-nine, fifty—spits out the mouthful of toothpaste and sucks clean water from his toothbrush before leaning close to the mirror*

*and smiles knowingly at his image and thinks Sheetz doesn't know
who he's dealing with, I can be dangerous too. . . .*

10

Don Sheetz two-fingered the last entry in the computer spread-
sheet, saved it, and closed down the machine for the night. It was
close to eleven o'clock. He rubbed his eyes with the palms of his
hands until his eyelids hurt. Got up wearily from his cluttered
desk, stretched, yawned. He wondered if he had enough energy
left to stop for a beer at the Triangle Tavern; he decided he
didn't, he better just go home. Five-thirty in the morning came
awfully early these days. He left a note for Marie, the bookkeeper,
when she came in in the morning, turned off the lights in the
office, and went down the wood stairs from his office into the
shop.

His last worker had left a couple of hours earlier. He realized
he still had on the blue bandana he wore under his hardhat or
welding hood to protect his shaved head while he worked; he took
it off and idly rubbed his head as he wandered through the empty
shop. The business was a lot of work, but he was still proud of
what he'd made out of it. Buchanan Steel might have shut down,
but his little shop was holding its own. And he didn't have to
answer to anyone—bosses, that is—didn't have to kiss some fore-
man's ass to keep his job. He did quality work, he had enough
orders that he could turn away most of the troublesome clients,
the long hours were worth it for the feeling of being his own man.
He lit a cigarette and twirled the bandana on the end of his finger
a couple of times as he headed for the switch box and turned off
the banks of overhead lights.

Something moved in the darkness between the racks of angle
stock. Sheetz froze, ready. A soft laugh came from the shadows;
then Kim stepped closer to the circle of light from one of the few
bare bulbs left burning in the shop.

"Not bad," Kim said, referring to the fighting posture Sheetz had taken. Crouched slightly, at an angle, with his left hand in front of him like a claw, his right hand clenched in front of his crotch, both ready as much as protection as to strike. "Probably be a little more threatening without the rag in your hand. And the cigarette."

"Shit," Sheetz said, straightening up. He stuffed the bandana in his rear pocket, took the cigarette from his mouth and flipped it away. "What are you doing, going around scaring people like that?"

"Not bad, though, for someone as out of practice as you are. And out of shape. Of course, if I was serious, you'd be dead."

"We'd have to see about that," Sheetz said. But he knew Kim was right. "Come on up to the office. I've got some Jack Daniel's for emergencies."

"Not tonight," Kim said. He took a few more steps into the circle of light, moving silently in the soft black shoes, looking around the shop. Then looked at Sheetz. "You had a visitor today."

"I had a number of visitors today, you count all the deliveries. Which one you referring to?"

"Julian Lyle."

"Oh. Yeah." Sheetz pulled a face, spit on the oil-soaked floor.

"You don't like Lyle, do you?"

"I told you before. I think he's a phony. He's like a groupie. I think he hangs around you because it gives him a kick, gives him a thrill. Like a kind of slumming. Ah, I don't know. Maybe I just don't like his type." Sheetz spit again.

"Slumming," Kim repeated. He thought of something for a moment, then said, "You may be right."

Sheetz looked at Kim and noted a touch of sadness cross his face. He was about to ask him why he wanted to know about Lyle when Kim continued.

"He asked you about a guy named Stratton."

"Yeah, he wanted to know where Stratton lives and if I knew if he was hanging around any young cunt." It hit him like a blow to the stomach. "Jesus, Kim. Did he mean Cory? Ah, Jesus, I never thought. . . ."

"It's possible," Kim said. Looking away again. "She's been gone a few days now, and I guess the last person she was seen with was Stratton. Lyle doesn't want me to get involved because he's afraid it might affect the outcome of the custody hearing but. . . ."

"You don't worry about it, Kim. I'll find Stratton. I'll find out if he's with Cory, and if he is I'll take care of him."

"No," Kim said sharply, his eyes narrowing, focused. Then he caught himself. "No, not you. Thank you, but he's not for you. If you find out where Stratton is, just call Lyle at his office and tell him."

"I know Stratton's got a place out at Indian Camp, an old cabin or something. And I think there's someplace he stays at here in town when he doesn't want to make the drive but I'm not sure where. I didn't tell Lyle because—"

"I understand. It doesn't matter. Just let Lyle know the first thing tomorrow. I'll let him take care of it for now. Later, there will be time to see Stratton. If that's where Cory is."

"Whatever you say. But keep in mind, if you need any help. . . ."

Kim smiled slightly. "I appreciate it. But I won't need any help."

"No, probably not," Sheetz said. He picked up a tab of scrap metal from the floor and tossed it in the waste bin. "He also got real touchy when I mentioned you told me about the dealings between him and Dickie Sutcliff."

"How did that come up?"

Sheetz shrugged. "I don't know. Sutcliff just died, didn't he?"

"Yeah. Over the weekend. Fell and hit his head."

"Lyle seemed uneasy about something when I mentioned him. Like he was defensive about something. Maybe he thinks you had something to do with it," Sheetz said and grinned at the absurdity.

Kim thought a moment and turned to leave, back into the shadows again, then stopped and looked at Sheetz. "You were always a good friend."

Sheetz shrugged, uncomfortable, not knowing what to say.

"We go back a long way," Kim said. "Back to that time you helped me in junior high."

"The only reason I helped you then was that I figured you'd grow up and be able to whip my ass forty ways to Sunday."

The two grinned at each other. Before Kim left, Sheetz added, "And the stuff you taught me, Sifu, saved my life in 'Nam. A couple of times."

"I wish we had been there together," Kim said, thinking of something. "Maybe it would have made it easier."

"We were, one way you think about it. But nothing would have made it easier."

"No, I guess you're right," Kim said. They looked at each other a moment, understanding something between them, nodding slightly; then Kim disappeared again into the shadows of the shop.

Sheetz looked at the spot where Kim had been standing a few seconds earlier. Thinking, Like some goddamned ghost. A haunted man. Poor Stratton. If he's with Cory, I better start looking for another welder. And I've got to get a better lock on that side door. . . .

PART TWO

11

"So. What brings you to town?" Julian looked at Bryce, his fingertips pressed together in front of his mouth like a small cage, swiveled in his tall-backed leather chair thirty-three degrees to the left, sixty-six degrees to the right, and back to neutral. "To what do we owe this august pleasure? What auspicious occasion has precipitated our good fortune?"

Bryce resisted the temptation to say what he was thinking: Julian, you always were full of so much shit. "August. Isn't that Pappy's first name?"

"August. Augustus. It's also my middle name. What made you think of that?"

"You're the one who said 'august.' "

Julian flexed his fingers, and thought of the joke when they were kids, a sideways version of a spider on a mirror doing push-ups. "My father is Augustus the Second, to be exact. Though most people in town knew him as Mal."

"And on Orchard Hill we called him Pappy."

Julian closed his eyes. "That was the family name for him. And us kids."

"Ol' Pappy. Too much." Listening to Julian spout off about his family's high-faluting names brought out his hipster lingo. "Far out. Was there an Augustus the First?"

"His father." By way of explanation, Julian nodded to a large painting on the wall of his office.

"They sound like Roman emperors or something." Bryce, always restless, was up out of his chair and across the room to take a look at it. "Groovy. But I guess your family was always into that kind of stuff, weren't they? Why else would you name a poor kid something like Augustus the Second? Why not just Junior? 'Hey, Junior!' Instead of, 'Hey, The Second!' You know?"

Julian shrugged, ignored Bryce's attempts at humor at his family's expense.

It was more of a colored drawing or illustration than a painting, a schematic of the Keystone Steam Works at the turn of the twentieth century, a view as if seen from the air, from over the river, the cluster of reddish-orange brick buildings with their distinctive sawtoothed clerestory windows along the roofs, the buildings of Buchanan Steel beside it on the riverbank, behind the mills the town of Furnass climbing the slope of the tree-covered valley. It was during the heyday of the plant, when the Keystone Works rivaled Buchanan Steel as the largest employer in town; around the edge of the painting was a border of medallions, inset drawings of manufacturing processes going on in the plant—the stamping mill, the mammoth forge, the annealing furnaces—as well as scenes of various Keystone Steamers at work in the field— a mobile well driller, a steam shovel, a steam tractor—scenes of the supposed genteel fin de siècle life of Furnass, ladies with parasols and men in top hats promenading under fashionably spindly trees along the sidewalks in front of the plant.

"I remember this picture," Bryce said, examining the scenes one by one. "It used to hang in Ol' Pappy's study."

"Before that it hung in the office of the Keystone Steam Works. In fact I have a lot of things here that were part of that office. Those barrister bookcases. This desk and chair."

"And it all went down."

"That's one way to put it. Yes, it all went down." Julian studied his arrangement of fingertips in front of his face, touched the sides of his index fingers to his lips. "Eventually Buchanan Steel took over the buildings when Keystone went out of business. And now Buchanan is out of business as well. Things change."

Bryce retook his seat in the molded wood chair in front of the desk. "Ol' Pappy. He was a righteous cat. The way he used to back you up against a wall and make you stand at attention until you learned to recite poetry."

Julian closed his eyes and intoned:

"Tell me not, in mournful numbers,
Life is but an empty dream!
For the soul is dead that slumbers,
And things are not what they seem.

Life is real! Life is earnest!
And the grave is not its goal;
Dust thou are, to dust returnest,
Was not spoken of the soul.

"Etcetera, etcetera, ad infinitum. Yes, I remember very well. And I remember he did the same to you until you learned to read."

"You're right. I had that lazy-eye thing. I used to think I was stupid in school because I couldn't read like everybody else. But Ol' Pappy would put me up against that wall and drilled me until both eyes learned to work together. Fascinating rhythm, when you think about it. Him taking the time to do that. I guess I owe everything to him. He got me reading, and that got me interested in books and that led to philosophy and then theology, and here I am today. Copacetic."

"I'm not sure his teaching you to read was a blessing or a curse. For the rest of us, I mean." Julian smiled, raised his eyebrows, trying for clever.

"Ah Julian. Always the funnyman."

Julian's cage of fingers became a double-hammered gun that he sighted down his fingers at Bryce. "You still haven't told me what brings you to town today. The only time we see you, it seems, is when there's some sort of problem or tragedy. Something that you think I need to be counseled about."

"It's an occupational hazard of being a minister. I'm sort of a dial-a-tragedy service. But I did want to thank you again for asking me to conduct the service the other day for the Dickie-Bird. Even if it was a kind of *Beat the Clock* type of funeral."

"And I thank you for doing it on such short notice. I thought your officiating was the appropriate thing to do, with our background and all."

Bryce snuffled his sinuses.

"And Tinker wanted to keep it as short as possible. No sense dwelling on the past, if you know what I mean."

"The dead and the quick, as it were."

Julian wagged his head.

"It seems like everything after Dickie died was speeded up."

"How do you mean?"

"All that rush-rush at the funeral home. Dickie died on Friday night, might as well have been Saturday, and then the burial on Monday. And no viewing. The Dickie-Bird was no sooner dead than we were sticking him in the ground. And there doesn't seem to be much of an investigation into the circumstances of how he died either."

"Why would there be an investigation at all?"

"I don't know. It just seems a little odd, don't you think? A guy in good health, in the prime of life, supposedly falls and hits his head on the edge of his desk, all alone, late at night, and it kills him. Doesn't that sound suspicious to you?"

"Not particularly. That's apparently what happened."

"My point exactly. 'Apparently' being the operative word. We don't really know, do we? From what I heard, I'm not sure there was even an autopsy. Do you know if they did one?"

"Who were you talking to about an autopsy?"

Bryce shifted in the chair; the molded wood looked official and lawyerly but it was certainly uncomfortable on his tailbone. I wonder if they do that on purpose. Make 'em squirm when they talk to attorneys. "Well, there was Jennifer and Tinker, and Harry Todd—"

"Bryce." Julian sounded distressed. "What are you doing, going around asking people about an autopsy on Dickie? What business is it of yours? These people have just lost a loved one—"

"Not the way I hear it. Okay, maybe Jennifer, she seems to have genuinely cared about her father. But I sure can't say that about Tinker or Harry Todd, not after talking to them."

"When were you talking to them?"

"Yesterday."

"Bryce. . . ."

"I went to offer my condolences, but I have to say that neither one sounded all that sad to see Dickie dead and gone. And nobody seemed to care whether there was an autopsy or not."

"If there was no autopsy it was because there was no need for one. There was a dent in Dickie's skull, to put it crudely, an open wound. It was very obvious what happened."

"But did he fall or trip? Was he sick? Drunk?"

"Bryce. . . ."

"Did you actually see the wound?"

"Yes. Well, no. But both Howard Griffith and Perry Sykes said—"

"Perry Sykes, Furnass' illustrious chief of police? In high school Perry Sykes was a pimply blob who couldn't tell that a stoplight was red unless somebody told him."

"Not very charitable there, Pastor."

"You know it's true."

"As I was saying, both men handled the body and made the determination that—"

"So there was no autopsy."

"I didn't say that. I don't know if there was one or not, to be quite honest. I do know a death certificate was issued—"

"Epidural hematoma."

Julian just looked at him for a moment. "Yes. The result of blunt-force trauma. I think that's the end of the story. Or it should be, as far as you're concerned."

"But—"

"I think you should really stop and consider what you're doing. Particularly when it comes to Tinker. She may not demonstrate a sufficient amount of grief to your high standards, but the woman has just lost her husband. And you're going around dredging up all sorts of unpleasantries and making all sorts of insinuations. You're acting like this is some sort of game put on for your benefit, and it's not. It's real, it's real life with real people and real feelings. If you can't respect that, you should. Being a minister doesn't give you a free pass on reality."

"And you're sitting here making all these determinations like you're an important person in this town and you're not. You're a small-time lawyer with a few clients and list of failed projects. . . ." Bryce caught himself: Oh man, did I just say that? I can't believe I did that. "Look, I didn't mean. . . ."

"Yes, you probably did." Julian got up from his desk and walked to the door. "And it's probably better to get it out in the open, seeing as how that's the way you feel. I hope you will at least consider what I said about Tinker. On your supposed list of suspects, I would say she's the least culpable. But then what do I know, right Bryce?" He opened the door and stood beside it as Bryce got up and shrugged at Julian as he passed—You know me—and heard the door definitely click behind him.

12

Oh man, I should never have said those things to ol' Julian. Even if they are true. All right to think them, just don't say them out loud. Sorry, Lord. Not charitable. But the guy drives me nuts. All that superiority crap. Just because of his family, and the truth is his family was a mess. And he said he didn't know if there was an autopsy or not. I wonder what he does know. He sure did get protective there for a bit, defensive to say the least. Funny, when he gets upset the veins stick out on his forehead, always did, those times playing basketball in the alley and Sonny Rourke would outjump him every time. Julian would try to make his case and talk it to death until we all fell down laughing and the veins would stick out on his forehead and that made us laugh harder. Ol' Julian. And he was sure protective of Tinker, he certainly slanted it to imply that if anything suspicious went on it had to involve Harry Todd, not Tinker. I wonder what Julian knows that he's not telling. I wonder if he's hiding something. . . .

Bryce decided that, seeing as how he got nowhere talking to other people, he should go directly to the source. When he stopped for diesel fuel at a station off 79 North, he called Shirley at the church office who, after making several calls of her own, called him back with an address for a P. DiCello on Whippoorwill Drive in Seneca. Whippoorwill Drive turned out to be a private road circling the Senecan, a townhouse community close by the Seneca Towne Centre that sported a billboard near the entrance that read:

ANOTHER SUTCLIFF REALTY DEVELOPMENT
FOR LEASING INFORMATION CALL . . .

He recognized the midnight blue Corvette parked in the space marked 204. Bryce parked in a visitor space and shuffled across the artificial hillocks on the lawn.

Pamela answered the door in a baggy sweatshirt and cargo pants, her thick black hair unbrushed, unruly about her head. She looked drawn, not as if she had been crying exactly, but as if she hadn't slept much lately. Or maybe too much.

"Hello, Pam—, Miss DiCello, my name is Reverend Orr, I hope I'm not disturbing you, I was a friend of Dickie Sutcliff's, maybe you remember me from the funeral. . . ."

"Rachel's husband."

"Yes, well, that's one distinction, isn't it? Always a bit strange when a husband is known by his wife's associations but I guess that's the way of the world these days, isn't it?" He knew he was rambling; he coughed, trying to get his thoughts together. Even disheveled she was strikingly beautiful, olive skin that appeared hopelessly soft, large brown eyes that seemed to drink him in. He was in love.

"How can I help you, Reverend?"

"Is this a bad time?"

"There's probably no good time."

"No, I suppose there isn't. You know, you saying that, I just realized that I didn't come out here to see you to offer you comfort or anything. I came to see you to help comfort me. Isn't that crazy?" Thinking, She's another one, looking at me like I'm an idiot. I get that look a lot. "Could I speak to you for a few minutes? I guess I'm still trying to make sense of Dickie's death."

"There is no sense to Dickie's death." But she stood aside to let him inside.

The place felt as if she was still moving in, not quite settled. In the living room was a large taupe-colored sofa, a matching overstuffed chair and ottoman, a stand with a television set, and little else; taking up the other end of the room, in view of the television, was a large exercise ball, the kind you could sit or roll on, and a yoga mat. The dining room was empty, only an open area on the way to the kitchen. Of course, Bryce thought, she was waiting for Dickie to move in, to see the furniture he wanted, so they could get their furniture together. A wave of sadness washed over him, caught him in its undertow and dragged him under: for the first time the full impact struck him that Dickie

Sutcliff was truly dead. Gone. Forever. I'm supposed to be taking comfort in thoughts of the afterlife about now, aren't I Lord? Why don't I? He looked around, helpless. Pamela motioned him to sit on the sofa and he obeyed, momentarily unable to think.

"You were a friend of Dickie's," she said, sitting cross-legged on the ottoman. "I wasn't aware of that."

"We grew up together on Orchard Hill." He didn't know whether to remove his raincoat or not. He decided to keep it on, rubbing his hands together as if to show he was still chilled. "There were a bunch of us. . . ."

She nodded. "I've heard some of the stories. I guess Julian Lyle was part of your group too."

"So, Dickie talked about ol' Julian and not me," Bryce said, trying to make a joke. "I don't know whether to take that as a compliment or an oversight."

"I'd take it as a compliment. I don't want to say anything bad about a friend of yours, but Dickie wasn't very . . . complimentary about Julian."

"I'm sure he never said anything that I haven't said myself at some time or other. Julian and I grew up together, but I wouldn't call us friends now. For that matter, Dickie and I certainly knew each other back then, but I have to admit we were never that close either. You know how you are when you grow up in the same neighborhood. . . ."

Pamela thought a moment, tried to set her thick hair with a flick of her head. "I don't think Dickie thought much of Julian's . . . abilities."

"I'm told he thought he was Dickie's attorney."

"Not hardly." Pamela smiled sadly. "Not for the important things anyway. As I understand it, they were involved in a few business deals, but I think it was more of Dickie cleaning up something that Julian got himself into."

"That sounds like the Julian I know," Bryce said.

"A lot of people would say that Dickie took advantage of Julian's bad situations. But you know Dickie: if an opportunity presented itself, he would take advantage of it." She smiled a bit wistfully. "With everything he had."

"And that sounds like the Dickie I know. Knew," Bryce said, leaning forward, thinking, That's the way I want to be. Going after everything I do with everything I have. "I'm sorry to be blunt about this, but there's something I want to ask you. I heard you think somebody murdered Dickie. Why do you think that?"

"Where did you hear that?" Pamela looked at him, then softened a little. "Oh, of course. Rachel. I'm sure what I said must have traveled around the hospital."

"Please don't say anything to her. If she finds out I told you, or that I even talked to you about this. . . ."

Pamela shook her head, closed her eyes, then looked at him again. Bryce thought, For eyes like those, for a look of love from eyes like those, I would cross a desert.

"Don't worry, I won't say anything to her. I can imagine that Rachel can be rather formidable to be married to. No disrespect intended. At the hospital she's a formidable presence, and respected for it."

Bryce wagged his head. Don't say a word, just leave it. You already sold out your friend. . . .

"And it's my own fault for saying it about Dickie. I should learn to keep my mouth shut." Bryce smiled, sympathetically. Thinking, Welcome to the club. Nice to know pretty girls have the same problems as ordinary guys. Even ordinary-looking middle-aged guys. . . . "So, you no longer think somebody might have killed Dickie?"

"I didn't say that." Pamela fixed him with those same brown eyes. "I'm sure somebody did. I should just learn not to talk about it, seeing as how nobody seems to want to find out who it was, or even admit that it's true."

"But what makes you think so?"

She unwound her legs, sat with her feet on the floor. "Do you know how Dickie died?"

"They said he fell and hit his head. . . ."

"There was a dent in his skull, an open wound, the edge of the desk punctured his skull. Do you have any idea how much force it would take to create a wound like that? And you're telling me that it came from a simple fall?" She shook her head.

"It wasn't me who said it," Bryce said, opening his palms in front of him to show there was nothing there. "It's just what I heard. . . ."

"Well, I don't believe it. I don't believe he was clumsy enough to fall like that, not with that kind of force. Someone either slammed his head into the edge of the desk, or slammed him and down he went. But nobody wants to consider that. And they buried him as quickly as they could so nobody would. Of course, I didn't have the authority or the rights to delay the proceedings. . . ."

"I'm sorry," Bryce said, wanting to reach out and touch her. And not daring to. "I thought it strange too, that they buried him so quickly. I asked about an autopsy but nobody seems to know if there was one or not. It's beginning to sound like there wasn't."

She looked at him as if to say, Of course not. What would you expect?

"Was that Tinker's doing? That everything happened so quickly?"

"It could be. I'm not really sure what the legalities are. Dickie had served her with papers for a divorce; would she still be the next of kin? I don't know, I guess so. If it wasn't her, then it would have been Harry Todd. Or even the two of them."

"What about Harry Todd? I didn't know there was so much bad blood between the brothers. Harry Todd said that Dickie was going to bounce him out of the Big House to make a point, I guess to show that he had the means to do it."

Pamela shook her head, smiled sadly. "I know that he said that to Harry Todd, but he wasn't actually going to do it. He was only trying to shake Harry Todd up, to get him focused on his work. Dickie wanted him to think about what he'd do if he lost the house so he'd appreciate what he had. He wanted Harry Todd to keep on living in the house."

"Harry Todd thinks Dickie hated him. He thinks Dickie thought he was a total waste of time."

"Dickie would have supported Harry Todd if for no other reason than it was so important to their mother. If Kitty loved him, that was enough for Dickie. But I know for a fact Dickie was committed to taking care of Harry Todd regardless how his work with Sutcliff Realty worked out. He told me he was setting up a trust fund that would cover the expenses of living in the house as well as provide an income, if it came to that. He wasn't going to see his brother out on the street."

"Really? I'm pretty sure all that would be a surprise to Harry Todd. He also said that when he came back here he never had any intention of going into the business, but that he's thinking now of trying to get control of it, depending on what Dickie's will says, so he can sell it for the money. Maybe even sell it to Tinker, if she wants it that badly."

"Oh, I'm sure she wants it that badly. Tinker." Pamela thought of something, then shook her head sharply again, her hair resettling along her shoulders. Bryce thought, It's not that feminine thing, the flicking of the hair that women do to make sure they look good, it's like a reflex, involuntary, to try to clear her head, to dodge or drive away something she doesn't want to think about or can't.

"As for Harry Todd's intentions," Pamela was saying, "Dickie was afraid that Harry Todd wouldn't do well in the business. No, the troubles between the brothers went back further than Harry Todd's coming back to Furnass, maybe as far back as their sister Kathleen. Or maybe as recent as Jennifer."

"Dickie's daughter Jennifer? Don't tell me Harry Todd. . . ."

"I don't know the whole story. But I do know that when Harry Todd first came back to town, Dickie wasn't concerned so much with Harry Todd's possible involvement with the business as he was with Harry Todd's possible involvement with Jennifer. It seems that Dickie knew his brother very well. He probably also knew Jennifer very well."

He almost said something about the sexual reputation of Sutcliff males in town, starting with their father, but caught himself in time. His mind was, if not reeling, at least spinning a bit; the sexual references, as meager as they were, in his overactive imagination were getting to him. Harry Todd and Jennifer? Dickie and Pamela. All this stuff going on and it's like I'm on a different planet. Dickie was my age, here's an attractive, no, beautiful younger woman who was attracted to him, not only attracted but they were lovers, they made love, they climbed into bed together and . . . It's not out of the question that a beautiful young woman might—no, I can't even start to think like that, it's never going to happen, never, that's gone forever too. . . .

He stood up abruptly, taking both him and Pamela by surprise. He dug his hands into his raincoat pockets. "I should be going. Really. Thank you for your time."

"I don't know if I said anything to help." Pamela stood up, much too close for Bryce's comfort level. Before he could move away, she stepped closer and gave him a brief hug—his chin was in her thick hair, the animal smell of it and the sweetness of herbs and shampoo—he didn't have the chance to even remove his hands from his pockets; then she turned and led the way toward the front door. Afraid he was getting an erection—No, Lord, please not now, why now, no, please—he kept his hands in his pockets, wrapped the raincoat tighter about himself.

"I'll let you know if I turn up anything," he said at the door.

Pamela smiled. "And I won't mention to Rachel that we were talking."

"Good. Wouldn't want her to get the wrong idea. Heh heh."

"Or the right one. Good-bye, Reverend."

13

"Your guy Stratton has a place out at Indian Camp," Sheetz said on the phone. "It's a cabin of some sort, I've never been out there. The address is 112 Indian Camp Road. I'm told it's near the intersection with County Road 47."

Julian hurried to get it all scribbled down on the first piece of paper he could get his hands on, the back of the envelope for an Equitable Gas bill, the receiver tucked under his chin. "Hold on. County Road 47?"

"Yeah. Forty-seven. Other than that I don't know a thing about the place."

"That's quite a lot," Julian said, taking the receiver in hand again. "Seeing as how when we talked last evening you couldn't remember anything about it."

"Yeah, well, like I said, I started thinking."

Julian didn't want to push him too far on it; at least he got this much information. Wonder why this morning he can suddenly remember. Wonder what made him change his mind.

"Regardless, I really appreciate your help. And I'm assuming that you haven't heard anything from him, or who might be with him."

"Nope."

"I also don't suppose you happened to remember about his place here in town, where it is?"

"I never knew anything about that, Stratton was always careful not to talk about that. I wouldn't know about his Indian Camp place except one time he asked me to have one of my guys deliver his check to him, after he was off a couple weeks when he got hurt."

And last night he said Stratton always picked up his check. Something really gave Sheetz a change of heart. Wonder what else he knows and isn't telling me? "Well, I really appreciate your help, Don. Please let me know if you happen to remember anything else."

"Yeah. Sure."

"And would you do me one other favor? Please don't mention our conversation or give Stratton's address to Kim."

There was silence on the phone. Julian went on. "The reason I say that is Kim is very concerned about Cory and her well-being, you can understand, and I wouldn't want him to overreact and do something that . . . er, he might regret later. You know Kim." He tried to mitigate it with a little laugh.

"Yes," Sheetz said after a moment. "I know Kim. You take care, Lyle."

Julian hung up the phone and looked at his notes on the back of the envelope. He supposed now he'd have to take a drive out there, to see if Stratton—and possibly Cory—was there. It was certainly safer for Stratton if he went, and not Kim; he'd have to be careful not to tell Kim about the location of Stratton's place. He was worried about Kim. Worried about what his friend was capable of. Julian knew, if anyone in town did, the violence that lay beneath the surface of the man; it was one of the things that interested Julian about Kim in the first place, when he first agreed to represent him in the murder charge for the fight with his father. As he got to know Kim better, over the months of the trial and then later, as Kim gradually began to trust him in some measure, Julian learned how deep that violence was part of Kim's nature, how much Kim struggled to keep it in check—to live with what he had learned about his capability for violence while in Vietnam, to deal now with being known in town as "that Oriental-looking guy who killed his father."

Julian was proud to be seen with Kim, knowing that most people in town—with good reason, if the truth be known—were afraid of him; if anything the air of danger that surrounded Kim, the sense of violence right below the surface, only increased Julian's pleasure and pride in the friendship. A feeling, he sometimes thought, like walking around town with a wild animal on a leash. A cheetah or leopard.

But it wasn't Kim who was his main concern this morning. He was still thinking about Bryce's visit earlier—thinking, He said, You're sitting here like you think you're an important person in town, and you're not, you're just a two-bit lawyer with hardly any clients and a list of failed projects—and what Bryce might turn up with all his questions. All his sniffing around could only end badly. Why can't the guy leave well enough alone? Why does he always push push push, stirring up trouble for everyone else. He says he's a dial-a-tragedy service but the truth is he loves the tragedies, he loves to be involved in them, they make him feel special, like he is someone; if there isn't a problem or situation that he can minister to he invents one, he was always like that. Julian remembered Bryce said he talked to Tinker. He thought of going to see her but realized that if someone saw him at her shop it might raise a whole new set of questions. He picked up the receiver and dialed her number.

"Did you find the will?" Tinker said, after one of her shop girls called her to the phone.

"Hello to you too," he said, trying to be friendly.

"I know you didn't call because you missed me, Julian," she said. He could hear her take a drag on her cigarette—another reason why he was glad he didn't go see her in person. He thought, She must be the only florist whose bouquets smell like tobacco. "What's up? I'm very busy today."

"Bryce was here asking a lot of questions. He said he'd also been to see you."

"He stopped by Dickie's office yesterday while I was there. Said it was a pastoral visit to offer his condolences, but you know Bryce. Who knows what he really wanted. He may be a minister, but he still acts like the same doofus he did in high school. I never did understand how Rachel puts up with him."

"Not well, I suspect," Julian said. "What all did he ask you about?"

"How Dickie died. That he was sorry it happened. That sort of thing."

"Did he ask you whether there was an autopsy?"

"Yes, which I thought was strange." She took another long drag on a cigarette, blowing it out in a hiss. "I was rather blunt with him, told him in effect that he should mind his own business. I can only take so much of the guy."

Julian sat back from his desk, slouched in his chair, one leg crossed at the knee over the other, his free arm resting across the top of his head as if expecting the ceiling to fall in. "No, I think that was the right thing to do. We can't afford to have somebody going around stirring up questions. We never should have asked him to do the service at the funeral. I thought at the time that was a mistake. . . ."

"Don't get your tit in a wringer, Julian. When Bryce left here I had him convinced it was Harry Todd that he should be talking to."

"That's good, that's good."

"Bryce isn't going to find out anything about anything. Even if he did, he wouldn't recognize it if it jumped up and bit him in the butt. Besides, there's nothing to find out about, as far as I'm concerned."

"No, no. Of course not." Julian uncrossed his legs, sat up straight at his desk, elbows on his blotter, a more official-looking posture. "I think we need to get together to decide our next steps."

"What next steps are you referring to?"

"Well, you know . . . moving forward. . . ."

"I am moving forward, Julian. I'm getting on with my life."

Julian was taken aback. Maybe she was talking this way because there was somebody with her, somebody had come into the room. Or maybe she was afraid her phone was tapped?

"Yes, well, of course. Suppose I stop by your shop this afternoon. . . ."

"There's no need for that, Counselor. If something comes up be sure to let me know—especially if it's something to do with Dickie's missing will. Otherwise, I'll let you know if there are any business matters that we need to discuss. Nice talking to you." And the phone clicked dead.

Julian hung up the receiver and leaned back in his chair. What was all that about? What just happened here? She brushed him off as if there was nothing between them, as if none of their discussions had taken place. What was going on? Whatever it was, he knew enough not to push her. Give her some time. Some space. Have to remember she just buried her husband. For all her bluster, that's probably more of a shock than she'd like to admit. He'd wait a couple of days, let things settle down a bit, then go to see her. See how things stood. But he had a sinking feeling, an all-too-familiar sensation, the presentiment that his hopes and dreams were once again sinking slowly out of sight. Disappearing before his eyes no matter how he tried to hold on to them, to make them real.

He sat with his elbows pointed on the arms of his chair, his hands before his face, touching his lips, one hand cupping the fist of the other, looking slowly around his office, surveying his surroundings. It had been the manager's office when the Alhambra was still a functioning theater, from the time when it was a vaudeville palace as much as a movie house, the decor appropriate to the extravagances of its age from the early 1920s, red-flocked wallpaper and seashell sconces, a five-globe chandelier of cast-iron tendrils hanging in the center, all decorations he had planned to replace but needed to put the money instead toward the renovations for the Shoppers Bazaar. He had done what he could to make the room his own—the large picture of the Keystone Steam Works, the wood cabinets and shelves from his father's office—but it still seemed like a borrowed space; the red-flocked wallpaper was peeling off the walls, the sconces were askew, and there was the undeniable odor of mold, a mustiness about everything in the place. He thought, I bet when I leave here I even have it on my clothes. Without realizing he was doing it, he sniffed at the sleeve of his tweed sport coat. The one window from where he sat showed the backs of the old brick buildings along the main street, back stairways and trash bins and fire escapes. He had to get out of here. He took his scarf from the coat tree beside the door and, winding it about his neck, hurried through the empty outer office—thinking, One advantage of having an unreliable secretary who takes off all the time without telling me is that there's rarely anyone around to tell where I'm going, or make an excuse to for going out, because most of the time I don't really have anyplace to go—and along the corridor of empty boutiques, pushing through the padded doors to the foyer and out the main doors to the street, biting a mouthful of the chill air like a swimmer popping to the surface.

14

Augie's Kwik Dog was on a steep side street below the main street next to the alley, a small place with only a half dozen tables, a half dozen stools at the counter. Julian knew Kim preferred the Kwik Dog to the Furnass Grill because most people who were out at this time of day, pensioners and the elderly, the few salespeople and office workers who were still in town, didn't like the climb back up the hill to the main street afterward, so it attracted an out-of-the-way clientele. He found Kim at his usual table at the back, having a cup of the tea that Kim bought and kept at the restaurant so Augie and Ada would have it when he came in.

"I wasn't sure if you'd make it or not today," Kim said, looking up at Julian as he got seated across from him.

"Sure, why wouldn't I?"

"I thought you might have a lot going on. Lots of calls to make."

"I've got my share," Julian said, smiling to Ada as she brought his coffee, checked that there was cream in the pitcher by the napkins. "I'll take a cinnamon roll too, if you have it."

"I made fresh last night," Ada said and headed back to the counter. Julian as always studied her ass in the blue jeans, the distinct space between her legs, several inches wide, as if her hips were a mechanical apparatus, formed a crossbeam or trestle for her legs. Then turned back to find Kim watching him. Julian grinned, shrugged.

"So," Kim said, bringing his hands together in front of his forehead, almost like a supplication or prayer, then sweeping them back over his long sleek hair, setting it around his shoulders, "I guess there's no word on Cory."

"Nothing so far. But I haven't given up."

"And nothing about Stratton. Where he lives or how to contact him."

"No, not a word." Julian smiled at Ada as she brought the roll, then watched her return again to the counter. "But I'm staying with it. I'll let you know the minute I learn anything. And don't worry, we'll find her okay."

Kim nodded once to the side, looked disappointed, sad, staring into his tea, wistful even; Julian thought he understood. He hated to keep the information from his friend that Sheetz had called about, the location of Stratton's place out at Indian Camp, but Julian couldn't take the chance. He didn't know what Kim might do, he couldn't take the chance that Kim might do to Stratton what he was increasingly afraid he did to Dickie Sutcliff.

Kim took the mug of tea in his two hands, touching it only with his fingertips, almost like a prayer, an offering, to take a drink. He placed it back on the table in front of him, carefully, setting it down precisely where it had been, then looked at Julian again.

"I'm sure Don would tell you, if he knew where Stratton was."

"I guess you two go back a long way."

"Yes, a long way." Kim smiled a little to himself. Repeated taking a drink of his tea holding the mug only with his fingertips. Julian thought, It's like he knows he has to be careful with everything he touches, it's like he knows if he's not careful he could crush that mug without even trying, without even meaning to.

"When my family first moved here, when my brother, Tom, and I were only in junior high school, Don was the only one to stand up for us. We had trouble because we looked different, the other kids wouldn't have anything to do with us, or if they did, it was to call us names, try to start something. This one time, Tom and I went for a walk along the river, I guess he was in the ninth grade, I was in seventh, we followed the railroad tracks up past the mills and the rail yard at the foot of Orchard Hill to a wooded area between the bluffs and the rivers, there were a couple ponds there—"

Julian nodded. "Big Goosey and Little Goosey."

"What?"

"That's the name of those ponds. Big Goosey and Little Goosey. We used to go there too, when we were kids." Julian took another bite of his cinnamon roll.

Kim nodded sideways. "I didn't know they had names. So you know it's pretty isolated there."

"Oh yes," Julian said, remembering.

"Well, this day we ran into a group of guys from Locust Street. This was before I took seriously any of the training my father tried to teach me, I thought it was all sort of pointless, but Tom had some training and when the guys came after us Tom tried to defend us. Defend me, I guess. But there was just too many of them, they got him down and started kicking him and then dragged him off into the grass, a couple of them grabbed me and held me because I was smaller, I'll never forget, I could hear them hitting Tom and these two guys kept taunting me, 'What are you going to do about it, gook-face?' I tried kicking at them and everything but they just laughed. And then Don came along and he told them to let me go and they did and then he went with me to find Tom. They had left him in a storm drain, he was bleeding really bad, but Don helped me get him home. Tom was never right after that, he must have had a bad concussion but we didn't have money for doctors or anything. After that, I began to train seriously, I learned everything my father could teach me, any of his students could teach me, and then I'd teach Don as a favor for what he did for me. For Tom." Kim smiled again to himself. "Don got pretty good."

"I never heard that story before."

"I don't like to remember that stuff. But thinking of Don. . . ."

"And after you got good at what your father taught you, you paid a visit to those guys from Locust Street."

Kim just looked at him and didn't say anything. Blinked slowly, almost sleepily. Expressionless.

Of course he wouldn't say anything, Julian thought. It was a mission for Tom. Any more than he'd say if I asked him if he had anything to do with what happened to Dickie Sutcliff. Like some avenging angel.

Ada was beside the table, another small pot of hot water in one hand, the coffee pot in the other. "I thought you might need a warm-up, hon," she said, smiling at Kim.

"Thanks, Ada," Kim said abstractly. Then tried to be more sociable. "Where's Augie today?"

"Little Augie forgot his release for a field trip tomorrow, so Augie took it over to the school."

"And he left you to run the whole place."

"We're never that busy around this time. Just you guys."

"See that, Julian?" Kim said. "Augie's smart enough to know who he can trust."

"Absolutely," Julian said. But Ada had yet to look in his direction since she'd returned. She seemed ready at any instant to reach out and touch Kim's hair.

"I meant to tell you," Ada went on. "The boys can't stop talking about the move you showed them the other night in class. I guess you did a demonstration."

"Just to show them what it was supposed to look like." Kim looked at Julian, embarrassed.

"Well, whatever it was, it sure left a big impression."

"That's good. Maybe it'll come in handy someday. Your boys are doing real good."

"Honest?"

"Honest."

Ada beamed and headed back to the counter without giving Julian a warm-up to his coffee. Julian cupped the top of his head and sighed.

"Are they really? Doing good?" he asked Kim.

Kim nodded sideways, attending to his tea bag. "So what else is going on?"

"Lots of little annoying things." Julian still had hopes of catching Ada's eye. "I had a visit the first thing this morning from the Reverend Orr."

"Your friend Bryce."

"The-guy-I-grew-up-with Bryce."

"What did he want?"

"He always seems to turn up when he thinks I need counseling about something."

Kim looked at him, waiting for him to go on.

"This time he thinks there are some suspicious things about the way Dickie Sutcliff died that I should be concerned about."

Kim nodded sideways and sipped his tea.

Christ, I can't tell him that, can I? The next thing you know he'll be going after Bryce to protect me. Then it occurred to Julian that, if he was careful in the way he presented the information, the way Kim reacted might tell him if Kim in fact had something to do with Dickie's death, or if he was letting his imagination get the better of him, if Bryce's nutsy suspicions were starting to rub off on him. Julian pushed his chair back from the table and sat sideways, crossed one leg over his knee, still keeping an eye out for Ada.

"Bryce thinks it's suspicious that Dickie would fall in his office that way. That a simple fall like that would be enough to kill him." Julian smiled to himself, shook his head in disbelief—he thought it was a nice touch. "He's got some idea that maybe there was somebody else in the office that night with Dickie. And he's all fussed up that there wasn't an autopsy or more of an investigation into the circumstances. Crazy Bryce."

"Does he think you had something to do with it?" Kim said, watching Julian.

"No, no, nothing like that," Julian laughed, brushing away such an idea with the back of his hand. "If anything he thinks Harry Todd might have something to do with it, if in fact there was something suspicious in how Dickie died."

"Still, I can see how it would be upsetting for you. To have yourself questioned like that by a friend. Someone you trust."

"Well, yes, a little. Though as I said, Bryce and I aren't particularly . . . friendly, you might say."

"But there's a loyalty there," Kim said, again brushing his hair back over his head, resetting it on his shoulders.

"Yes, I guess you're right." Julian was touched that Kim would be concerned about Bryce's loyalty to him; he was used to thinking of Kim as a killer, not as a model of empathy. Ada came from the back along the counter and Julian motioned to her that he needed more coffee. She nodded but before she got to the table Kim stood up abruptly.

"I've got to be getting back. I forgot something at the studio. I'll talk to you later." Before Julian could say anything, Kim was heading toward the door, tucking some bills in Ada's apron pocket as he passed her. Ada laughed and watched him out the front window as he headed back up the sidewalk out of sight, then continued to Julian's table.

"He sure seemed in a hurry about something, didn't he?" Ada said, filling Julian's cup.

"Yes, he did," Julian said. Unable to judge whether it had anything to do with what he said about Dickie's death. I better talk to him again later, make sure he doesn't think Bryce is really a threat. Don't want to be defending him again on another murder charge, he thought, only half joking with himself. He didn't really want any more coffee, he only intended to keep Kim company, but as long as Ada brought it he decided to finish it as he picked with a tongue-moistened fingertip at the crumbs of cinnamon and sugar on the plate.

15

Bryce hadn't seen or talked to Perry Sykes since high school, not that they ever talked back then either. Sykes had lived in the area of town below the main street, below Seventh Avenue, on the slopes between the main street and the mills along the river, one of the group of boys who hung out together, in the same way that the Orchard Hill boys hung out together, whom Bryce never quite understood or got along with that well: the downtown boys were large and fleshy—Bryce remembered Sykes as one of the largest and fleshiest, a kid who even in the tenth grade walked with a flat-footed limp while sucking air—and were on the football team, linemen, of course. Bryce's friends—the Orchard Hill kids—tended more to be basketball players, even though Bryce himself was rather squat. Bryce's claim to fame on the basketball team came from his ability to distract; as the players ran back and forth, up and down the court, Bryce maintained a steady monologue, in an undertone just within the range of hearing, an ongoing commentary on the progress of the game and the play of whomever he was guarding, as well as the attributes of various cheerleaders, the latest record by the Everly Brothers or Fats Domino, questions about the player's family, even where his opponent was thinking of applying to college. Odds were that sometime during the game, at least once—and once it happened, it usually became an increasing distraction—the player across from him would stop in mid-dribble or looking to make a shot, caught involuntarily in Bryce's barely audible flurry of questions or comments, and say, "Huh?" just long enough for Bryce to steal the ball and get it to one of his teammates who could actually make baskets. His reputation for these monologues was such that students in the bleachers often sent up cheers of "Talk to him, Bryce! Talk to him, Bryce!" which in itself was a distraction to opposing players.

All Fall Down

Bryce left his car in the alley across from the police station and the back of city hall, entering the building through the narrow entrance off the alley he remembered passing through as a teenager when once he and Julian and a couple others from Orchard Hill were dumped in the back of a police cruiser and brought to the station for throwing crabapples at Mrs. Blackstone's front porch, brought here more to scare them than anything else. The scaring had certainly worked: walking into the building now he got a sinking feeling in his stomach, the old fear of uniforms and authority that he sometimes wondered was the reason he went into the ministry after college to stay out of the army—at the age of twenty-two he wasn't afraid of dying in Vietnam because the concepts, either dying or Vietnam, had no meaning for him, but he was sure enough afraid, terrorized is more like it, of being told what to do by a screaming, mean-faced drill sergeant. In the crowded reception area, Perry Sykes was talking to another officer who was seated at a desk behind the counter, reaming out the officer about what seemed to be an incorrectly filled-out form. Bryce had kept track of Sykes's law enforcement career in Furnass through the local papers but he was unprepared for the changes in the man. Sykes was still supersized and fleshy, but the flesh seemed stretched over solid muscle; his puffy face had slipped a few degrees into heavy jowls that seemed meant for clamping and holding on. When Sykes turned and saw Bryce, when Bryce saw the look on Sykes's face when he recognized Bryce, the sinking sensation in his stomach turned into an outright gurgle. Why am I doing this again? Be with me, Lord.

"Bryce. Dicey-Brycey. I guess it's Revered Bryce now."

"Perry. Hail to the chief. How ya doin'?"

Sykes offered his hand across the counter and absorbed Bryce's. "I'm good, I'm good. Yourself? We never see you at the class reunions, Reverend. I never realized Drumlins was that far away from poor ol' Furnass."

Bryce laughed a little, snuffled. "You know how it is, Perry. Things keep piling up."

"Yeah. I do know how it is. How is Rachel these days? You have a couple of kids—Mary, she's in CMU, isn't she? And Brian's out in California."

"Wow, that's impressive. The long arm of the law, keeping track of people. And we don't even live here."

"I'd like to take credit for our police work. But it's from being on the reunion committee. Still, it always helps, knowing who's around, what they're doing these days. Come on back to my office. What brings you to town?"

Bryce walked around the end of the counter and followed Sykes down the corridor—he noticed Sykes still had the flat-footed limp though now it seemed more of a swagger than a limitation, an affectation like a dare for someone to try to take advantage—past a row of empty cells, thinking, They brought us all back here, that big cop, Officer Martin, he never liked us Orchard Hill kids anyway, pushed us into one of these cells and laughed, for of all things winging crabapples at Mrs. Blackstone's porch, but the crabapples were meant for some of the Locust Street kids who came up on the hill, the ones hitting her porch only because Herman the German couldn't aim—funny, Dickie Sutcliff was there with us that time, it was his dad who came and got us out, told Officer Martin to leave us alone or there'd be real trouble and darned if he didn't—to Sykes's office. It was a cramped space with cream-colored walls covered with flyers and notes and smudged with soot from the mills, grease spots from suspects leaning back in their chairs, the furniture in shades of procedural gray; Sykes seemed to fill the room as he took his place behind the desk, motioned for Bryce to sit down.

"Like I say, what brings you to town, Bryce? To the police station? I'm not fixing any parking tickets for old time's sake, in case you're wondering."

"I wouldn't expect you would." Hmm, that didn't come out right. "No, I'm here about something a little more important than parking tickets."

"Parking tickets are a serious business, Reverend. They're nothing to take lightly, they're the law and it's my job to uphold that law."

Oh for Christ's sake—excuse me, Lord. Can I say anything right to this guy? Probably not.

"No offense intended, Perry. Or do I call you Chief? Heh heh." Perry Sykes looked at him blankly, not friendly. "Yes, well, what I came to talk to you about, what I came to ask you about, was Dickie Sutcliff's death."

"Yes, Pastor, a death would be considered more important than a parking ticket. Terrible thing about Dickie dying that way and all. I just saw him the day before, actually the night before, at the city council meeting. He was in his usual form, you know Dickie, glad-handing everybody, working the room. Acting like he was everybody's best friend."

"Did he usually go to city council meetings?"

"Sometimes, I guess." Perry Sykes took the measure of Bryce. "Why?"

"I was wondering if there was anything particularly going on. Anything that might get somebody riled up against him."

"Like I said, why?"

"Well, I was wondering if somebody had a particular grudge against Dickie about something."

"Somebody always had a grudge against Dickie Sutcliff about something. Everybody knew Dickie, and most knew not to trust him. He could be a real bastard. May he rest in peace."

Bryce snorted, pleased, thinking he finally had a good opening to make a connection with Perry, share a laugh about the indiscretions of their youth. "Don't tell me you're still mad at Dickie about Judy DiBona, are you?"

"What about Judy DiBona?"

"Wasn't there something about you at the prom, you took her to the prom and then she disappeared with Dickie for a while after we got to the country club. Somebody saw the two of them in the back seat of Dickie's car, something like that? Dickie being Dickie."

Perry Sykes studied him. "You're a funny guy, Pastor."

What? "People say that. I try to keep it light. Light and fluid."

"I'm trying to figure out what you're trying to get at. Or are you just thick?"

"What, you mean because I think that's a funny story? Well, I enjoy a good story as much as the next guy. I may be a minister, but I'm still human. And what's more human than teenagers in the back seat of a car? We all did some crazy things back—"

"So you really don't know that Judy DiBona and I are married. That that's my wife you're talking about."

Bryce looked at him—Did it again. Fascinating, without even trying—pinched the end of his nose to try to clear it, the dampness of the building was clogging up his sinuses. "Really. Well, that's great. I always liked Judy, a real live wire that girl. Any kids? I guess so, that's them in the picture on your desk, right? Well, that's what I get for not attending the class reunions, isn't it? Please say hello to her for me." I'm such an asshole. A fool. Holy or otherwise.

Perry Sykes seemed to be looming larger behind his desk by the minute, looking at Bryce steadily under his ridge of eyebrow. "What did you want to know about Dickie's death?"

"There was some talk . . . somebody indicated, er, thought . . . that there might have been foul play involved, if you know what I mean. And I thought, well, if anybody would know about foul play . . . er, I mean, that you would certainly know if. . . ."

"What sort of foul play, Pastor?"

"As in, that Dickie might have been murdered."

"Murdered." Perry Sykes rolled the word over in his mouth, sampling it, as if he wanted to get its full taste. "Would you care to tell me who suggested that Dickie may have been murdered?"

"I don't think I should. It was spoken in confidence. . . ."

"I didn't 'spect so." Having swallowed the word, Perry Sykes was now focused on the aftertaste. "So somebody thinks Dickie might have been murdered. I don't suppose you have any idea as to who might have murdered him, do you? No, I didn't 'spect so either."

"I thought maybe you might have uncovered some clues or evidence that might support such an idea. Or put it to rest, if that's the case."

"If I had, don't you think I'd be conducting an investigation?"

"Absolutely." Bryce puffed air in and out of his nose several times, trying to clear it. "I thought maybe you were and were downplaying it. Keeping it under your hat, as it were."

"I can tell you, Pastor, that I've got nothing under my hat"— Bryce thought Oh please don't let me smile please don't let me smile—"I've got nothing up my sleeve. The case is closed. Dickie fell in his office and hit his head on the edge of the desk. End of story. I saw the body, there was a dent, an actual hole in his skull you could stick your thumb into."

"I heard you saw the body."

"It wasn't pretty, Pastor."

"I'm sure." Bryce puckered his lips, kissing air. "Did the autopsy indicate any drugs or alcohol in his system? Any reason why he fell?"

"What autopsy?"

"That's what I was wondering. Was there an autopsy?"

"The death certificate said—"

"Yeah, I know. But what about an autopsy? Wouldn't you need an autopsy in a case like this in order to get a death certificate? Nobody seems to know anything about it. Wouldn't it be law enforcement's role to make sure the cause of death was confirmed? To make sure nothing was overlooked?"

"So you're saying I maybe didn't do my job, Pastor? I'd be careful—"

"No, no, I didn't mean that at all," Bryce shifted in his chair. "But if you didn't see an autopsy or call for one, who would? The medical examiner? The coroner?"

"Yes."

"And if there wasn't one before, I guess the only way to get one now would be to exhume the body—"

Perry Sykes stood up so quickly that Bryce juked, stood as a reflex. "You always were a nut case, Brycey. Sorry to see you have to leave so soon."

Before he could say anything, Sykes put his hand on the back of Bryce's neck like a large C-clamp and guided him out of the office and back down the hallway toward the front, jostling him a little in a way that might have appeared playful but wasn't, as if Bryce were a puppet and Sykes the puppeteer, his grip strong enough to lift Bryce slightly on his toes—as they passed the row of cells, Bryce thought Is he going to throw me in jail? Can he do that?—saying, "Brycey, Brycey, Brycey, you always did talk so much shit." When they reached the reception area, Sykes said to the officer at the counter, releasing Bryce with a push, "You better keep an eye on this character when he's around town, Sergeant. I think he's a troublemaker." Grinning without humor.

"I'm already on it, Chief," the officer said.

Bryce thought he understood what the sergeant meant when he got back to his car in the alley: there was a parking ticket on his windshield. At least, he hoped that's what the sergeant meant.

16

Bryce was shaken, visibly shaking, when he left the police station. Can he do that, he thought, treat people like that? Yeah, I guess he can, who am I going to report him to? The strong arm of the law. The strong breath of the law too, Lord, his breath was terrible up close, breathing down my neck, like he'd been eating raw flesh or something. Bryce checked in his rearview mirror to make sure he wasn't being followed, that there wasn't a police car trailing somewhere behind him, but he didn't see one. He kept driving.

There were flurries in the air, the sky featureless, low, no space above the valley's hills, as if the valley were wrapped in wax paper, hermetically sealed, impenetrable, the light that filtered through from no one source but everywhere, or rather, nowhere, shadowless, featureless, cold. He was driving aimlessly, he knew that, just to drive, to try to shake off the talk with Sykes, the feeling it gave him in his stomach, the threat of violence just below the surface, that something brutal could break out at any time aimed at him—I guess the police have to be like that, live like that, ready to be hurt and hurt in return at any time, never able to relax, ready for it whatever it is, but why me, why did Sykes react like that? I didn't mean he didn't do his job even though it looks like he didn't, but I wonder why, what did he have to gain, did somebody tell him or pay him to overlook the obvious about Dickie's death, or would he still hate the Dickie-Bird that much from so long ago that he just wouldn't care if the man was killed or not? Yeah, maybe so, I guess Sykes is human, that's probably what I dislike most about him. Scary dude. Far out. Fascinating rhythm. You sure make all sorts, Lord. He was on Eighth Avenue, on the slope above the main drag, where the nicer homes downtown were or used to be, before they were zoned commercial or divided up into apartments or doctors' and dentists' offices. Half a block ahead, double-parked in front of Griffith's Funeral Home, the large orange brick building that was once the house of a mill official, was a large white unmarked box truck. J. Howard Griffith, in a camel hair sweater vest over his white shirt and tie, was in the middle of the street beside the truck, directing the occasional car around the truck as the driver and helper unloaded new caskets from the rear, the caskets wrapped in plain brown paper as if that were enough to disguise the contents, wheeling them on a gurney down a ramp into the lower level of the funeral home. When Griffith recognized the car he smiled broadly and waited while Bryce pulled alongside him and rolled down the window.

"Wow, that was quick, Reverend. I just left that message on your machine less than a half hour ago."

"I fly on the wings of angels, Howie," Bryce said, looking into the buttons of the man's sweater, having no idea what he was talking about. "The business of the Lord can't wait."

"I was thinking we could just discuss it on the phone, but I'm glad you came down. Park in the lot and we'll go inside."

Bryce pulled into the empty lot beside the funeral home— thinking, Never considered that, he has to stock his inventory like every good merchant. And here's this big empty lot when deaths are slow, I wonder if he gets a tax break like a church, the over- head would be a killer, heh heh, that's a good line, I have to remember that one—and walked back to the front steps. Griffith left his post in the street and ushered him inside. There were no funerals at present, no viewings, but the soft organ music played nonetheless, the smell of too-sweet flowers permanently embed- ded in the carpets, the floral wallpaper, the cushions of the taste- fully appointed straight and overstuffed chairs. All the coziness made Bryce slightly queasy. He followed Griffith to the rear, then through a door and down a set of steps, past a picture of a roiling seascape, along a short maze of corridors to the office. In another part of the basement he could hear the men unloading the caskets, a series of thumps and squeaky wheels, a distant hollow voice saying, "Damn it Charlie, that was my foot!" Griffith smiled and took his place at a spindly-legged table that he used for his desk, motioning Bryce opposite to the couch.

"I thought the Sutcliff funeral went very well, didn't you?" Griffith said. "Did you hear anything . . . er, to the contrary?"

"No, nothing at all. Though everyone seemed in a hurry to get out of there."

"They did, didn't they?" Griffith said. "But I don't think that was a comment on the proceedings."

"No, I don't think so either." Bryce worked his nose up and down, side to side; he wondered if they piped in the flower smell along with the music. "They certainly couldn't complain because it took too long. I think we set a record there for the hundred-yard funeral dash."

Griffith laughed like a compressor starting up. "Matter of fact, that's what I wanted to talk to you about. I've found there aren't too many pastors who can conduct a service, shall we say speedily, and still keep it poignant. I was impressed that you did so."

"I like to keep things moving along. Though it certainly helped in Dickie's case with your folks ready to wheel the casket out if I stopped for a breath."

"We like to keep things moving as well. But despite the constraints, you were able to work in some human touches, little stories about the deceased to make the service more personal."

"My wife thought my story about Dickie in the shower room was too personal."

Griffith laughed. "Perhaps that could have been . . . toned down a bit for the occasion. But no matter. As I said, I was impressed at how you handled it all. I was wondering if you'd consider taking a position with us, accept a retainer for your services."

"A retainer. Really."

"We occasionally have requests for a nondenominational service that is nonetheless officiated by a member of the clergy. Having listened to you—I hope you aren't offended by this—you sound like you could be just about anything when it comes to a religious affiliation—I mean that in a good way. And because you don't have a church here in town, it would help avoid any territorial squabbles. As for my end of the deal, I need somebody who can conduct a quality service but keep it moving, somebody who understands the reality that I'm running a business here, that even when it comes to honoring the deceased time is money."

God's hired gun. Fastest eulogy in the West. "Well, that certainly sounds interesting. Let me think about it. . . ."

"I'll pay eight hundred dollars a service."

"We have a deal."

"Good, good. I'll try to give you as much notice as possible, but you realize that these things pop up unexpectedly."

"Death has a funny way of doing that. Give me a call and I'll be there." Have Bible, will travel.

"Good, good." Griffith stood up, rubbed his hands together, pulled down his camel hair sweater vest over his tummy. In the distance came the sound of an overhead door clattering shut. "Do you have any questions?"

Bryce remained seated. "Hmm, well, matter of fact I do. About Dickie's death. I had some questions about it but everyone I ask seems to give me the runaround."

Griffith sat back down again. Though less like a man who was interested in the topic and more like a man who was ready for bad news. He applied his smile again as if he had forgotten an important accessory to his outfit.

Bryce took it as an indication to proceed: "Who is the coroner in town?"

"Actually, it's an elected official on the county level. John Somerset. Of Somerset and Sons, the funeral home in Onagona. That's one of those things you supposedly vote on every four years. Though I admit he's held the position so long he might as well have been appointed. Why do you ask?"

"Is it the coroner's job to issue a death certificate?"

"The coroner or attending physician or the funeral director— usually it's some combination of the three."

"Then who determines if there should be an autopsy?"

"Under normal circumstances that's the family or the doctor attending the person at the time of death. If the attending physician can't determine the cause of death, or if the circumstances are suspicious, the police and the coroner are notified and then yes, the coroner will call for one. But he still has to have the permission of the family. The autopsy permit has to be signed by the next of kin. What's all this about, Reverend?"

"So who issued the death certificate for Dickie? And why wasn't there an autopsy?"

"The coroner issued the death certificate in this case, because he was called in by the medics and the police who first arrived on the scene." Griffith paused a moment before proceeding. He sat studying his hands folded on his spindly-legged table, his legs crossed underneath as if they were tied at the ankles. "And I don't know why there wasn't an autopsy."

"Do you think there should have been?"

"It's really not my job to question these things."

"But if you were going to question. . . ."

"Yes," Griffith said, looking pained. "I think there were enough questions involved to warrant an autopsy. Enough unanswered questions."

"Such as?"

Griffith looked like a man ready to step into a dark and unfamiliar room; all that was missing were his arms stretched out in front of him, fully expecting to bump into something. "Such as a large bruise on the other side of his head. On the opposite side of his head from where he hit his head on the edge of the desk."

"Are you sure?" Bryce said. Griffith looked at him. "Yes," Bryce said, "You're sure."

"I thought I noticed it at Dickie's office, and examined the body more carefully when we got it here." Griffith sighed, took a deep breath. "There was definitely a blow to the other side of his head. A very hard blow with something blunt, maybe even a fist. There was a large bruise. A blow like that, if it hit just right, I suppose could have killed him on its own, or at least rendered him unconscious. He could have been close to dead even before he hit the desk. The point is I don't know. For that matter, I don't know that the blow to the other side of his head didn't happen earlier in the evening and had nothing to do with his fall against the desk. Or that it made him woozy and that was why he fell later against his desk. That's what autopsies are for. To determine such things."

"So I'm back to my original question: Why wasn't there an autopsy? Was the coroner aware of the second blow to his head?"

"I don't know that either. It would have been hard to miss, but, on the other hand, the open wound on the other side of his head, the obvious connection to the edge of the desk, was so blatant that everyone including the coroner might have taken it for granted. People take shortcuts, don't want to work too hard."

"I take it you're not a fan of Somerset."

"In this business it's easy to cut a lot of corners, if you're so inclined." Griffith considered what he wanted to say, how he wanted to say it. "I don't know if the standards of his private practice extend to his public duties."

Shortcuts, Bryce thought. Like hiring a minister who can rush a service through so the hearse and limousines are ready for the next funeral of the day. Judge not less ye be. "But someone else could have asked for more investigation and/or an autopsy."

"That's true."

"And they didn't."

"Apparently not."

Bryce was sitting on the edge of his chair. Fascinating. Absolutely fascinating. So I was right. "So, there must have been someone else with Dickie in his office at the time it happened, and it must have been someone strong enough to hit him hard enough to send him careening against the edge of the desk."

"It's not a definite, like I said, there could be other scenarios, but it's certainly a possibility, a strong possibility. . . ."

"Well, if you consider the people we know about who had a motive, I'd say that leaves Tinker out of it. It doesn't sound like she'd be strong enough to hit him that hard."

"Probably not. . . ." Griffith was obviously uncomfortable speculating like this.

"That would leave Harry Todd."

"I don't know. . . ."

"He certainly had enough reason to want Dickie out of the way."

"I wouldn't know about that," Griffith said. "I do know that he met Tinker here when she came to make the arrangements. It's obvious there's no love between the two of them, but I guess he wanted to be involved with the arrangements. I do have to say that neither one seemed that disturbed about Dickie's passing. It was like a business transaction that needed to be fulfilled. It made my job easier, certainly, but still . . . you expect. . . ."

"Did they ask to see the body?"

"I asked Tinker to make the official identification. Harry Todd said he didn't care to."

"Or need to. Because he could have already known what Dickie looked like, being the one to hit him."

"I couldn't say that at all."

"But I can. And the police didn't have any further questions?"

"I gather they pretty much went along with the coroner's evaluation and left it at that."

Bryce thought a moment. "I have to ask this. If you knew about the second blow, the earlier blow, why didn't you say something?"

"I'm not proud of it. But it's as I said: that's not my job. It's not my place to add to the sorrow of the bereaved. Even if they appear not that bereaved. I have a reputation to maintain in the community for giving comfort to those in need. How is it going to look if I go against all the official declarations and start talking about the cause of death, even murder? A murder no one else is concerned about or considers worth investigating. People would think I'm crazy, or worse. The same is true for yourself. It's all well and good that you have these suspicions about how Dickie died or who might have had a hand in it. But then what? Who are you going to talk to about it? The police?"

"I was just there. Perry Sykes literally tossed me out of his office at the suggestion he might have missed something."

"There you are. So who else is there? The media? You have nothing to substantiate your suspicions, other than my say-so and that's only hearsay at this point, and I don't want to be included in any actions. The only way to get evidence to back up such claims would be to exhume the body, and you'd need evidence to get a court order to make that happen. A catch-22. Plus the permission of the family that seems very content to have the man buried and forgotten. My advice, Reverend, is to accept that there are some things that we'll never know, that are best left unresolved, and get on with the business of living. You know?"

17

But he couldn't forget about it, it wasn't in his nature to leave something alone once he started to worry it, not from some passionate intent to find truth or clarity or justice—though in fact he did possess that intent, did in fact seek truth or clarity or justice, or any combination of the three if he could find them, it was just that the intent for any of those qualities wasn't part of this search, though he couldn't have said what the intent of this search actually was—but because he simply didn't know when to let something go; once an idea occurred to him it would stay with him, haunt him like an old song that he couldn't get out of his head. The question was: Where could he go from here? He sat in his car in the empty parking lot of the funeral home, watching abstractly as his breath slowly fogged the windshield, the side of the orange brick building in front of him, the white window frames and the closed venetian blinds, the bare bushes along the foundation and the frozen, decimated flower beds, all becoming less distinct, gradually disappearing, until he turned on the engine to get the heater going. The afternoon was growing late; he should be heading back to Drumlins before it was dark—the flurries had stopped but there was a skiff of snow, it was getting colder and the roads could be icy; the wind had come up and small veils of snow lifted from the black asphalt, drifting over the expanse of the lot before disappearing again—but he wasn't ready to leave yet, he wasn't ready to give up, as long as he was here in town there had to be something else he could do to find out what happened to the Dickie-Bird, there had to be someone else to talk to.

Admittedly, he was beginning to wonder what could possibly happen as a result of his asking around. He couldn't imagine that the authorities would actually exhume Dickie's body, no matter what he discovered about the circumstances of Dickie's death;

and suppose they did decide to, there was still the matter of getting the family's approval for an autopsy, and from what he'd
seen and heard so far, that would be hard to obtain, either from
disinterest or from someone having something to hide. Except, he
thought, Jennifer. It was obvious she loved her father, she would
want to do anything she could to find out what happened that
night in Dickie's office. Yay! he thought. I don't have to go back
just yet! Excited all over again, filled with a new sense of purpose,
humming tunelessly to himself in his monotone—Thanks, Lord,
tell Dickie to hold on, I'll get to the bottom of this thing yet—he
ground the car into gear and headed out of the parking lot, down
the steep side street past the main drag, and on down the hill to
Third Avenue, across the railroad tracks and along the cyclone
fence to the entrance of what was to be Furnass Landing.

He checked his watch: it was only four o'clock, it seemed too
early for quitting time, but no one appeared to be around, the
construction site looked abandoned. A few pieces of heavy equipment were parked here and there, bulldozers and a front loader,
a couple of earthmoving trucks, a crane with its boom lying on
the ground as if it were broken, but the operators were nowhere
to be seen, the place deathly still. Where the mill buildings used
to be—Bryce remembered them when he was a kid, he played
baseball at the field right outside the fence, the buildings seemed
huge, forbidding and forbidden places, enveloped in smoke and
steam, churning with the sounds of machinery, the ringing of steel
on steel—were now empty spaces, sudden and surprising views of
the bluffs of the valley's hills rising across the river, perspectives
he'd never seen before. He bounced slowly in and out of the ruts
of the makeshift road, threading his way between mounds of dirt
frosted with old snow, tangles of rusted pipes, large tanks still
crusted with dirt from being unearthed, looking vulnerable and
out of place exposed to the air. Close to the river was a phalanx
of five tall smokestacks like the pipes of a giant organ but with

nothing attached to them. Further on some of the buildings were still standing but appeared in the last stages of decay, their windows broken out, the walls rusting away and overgrown with weeds and vines.

Midway across the industrial wasteland was a row of white trailers linked by a wood porch. A black pickup truck was parked in front of the only trailer with lights in the windows. Bryce thought the truck was the same one he saw at Dickie's house in Highland Hills. He parked and walked around it, both to admire it—the truck was huge with oversized tires, a step-bar to help the climb up into the cab, a brace of spotlights across the roof— and to see if there was anything to indicate that it belonged to Jennifer. In the back window were Grateful Dead decals, a dancing skeleton in a top hat, a lightning bolt cracking a skull; the passenger's seat was taken up by a portable desk; a Native American dream catcher and prayer feathers dangled from the rearview mirror. He was peering in the side window—he felt like he needed to stand on tiptoe—when Jennifer came out the door of the trailer and stood at the top of the steps. She was wearing a black and green wool shirt with the shirttail hanging out, jeans and cowboy boots, and a white hardhat, her red hair streaming down around her shoulders like a cowl, like a war bonnet.

"Oh hey, Jennifer." He walked over to the steps, hands tucked in the pockets of his raincoat, feeling he'd been caught red-handed at something, but she held her position at the top, seeming to block the way and he didn't want to try it.

"That your truck? It's a beaut. I wasn't sure if you were here or not, if anybody was here or not, things seem a little quiet."

"It's a little late in the day. The guys who were here have all left."

"Ah," Bryce said. Looking around, stalling for time to get his thoughts together.

"But you're right," the young woman said, as if aware she might have come off as unfriendly. "Things are a little quiet right now. We've had to pull back operations until things settle down after my dad's death."

"How're you holding up with it all?"

She shrugged off the question, as if his concern was of no importance to her. "I thought you might be coming to see me again. I heard you've been asking a lot of questions around town about my dad and what might have happened that night."

"I must be making some people nervous, if the news traveled that fast," Bryce grinned, but realized she didn't see anything amusing about it. "Who'd you hear it from? Your mom?"

"Harry Todd called me. He thought I might want to know."

"Harry Todd called you. Fascinating. . . ."

"They still haven't found the will, in case you're wondering. But it's only a matter of time until it turns up. There's only a few places he would have kept it, and we're checking them out."

It's like we're in this little playlet, rehearsing our lines, her up there on her balcony, a workingman's Juliet. Wherefore art thou? "Your dad could be secretive, all right. Always had a plan, that guy. What I wanted to talk to you about. . . ." He put a foot on the first step but Jennifer wasn't moving and he pretended he was only resting it there, thinking, A rather tough Juliet. "I was talking to Howie Griffith at the funeral home. He said there were actually two blows to Dickie's head. There was a bruise on the other side, but nobody paid any attention to it. They just ignored it, if they saw it at all—"

"And you thought I'd really want to hear that?"

"Well, yes. Why wouldn't you?"

Jennifer shook her head, as if unable to comprehend him. "Nothing anybody does is going to bring back my dad. And all your poking around only brings back what happened to him all over again, just when we're starting to get used to him being . . .

gone. Besides, all you're talking about is speculation on some-body's part."

"But Griffith said he saw the bruise. With his own eyes."

"And if what you're saying is true, it means that my dad suf-fered more than I thought."

"But don't you see? It means that there could have been some-one else there in the office with him. Maybe somebody hit him and that's why he fell against the desk—"

"All I see is that you're stirring up things that don't concern you."

"But we owe it to Dickie to find out what happened. If there was somebody there with him they would have to be pretty strong, somebody who could hit him hard enough to hurt him that way. That certainly leaves out your mom, but I'm wondering about Harry Todd. That he told you about me asking him ques-tions only makes him more suspicious, doesn't it? I mean, it could mean he's bothered by it. Maybe he's the one who blocked the autopsy—"

"Julian Lyle blocked the autopsy."

Bryce pulled up short. "How could he do that? The only per-son who could deny permission was the next of kin. . . ."

"He told my mom that he was sure an autopsy wasn't neces-sary. And she went along with it, for whatever reasons."

"But you told me—"

"After you asked me, I started thinking and I remembered more about it."

"But why would your mother listen to Julian? I thought she had no use for him."

"She doesn't care for him, that's for sure, but they're in some business deal together. You know my mom, she'll make use of whatever or whomever is available. I suppose it has something to do with her trying to get control of the company and this project, but I don't much care. If she's depending on Julian Lyle to help her, I don't have anything to be concerned about."

"That still doesn't answer if there was someone with Dickie that night in his office. I think Harry Todd must have—"

"And I think you're a fool."

Bryce puttered, blinked up at her several times. Thinking, Did she just say that? To a minister? Wow!

"Harry Todd couldn't have had anything to do with it. Because that night Harry Todd was with me. Or I was with him. All evening. All night."

"Are you sure? Let's go inside, I'm freezing out here. . . ." He started up the steps but came to eye level with her crotch, Jennifer not moving.

"We don't have anything to discuss, Reverend."

"But wouldn't you let me—"

"It's time for you to leave. This is a construction site and you need a hardhat."

"You're kidding, right?" Her face said she wasn't. Bryce slowly retraced his steps, slipping at the bottom on a patch of ice that sent his arms and legs flying in different directions till he regained his balance. Great, I'm not only a fool, I look like one.

"I don't have anything to say to you, Reverend. I've probably said too much already. If you don't go now, I'll call the police. I think the response would be rather quick."

She nodded toward the entrance beyond the open field, toward the town mounting the slope of the hill. Parked across the street from the gate was a police car, across the railroad tracks, beside an abandoned grocery store, engine running, the exhaust in the cold air curling about the car like a tail. Bryce's stomach gurgled.

"Did you call them?"

Jennifer shook her head. "I didn't have to. I thought maybe you brought them with you."

Bryce chomped air a couple of times and got back in his car. As he drove out of the site and headed up the hill—as he passed the police car Bryce tried to see who was driving without being too obvious, telling himself maybe it was just a coincidence, to see if it was Sykes or the sergeant behind the wheel, but Bryce couldn't make out his face—the police car made a U-turn and followed him, half a block behind, staying with him as Bryce turned onto the main street and continued up through the town, before the dogleg that would take him to Orchard Avenue and up to Orchard Hill turning across the Twenty-Sixth Street Bridge over the Allehela and up the hill to Drumlins Road toward home. In his rearview mirror as he crossed the bridge Bryce saw the police car pull over and wait, watch while Bryce continued across the bridge and turned up the road on the other side across the slope of the valley, angling up and away from the town, leaving the lights of the town in the gray evening behind him, the remains of the snow on the streets and yards, smoke rising from the chimneys of the houses stacked up the opposite valley wall, the scene in monochrome, a cheerless place, past the Riverside Inn near the top of the hill, the building decorated in red and green lights for Christmas, the parking lot filling with cars and people walking toward the entrance carrying gifts, remembering that either the next night or the following night, he can't remember which and knows he'd be in trouble if Rachel knew he couldn't remember, he'll be coming here with Rachel for her department's own Christmas party, the headlights of the police car still there across the river though tiny now, far behind him now as Bryce gained the summit and headed home.

18

It had been twenty years at least since Julian was out this way, beyond Mingo Junction toward Indian Camp, probably not since his late teens when he and the Binder brothers and Danny Brehany—he remembered Bryce didn't come along on that trip, made a big to-do about not being interested, calling it a dumb idea; it was like Bryce to pooh-pooh the adventure when the truth was he didn't know how to swim—came out here to shoot the rapids on Little Berry Creek, but it looked the same as he remembered it, scrub country as he thought of it, the narrow road winding in and out of the tight little valleys—in southern Appalachia they would be known as hollows, but here in the northern fringe of the range they had no such colorful name—the second- and third-growth brush and trees close to the road, dried sticks at this time of year. The afternoon had turned dark—it certainly wasn't bright to begin with—snow flurries in the air, like a kind of fog, though nothing was sticking, the asphalt blacker from the moisture but not slick, the snow on the ground up the slopes of the ravines and among the trees old snow that wouldn't melt till spring.

He was sure this was a wild-goose chase. It seemed highly improbable that, given all the mystery about the man's whereabouts, Julian would simply walk up to his front door and find Stratton not only at home but that Cory was with him. And suppose Julian did find Cory there, what was he going to do about it? He certainly wasn't going to try to physically whisk her away from under Stratton's nose; Stratton with his drug dealing could be armed. Perhaps Julian could reason with the girl to contact her mother, and especially contact Kim, to tell them she was all right, persuade her to return home at least until the custody hearing was settled. But he didn't expect any of that to happen. The fact was the only reason he was doing this, making this trip out here, was to pacify Kim and keep him from coming here himself; when he got back to the office he would call Kim and tell him about Sheetz's call and say he had been out to Stratton's place and Cory wasn't there, that there was no reason for Kim to check it out for himself, and hope in the meantime that Cory had turned up on her own.

Julian felt it was his special province to do what he could to take care of Kim, help him get through the everyday stuff, protect him in a way from it—Kim might be a master of martial arts and violence but he was amazingly naïve about ordinary living, how the ordinary world worked—Julian felt it was his role, his function, the least he could do for a man he was proud to call his friend. Representing Kim in the trial for killing his father, the acquittal of all charges, was the proudest moment of Julian's career as a lawyer, and afterward he enjoyed the notoriety, that he was the guy who defended a killer, hoped that it showed that he amounted to something after all, that the name Lyle meant something again in the town. But the outcome of the trial did little to silence his detractors, any more than it silenced the doubts he had about himself. Try as he might, he knew that he had been terribly out of his league when it came to a criminal trial—most of his cases involved coal leases and boundary disputes, wills and divorces, petty things. He knew that when Kim's wife called him in the middle of the night to ask him to represent her husband— picked him out of the Yellow Pages because she worked in town and recognized his name—he agreed to take the case because it was flattering to have his name recognized under any circumstances. And he knew that the case had been decided, not because of his brilliant rebuttals to the evidence or his revealing cross-examination of the witnesses, but because Perry Sykes, the chief of police, testified that Kim's father, Tomi, was the meanest son-of-a-bitch he had ever encountered and that from his survey of the crime scene along with the statement of Kim's daughter who was in the house at the time, he went against the district attorney's assessment of the events and stated his conclusion that Kim acted in self-defense and therefore it was justifiable homicide, end of story. When Julian learned more about Kim after the trial, he sometimes wondered if Kim actually had acted in self-defense; there was certainly enough bad blood between father and son to trigger a fight between the two, enough to question Kim's motives and innocence in his father's death. But he didn't allow himself to think too long or too far along those lines.

Julian's concern today—an intellectual possibility that had grown over the days since Dickie's death into a gnawing apprehension—had to do with how far Kim might go to protect Julian, if he thought Julian was threatened or in trouble. Kim could be loyal and protective beyond reason in regard to those he cared about—the story Kim told today while they were having coffee about Don Sheetz when they were in junior high school, that he still felt gratitude to Don after all these years for helping Kim and his brother when they were attacked along the river, only reinforced his commitment to his friends. Julian had no doubt that when Kim got older and more accomplished, he tracked down and revenged each one of those kids who beat up his brother. What concerned Julian was whether Kim felt that same kind of loyalty to Julian in regard to Julian's troubled business affairs with Dickie, the same kind of protectiveness, the same willingness to enact revenge. From the moment Julian heard the details of Dickie's death, he thought there was no way that a simple fall could have caused that much damage to Dickie's skull, that there had to be someone else involved. True, any number of people could have been with Dickie in his office that night, there were any number of people in town who had a grudge against him, who might under the right (or wrong) circumstances have caused Dickie's death. But his first thought was Kim.

Under normal circumstances, he might not have been so quick to think Kim had something to do with such a thing—on the other hand, if he was honest with himself, he probably would have, because he associated Kim with anything having to do with violence—but earlier on the day Dickie died Julian had talked to

Kim about his business relations with Dickie—no, he had to admit it: he was complaining, as one friend would to another— telling Kim things about his relationship with Dickie that he should have kept to himself. Blaming Dickie, some of it justified, some of it not, for the precarious financial state that Julian found himself in. He thought it would be like Kim—in his loyalty to Julian for defending him in court, for being his friend when few others wanted to be seen with him—to want to take matters in his own hands; it would be like Kim, with his misguided view of the world—a world born and bred of violence; a world divided into friendlies and enemies; a world where you lashed out at your enemies, fought if need be to the death—to do what he could to make Julian's problems go away.

On the chance Kim actually had something to do with Dickie's death, Julian did everything he could to head off too much investigation into the circumstances of the death, assuming the role of Dickie's attorney and pooh-poohing any talk of foul play, counseling Tinker against having an autopsy; later, he wondered if he had jeopardized discovering if someone other than Kim had been involved. But he knew if he had to do things over, he wouldn't do them any differently, he couldn't take the chance, the more he thought about it the more he was afraid, almost certain, that Kim was involved in it, and it was Julian's job to protect him, that's what friends did, in the same way Kim must have thought he was helping Julian. When Bryce came sniffing around with all his questions, they only echoed, amplified the suspicions in Julian's own mind. The difference for Julian his nagging fear, his aching dread—was not only that Kim killed Dickie, but that in effect he had himself to blame for setting Kim to it.

The snow swirled and eddied before his windshield, at times almost a whiteout, though his wipers easily cleared it away, the road remained only damp in front of him, the snow not sticking.

"What's bothering you?" Kim had said.

"Is something bothering me?" Julian said.

"Seems to be," Kim said as they sat in his kitchen, having a beer, after Julian helped him move the chest of drawers Kim had refinished up to Cory's room. The room he hoped to be Cory's room.

Julian rested his forearm across the top of his head, his hand hanging down beside his ear like a five-fingered tassel. "I guess I could sum it up in two words: Dickie Sutcliff."

"Ah," Kim said. He put his bottle of Rolling Rock under his bottom lip and blew, producing a long low note like a foghorn, like a warning.

"Exactly," Julian laughed.

"What is your Orchard Hill friend up to this time?"

"He's another just-a-guy-I-happened-to-grow-up-with, not a friend. Not now, not then either, when we were growing up."

"I've gathered you're in some kind of business deal with him, but I never understood the connection."

"It's complicated. And not a relationship I would have chosen. Anyone who does business in Furnass or the surrounding area knows that you only get into a business deal with Dickie Sutcliff at your own risk. In my case I didn't have a choice. Dickie set it up that I either take the deal or lose my home and place of business. Dickie is always very thorough. When he screws you, he leaves you with a kiss."

"How did he screw you?" Kim placed his beer bottle on the kitchen table, holding it with his fingertips.

Julian sighed. "Well, if I'm honest with myself, I know it was my own fault for getting into such a position. No pun intended."

Kim closed his eyes, nodded to the side.

"A couple of years ago to help finance the Furnass Towers, I put up my house and the Alhambra Theater. But when Sycamore Savings & Loan went under, Dickie arranged to take over the mortgages for my house and the Alhambra in a scheme to use the

Towers to secure his loans for his Furnass Landing project. Like I said, it's complicated and involved some creative financing through his connections with the bank. The bottom line for me, however, is that he's been taking care of the mortgages on my house and the Alhambra."

"He's been paying them?"

"Yes."

Kim raised his eyebrows. "Actually, that sounds like a pretty good friend, if you ask me."

"Sounds like it, all right. But Dickie never does anything out of the goodness of his heart. He's like his father when he ran the business, Dickie's always got an angle. In this case, he more or less owns me, I'm like his in-house legal counsel. He throws a few cases my way but it's all shit-work, foreclosures and collections, and he expects it to be pro bono or out of the goodness of my heart, or if he does pay anything it's next to nothing. Now the latest thing is that he expects me to pay the property taxes on my house."

"Even though he holds the mortgage for the house."

"I know I shouldn't complain, but I also know that he could turn me out of the house at any time and we wouldn't have a roof over our heads."

"So he's just being a bastard."

"He's just being Dickie Sutcliff."

Kim thought a minute, watching his fingertips ripple up and down the sides of his beer bottle. "You know, I hear you talk about these guys that you grew up with on Orchard Hill as if they're old friends, or at least that there's some connection with them. But from all the things you tell me, it doesn't seem like most of them, like Bryce or Dickie Sutcliff, treat you very well. And it doesn't sound, from everything you say, that all things considered you really like them all that much. Nor should you."

"I'm afraid you're probably right." Julian laughed. It was funny, he had never pieced it all together before, seen those relationships in that light. It was one of the things he prized about Kim, the man might not have the credentials of advanced education, but he was able to see things at their most basic level, cut through all the bullshit.

"There ought to be something to do about people like that," Kim said, still watching his fingertips. "People who use other people. It's not right." Then he looked at Julian. His face blank. Expressionless. Blinking slowly, almost as if sleepy.

Was that conversation enough to send Kim after Dickie, to avenge his friend? Given Kim's simmering violence, his loyalty to those people important to him, Julian thought it possible. It was certainly enough to make Julian suspicious. More than that, fearful. At any rate with Cory missing, he had to be careful not to say or do anything that would send Kim after anyone else, such as Stratton. There was no question what that outcome would be.

The squall was over by the time he reached Indian Camp, the snow gone as quickly as it came. There was no town of Indian Camp—Julian remembered there used to be a general store with a post office somewhere in the area but he couldn't remember where—it was a series of cabins, vacation homes for summer people, with a few occupied year-round by particularly hearty souls, those who didn't need basic amenities such as insulated walls and bathrooms, strung along Little Berry Creek, some in clusters and others isolated, some within sight of the road and others tucked back behind fields and forests depending upon the curves of the creek and the road. Julian slowed when the numbers on the mailboxes started into the hundreds; 112 had a couple of bullet holes in it and sat cockeyed on its post as if it had been backed into. He turned down the gravel lane and followed it a hundred yards along the edge of a field—a trio of crows flew out of the dried cornstalks as he passed, complaining bitterly—then entered the woods. The cabin sat on a patch of bare earth close to the river. It was small, probably only one or two rooms, in a bad state of disrepair. An old Ford sat on cement blocks in the yard; around the side of the cabin were some empty chicken coops, a tank for fuel oil, a shed collapsed in upon itself, the outhouse. An oil stain between two ruts indicated where a vehicle was sometimes parked. The windows were dark but just in case someone was inside Julian tooted twice as a courtesy. He sat for a moment, then got out. There was the sound of wind in the branches of the bare trees, the ripple of the creek behind the house, his Jeep Cherokee ticking cool, nothing else.

He walked slowly to the front door, thinking, This is the way people get shot, and knocked. Waited, and knocked again. Tried the door: locked. He walked to the window and looked in, first only standing there, then, emboldened, he cupped his hands against the glass for a better look. There was one large room with several narrow beds or cots spaced around the walls, a dresser missing a drawer, a table and chairs, a pipe angled across a corner on which to hang clothes; beyond was a smaller room or alcove with an old stove, refrigerator, and sink. The interior looked about how he expected. The proverbial pigsty, he thought, except it gives pigs a bad name. Why would anyone live like this? Why would Cory want to be mixed up with anyone who lives like this? The only reason you'd live this far from civilization is if you didn't want civilized people to see what you were up to. He looked around the yard, to make sure no one was about, checked the surrounding woods—thinking, Yes, this is the way to get shot— and went around the cabin to the kitchen door. It was locked too but the door was loose in its frame, the old wood warped. He went back to the old Ford sitting on blocks. The trunk was open a crack; inside was a rusted tire iron. He took the tool back to the kitchen door and used the chisel end to pop it open. Am I really going to do this? Breaking and entering? Sure seems like it. He stepped inside, the tire iron in hand just in case.

"Hello? Anybody here?" He thought if someone had answered he would have shit himself. He walked carefully through the kitchen and stood in the doorway to the main room. The room was dark, the windows in late afternoon providing little light. The place had the dank smell of a basement, mold, a musk smell like animals or dead birds, like when he was a kid and uncovered old nests. All three beds appeared to have been slept in, though two of them were covered with dirty clothes, cardboard boxes, plastic bags from a Giant Eagle, miscellaneous tools. The table in the center of the room held dirty dishes, cereal boxes, half a loaf of bread. And drug paraphernalia, syringes, bags of white powder, a balance scale. Julian peered out the front window but saw only his Cherokee in the fading light. On top of the dresser next to the bed that appeared recently slept in was a saucer of small change, a crumpled pack of cigarettes, a handkerchief stiff with stains, a stack of receipts. And a collection of color Polaroid prints. Of Cory. Naked. Posing on a bed. A different bed than those in the cabin. One image looking down the chest of the man holding the camera, Cory with his erection in her mouth, looking up at him, her eyes compliant. Julian thinking, If Kim sees these he'll kill Stratton for sure. Whether it's Stratton in the pictures or not. And he should.

He had to get out of here. But on the chance he'd find something he went through the stack of receipts. Most of them were crinkled and faded as if jammed hastily into pockets. Giant Eagle. A state store. Several from gas stations. And one from the Grand Hotel. Made out to James Stratton. Two weeks' rent, dated the week before. Marked *Paid, Cash.* Julian thought of taking it but decided he didn't need to, he had seen enough. Too much. He had to get out of here. Now. He hurried back through the kitchen and out the door, around the side of the house toward his car, tossing the tire iron in the dead grass, expecting any moment to see the flash, hear the report, feel the thud of the bullet that knocked him from his feet, thinking, The guy's an animal, he deserves anything he gets, I'd like to be there if Kim got ahold of him, that would be something to see, no, I take that back, that's nothing I want to see. . . .

. . . the stories of the town exist seemingly outside of time and yet within time too, independent of time and yet dependent upon time in which to live, to live again each time in the retelling; the stories of the town exist seemingly outside of the lives of the town and yet through those lives too, dependent upon those lives in order to live, to live again, the stories then influencing the stories now, living again in the stories that are happening now, giving life to the town that seemingly exists outside and beyond that of the lives of those living here now . . . now as Julian heads back to Furnass in the veils of snow and growing darkness of the early winter evening he thinks of the story Kim told him earlier today about the time he and his brother were attacked near Big Goosey and Little Goosey by older boys from Locust Street, an attack for which he was sure those Locust Street kids paid for dearly when Kim got older and proficient at the martial arts his father taught him, tracking down his tormentors one by one, confronting them in alleyways or parking lots, after ball games or high school dances, by themselves or in twos or threes, all the better, his only concern that each boy recognized who he was and why he was there, and realized there was no escaping what was about to happen, no recourse, the lesson of the story to be played out with the inevitability of a Greek drama or a folktale recounted for generations around a fire . . . a story that brings to Julian's mind his own story that took place near Big Goosey and Little Goosey, between the river and the railroad tracks that run along the base

of the sandstone bluffs of Orchard Hill, an area of wetlands with a web of paths in and out of the scrub brush and sumac and trees of heaven, the ponds named so the story goes by early settlers who saw geese nesting here though those days are long gone now, the wildlife confined to frogs and box turtles, tadpoles and craw-dads, the area a kind of sylvan paradise, or if not that at least a woodsy refuge, particularly in those decades before the closing of the mills, in contrast to the small railroad yard and roundhouse at the Orchard Hill train station less than half a mile downstream, and beyond that the mills of Buchanan Steel, the smoke and steam and soot drifting up the valley with the prevailing winds, coating the leaves of the stunted trees and stiff grass with a grimy film that anyone who comes here accepts as a fact of nature or at least as the way the world is at the two Gooseys, like the small earthquakes that occur anytime one of the hundred-car coal trains comes along the tracks less than fifty yards away, the ground shaking enough that if you aren't ready it could knock you off your feet though by this time the blue jays and starlings and spar-rows are so used to it that they don't even stop singing, the hawks and owls and crows don't take wing but only hold on to their branches a little tighter till the roar and rumbling are past, the sound of the trains amplified from bouncing off the bluff of Or-chard Hill to the bluffs rising up on the other side of the river and back again, the steep wall of the valley across the river tree cov-ered with occasional outcroppings of sandstone, and the man-made outcropping not of rock but of hardened ash and cinder where trucks from the mill haul molten slag up the side of the slope and dump it over the side, the red-hot white-hot magma-like slag flowing down the wall of the valley like the world has burst a seam . . . the story that lives in the minds of certain boys from Orchard Hill called the Great Allehela Shootout, the story of Bryce and Julian, Herman the German and the Binder brothers, and Needle-Prick Brown the Insect Fucker following the crisscross trails down the bluffs of Orchard Hill to the Gooseys, to try out Brownie's father's new Remington bolt-action .300 Winchester Magnum rifle, Brownie wanting to show it off to Julian who recently made the high school rifle team, to see if the rifle is really as accurate as it is supposed to be—Brownie of course neglecting to tell his father that he is taking it—the column of boys making straight for the river where Brownie stands on a rock jutting out from the bank and takes a few shots at a tree trunk floating by in the current and then at a crow that happens to fly by—he misses both: "This fucking rifle isn't any more accurate than my .22," Brownie says, to which the others hoot— and Herman the German says, "So how far will it shoot?" and Bob Binder says, "Bet it's even less accurate then," and Brownie says, "See that tree across the river?" and Herman the German says, "There's a thousand trees across the river," and Brownie takes a shot, the boys all standing there trying to figure out which tree he was aiming for when there is a report from the opposite bank and an instantaneous whine and something slams into the ground at their feet, the boys standing stupefied for a moment until Herman the German says, "That was a bullet!" and the Binder brothers say in unison, "Somebody's shooting at us!" and Julian says "Run for it!" and the boys scramble back up the bank as another round hits a tree close to Brownie, and as they take cover in the tall grass Julian says, "We can't stay here, if whoever is over there climbs up the hill he can see us," and Bryce says, "Who would want to shoot at us?" and Bob Binder says, "Maybe somebody thought we were shooting at them," and Brownie says, "Wow, we're under fire, just like in the movies!" and Bryce says, "Who would want to shoot at us?" and Julian takes the rifle from Brownie and says, "There's a stack of railroad ties on the other side of Little Goosey up near the tracks, on the count of three split up and run for it, I'll try to cover you," and Brownie says, "Far out, just like in the movies," and Bryce says, "Why would anyone want to shoot at us?" and Julian says, "Just go. On the count of three: one, two—," but the Binder brothers are already up and running with Herman the German and Brownie close behind though Bryce is still lying there and Julian pushes him and works the bolt to eject the shell casing and bring a new round into the chamber and raises and fires across the river, taking aim high of the outcropping of rock on the other side where he thinks the shooter might be, shouting at Bryce, "Go! Go! Go!" firing a couple more rounds as Bryce finally gets into a crouch and runs off through the brush, another bullet hitting a rock nearby and Julian fires three more times then makes a run for it himself, through the brush and up a small rise and slides in the dirt behind the barricade of railroad ties, the boys laughing hysterically and punching each other with the exertion of running and the sheer terror of what just happened to them, what is still happening to them, though here the story, as stories are wont to do, diverges, takes on separate lives depending on who is reliving it, the basic actions not called into question but the motives behind those actions: in Julian's mind he remembers taking the gun from Brownie because there seemed no recourse, nothing else to be done, the fact being that somebody was shooting at them and they had to get out of there and he figured as the best shot of the bunch he had the best shot of not hitting anyone, aiming high each time of where he thought a shooter might possibly be, providing the cover he hoped that helped the others get out of there—though it was more than that too, though he couldn't have said it, put it into words: he was a Lyle; Lyles were supposed to take charge; it was their job and curse and birthright—remembering also later how Brownie kept laughing through it all, thought it was the funniest thing he had ever heard, somebody taking shots at them from across the river, as they sat hunched behind the wall of railroad ties, telling and retelling what had happened that day, embellishing it each time until it grew from a dangerous incident (which it was) to a grand adventure (which it wasn't), but that was Brownie, that's what everyone expected from Needle-Prick Brown the Insect Fucker, everyone knew Brownie was crazy, it was Bryce who disappointed Julian, showed his friend in a new light as Bryce sat there with a grin on his face listening to Brownie's exaggerations with the same rapt attention and enjoyment that Julian had seen on his face when they went to Crawford's Bar & Grill in the Hill District in Pittsburgh, the bar in the black ghetto they snuck into to hear Lou Donaldson and Art Blakey, Bryce digging Brownie's fabrications of the events as if what was happening to them was just another funny story to tell the other guys back on Orchard Hill—Julian wanted to shake him, scream at him This isn't a joke, this isn't funny, somebody could have been killed back there, and we're not out of this yet!—though to Bryce's way of thinking what happened was very different, the way Julian acted very different, the story taking on an entirely different life in Bryce's mind: what he remembered was Julian grabbing the rifle out of Brownie's hands as soon as they were sure someone had shot at them and firing back, loving it, acting like he was in charge, like he knew what to do as he always did about anything, overreacting like Julian always did, and loving the idea of shooting at someone too, Bryce just wanted them to get out of there as fast as they could but Julian acted like he was ready for a gunfight, actually wanted a gunfight, as if being on the rifle team gave him license to even shoot someone if it came to that, remembered as they hunkered down behind the barricade of railroad ties Brownie telling stories about what was happening to them, trying to keep them amused and their minds off how dangerous the situation was but all Julian wanted to do was keep shooting back, peeking up over the top of the ties to look across the river ready to shoot at anything that moved, he could have gotten them all killed, it was no thanks to Julian that they made it out of there safely—Bryce could never forget, or perhaps more

to the point, could never forgive Julian for not owning up after-
ward to his role in making the situation all the more dangerous
by the way he acted, for not taking responsibility for his actions,
an aspect of his friend's character that he had never experienced
before—the boys waiting till nightfall to run hunkered down back
over the railroad tracks and make their way up the trails in the
dark to Orchard Hill, the story of what happened that day quickly
making the rounds of high school and Shine's Pizza and Jerry's
Drive-In, the Great Allehela Shootout, though when the two
friends were present at either the telling or the listening of the
story, Bryce and Julian looked at each other, never sure who it
was they were looking at . . . and the stories live on in and around
Furnass this evening as well, stories within stories within stories,
winding in and out among themselves in counterpoint like voices
of a fugue . . . as at his studio on the main street in Furnass,
after his last student for the evening has left, after the last mother
picked up her son or daughter and he's reassured her that her
child is making excellent progress, Kim turns out the lights in the
studio and then crosses the dark empty space to sit cross-legged
on the floor in front of the wall-sized mirror, places the box shaped
like a dragon's head in front of him and removes a stick of in-
cense, places it in the holder between the dragon's eyes and lights
it, watching as the flame turns to coal and then to gray ash in
the darkness, the thin column of smoke trailing upward gray on
gray, watching it and its barely discernible reflection in the mir-
ror, thinking again of his conversation today with Julian at Au-
gie's Kwik Dog, of Julian telling him to his face that no, he hadn't
heard from Don Sheetz and no, he hadn't heard anything about
where Stratton and Cory might be, the lies constricting his heart
like a physical weight, a tightness in his chest, thinking that he
had trusted Julian, counted Julian as a true friend, never doubt-
ing that Sheetz contacted Julian because Kim had asked him to,
had trusted Julian but now he knows better, will not make that

mistake again, realizes just as he can trust Sheetz because of their shared experience growing up that Julian's loyalties lie elsewhere, his Orchard Hill friends, and after raising his palms-together hands to his forehead and to the image of himself before him in the mirror he stands upright all in one fluid motion, ties his hair up in a bun at the back of his neck as he used to for competitions before he was banned from participating, leaves the incense burning before the mirror as a reminder to whatever spirits might feel honored by it and, wearing his black satin jacket and black satin pants, in his black canvas shoes, moving with a slight whisper as the cloth rubs on cloth, leaves by the back door of the studio, down the back stairs and gets in his car parked in the alley, to go hunting . . . as at the Sutcliff House on the edge of Orchard Hill, the streetlights below delineating the dark town as it stretches to the viaduct at the end of the valley, the massive dark shapes and blank spaces along the river no longer to his mind marking where the mills used to be but the location of the project his brother Dickie was developing before he died that would have brought him fame and fortune, the project now Dickie's daughter Jennifer is working to complete, Harry Todd carries another armload of his mother's underwear and unmentionables, sweaters and blouses and a large wad of women's stockings, across the dark lawn to the fire already burning in the fire pit he's cleared to burn the things in the house he's determined he needs to get rid of rather than have hauled away, a fire pit like a sacred circle that he's lined with orange bricks that he found in the basement leftover from when the house was built, dumps the load onto the smoldering remains of his last armload of coats and suits and dresses from his mother's closet, the armload momentarily smothering the remains of the fire, and he wonders if he's defeated his own purpose and put out the fire, should have spaced out dropping the clothes onto the embers, but then slowly the fire catches again, at first heavy gray smoke leaking around the edges of the fresh pile of clothes and then flames, the wad of stockings the first to ignite, like patterns of glowing steel wool, and as the flames begin to take hold he moves around to the other side of the pit and uses the flathead rake he found in the garage to stoke the fire, spreading the burning material around until the flames are a satisfying several feet tall, thinking So my dead mother's life goes up in smoke, I wish it was that easy to get rid of the past for the living, looks through the flames toward his family's house, ghostly in the light of the flames and the corner streetlight and watches as the figure of a young woman separates from the shadows and comes toward him as if growing out of the flames and Jennifer stands across the fire pit from him watching the fire for a minute or so before she says, "Do you need any help?" and Harry Todd says, "No, that's okay, I've got it"; "I'd be glad to help carry down some— " "I really need to do this myself," and Jennifer nods, looking at him across the fire and says, "Yeah, I understand," the two of them watching the clothes curl and shift in the heat and turn to ash until Jennifer says, "You haven't started on my dad's room yet, have you?" and Harry Todd says, "No, I told you, I'd save it till the very last," "I really appreciate it," "But I will have to do it eventually, you know," and Jennifer nods, "I know," her lips pulled into a tight sad smile, mouths Thank you, turns and heads toward the house, Harry Todd watching her lithe, lovely form flickering with the dying flames of the fire cross the dark lawn and disappear into the shadows up the steps of the porch and disappear into the house and thinks Maybe, just maybe, for once I can do this one thing without screwing it up . . . as later in the evening, after she's heard her uncle come back into the house and move through the downstairs turning off the lights, climb the stairs to the second floor, use the bathroom, and then continue up to his room on the third floor, Jennifer lies in the darkness of her father's childhood room, the room where he grew up, lies in her father's bed, maybe the same sheet and blanket he used, it's possible, looking up at the dark forms of model planes hanging from the ceiling that her father once made, on the shelves more models, battleships and tanks that he built from kits, on the walls the pennants for the Furnass Stokers from high school, the Penn State wall hanging with the Nittany Lion logo, movie posters for Easy Rider, *Raquel Welch as a cave woman in* One Million Years B.C.—*thinks Oh Dad, how predictable—Bo Derek in a swimsuit and cornrows running on a beach in* 10—*well, of course—and after lying there for an hour or so, long enough to give her uncle plenty of time to get to sleep, she gets up from the bed and in her black panties and bra opens the door being careful not to make a sound, pauses for a moment as she listens for any sound in the dark house, then steps out into the hall, looking up the stairs to the third floor to see if she can see a light on, and when she doesn't proceeds to the main stairs and goes on tiptoe down to the first floor, goes first to a window on the side of the house to make sure the fire Harry Todd made from his mother's old clothes in the fire pit has burned itself out, though for a moment she thinks she sees a black form moving along the black trees at the edge of the hillside, looks again but there is nothing, laughs at herself, thinking You're seeing things, then goes into the kitchen to make sure all the burners on the gas stove are turned off, that there are no electric appliances left on, takes a can of Rolling Rock from the refrigerator from the several six-packs she brought to the house a few days ago and carries it back into the main part of the house, going from room to room in the dark downstairs to make sure everything is okay, aware that her uncle is not himself these days and needs some looking after, needs to know that there's someone else with him in the house, somebody to say good night to in the evenings and have breakfast with in the mornings, needs to know he has a friend and someone he can count on, family as it were, watching her shadow as she passes the windows in the half-light from the streetlight at the end of the street, watching her dark reflection in the mirrors, the tall lithe half-naked girl with long red hair down around her shoulders, ghostly white in the darkness of the old house, the rooms mostly empty now of furniture but enough pieces remaining to remind her of being here as a child with her grandmother and grandfather, the house a treasure of memories for her, finds the loose brick in the fireplace in the living room that she discovered originally as a child when she used the space behind it to hide her Milky Way bars and uses it now to hide a stash of rolled joints, takes one of the joints and the box of matches and lights the joint before returning the matches to their hiding place, then sits in the old wood straight-backed rocker she remembers her grandmother sitting in for hours at a time, sits there in the darkness of the house rocking slowly back and forth as she smokes the joint, chasing the soreness in her throat with swallows of beer, listening to the creaks and groans of the wood of the old house, the house like a living thing for all its noises, until she's completely relaxed and happy with herself, sticks the roach into the empty can and takes the can back to the kitchen then heads back upstairs, is taking one last look around the downstairs as she starts up the stairs when out of the corner of her eye she catches a glimpse of what appears to be a woman in white gossamer on the steps ahead of her, looking back down at her as the vision passes in front of the blackened stained-glass window and turns onto the second floor, Jennifer blinking, and hurries up the stairs after the woman but the second-floor hall is empty, there is no one there, and Jennifer laughs at herself as she heads into her father's old room, thinking Wow, the way she looked at me it's almost as if she was trying to tell me something, like she liked me or something, thinking I've got to cut back on that Guatemalan weed . . . as in his house on Upper Nineteenth Street Police Chief Perry Sykes is sitting in his living room, tilted back in his Barcalounger watching a taped segment of* Miami Vice *when he gets the call from the dispatcher,* the phone from long experience sitting on the end table next to his chair for just such late-night calls, and Sykes listens and sighs and then says, "Yeah, okay, I'm on my way," and he pushes himself up and straps on his gun belt and puts on his Eisenhower-style jacket that he's well aware if buttoned makes him look like an overbaked potato ready to split open and that accordingly no matter how cold out he leaves open, lumbers upstairs to where his wife in her curlers and nightdress sits under the covers reading one of her paperback romance novels, kisses her good night and says he won't be long, "Be careful, okay?" she says and he replies, "Yeah, I'll give it some thought," and grins and considers going in to check on his thirteen-year-old son but the last time he did so he inadvertently caught the boy masturbating and doesn't want to give the kid a complex, it's hard enough being the son of the chief of police, and goes back downstairs and out to his police car parked on the steep street with its tires dug into the curb and heads downtown, no flashing lights or siren, along the main street and then down to the Lower End, turning back toward the slope of the valley through the dark streets with the small frame houses of some of the town's poorest residents, black and white, who he knows are both the target of most of the crime in his town as well as most of its perpetrators, past the two-story development of linked dwellings called the Dwellings that were originally put up by Sutcliff Realty during World War II as lower-income housing and later taken over by the public housing authority not necessarily to its betterment, the streets quiet tonight with the cold of winter though on Ninth Avenue, the last street before the hillside, he pulls over to the curb beside a row of a half dozen or so choppers, the motorcycles all parked closely side by side as if nestled together for warmth or mutual support, in front of a bar called aptly enough the Hillside Tavern, a dingy cement-block building with a few beer signs aglow in the bunker-like glass-block windows, where a dozen men in motorcycle and gang jackets are standing *out front, some with pool cues in hand and others with a make-shift collection of chains and bottles ready in case of a fight, all looking down the broken sidewalk at the man sitting on the curb, the man dressed in a black satin jacket and matching workout pants, his long black hair tied in a bun at the back of his neck, and Sykes walks past the collection of bikers and walks over to Kim, standing over him as Kim slowly turns and looks up at him and says, "They call you?" nodding to the group of men in the doorway and Sykes says, "Yeah, they learned what to expect the last couple times you paid them a visit," and Kim says, "They locked the door on me and wouldn't let me in, then I guess they got scared I'd do something to their bikes," smiles wistfully to himself and gets up slowly, brushing off the back of his pants, the group of men almost comically taking a step backward as soon as Kim makes a move, and Sykes says, "You got your car here or do you need a ride?" and Kim says, "No, I've got my car," and nods to it parked down the street and Sykes nods a little and says, "You going to be okay?" and Kim says, "Yeah, I'll be okay," then adds with a little smile, "I promise I won't hurt any of your good citizens," and Sykes says, "I appreciate that," watches as Kim starts down the dark street of broken asphalt, the crown of the street too high so the cars parked along it are tilted cattywampus, and says after him, "Anytime you want to talk, you know, about anything . . ." and Kim looks back at him and smiles again and gives him a little salute and gets in his car and drives off, Sykes walking back to his police car past the men standing in the door-way to the bar, thinking Shit, I should have asked Kim to wait till I got out of here myself . . . as two hundred feet up the steep wooded hillside behind the bar, in Furnass Heights, the area of town on top of the valley's hills where the truly rich people of the town in the late nineteenth and early twentieth centuries made their home, the mill owners and officials and prosperous mer-chants who made their fortunes by trading on the misfortunes of the working classes—the Lyles never lived here, even during their best years when the Keystone Steam Works appeared ready to establish the way Americans and therefore the rest of the world would view transportation with the Lylemobile; the Lyle house was halfway up the slope, where it was built above and away from the rest of the town though by the time the family's fortune's failed the town had grown up the slope around it, Julian's grandfather burning it to the ground rather than see it divided up into apartments or otherwise occupied by those he considered unfit and unworthy—though now that there are no longer any truly rich in town the estates have been divided up into smaller lots and subdivisions, streets of well-kept orange and yellow brick houses on well-trimmed lawns, set back from the streets that are more like roads without curbs or sidewalks because where would anyone walk to in this area that they couldn't and wouldn't drive, a few of the original homes still to be found tucked away in odd corners, houses built in the mid-1800s when the area consisted of farms and orchards, an occasional old frame house that breaks the mold of respectability and in Julian's case proudly so, an air of not exactly seediness but definitely countrified about his place with the several storage sheds out back and the piles of lumber for some remodel project that is always half-done and the woodpile beside the house where he daily in the fall and winter splits logs to fuel his several wood stoves and fireplaces, the smell of wood smoke permeating the neighborhood so that when Julian drives home at night he can tell just by sniffing when he's almost there, to the house where now after eleven o'clock at night he makes his final tour through the downstairs to check the doors and see that all the fires are banked, from force of habit on the second floor checking the rooms of his five children though none of them live at home now, his brood scattered to the four winds either married or living elsewhere, then takes Reggie the basset hound who has followed him on his late-night rounds and slings the dog over his shoulder and climbs the drop-down stairs to the third floor where he and his wife, Marta, have their bedroom, Marta already sitting in bed watching Johnny Carson as Julian gains the floor and puts Reggie in his bed at the foot of their bed and then pulls the drop-down stairs up after him, which closes off the hole in the floor as well, the love nest and hideaway that he and Marta made for themselves at the top of the house as soon as the youngest of their children were old enough to fend for themselves during the night, deciding that it would be the only thing to keep them from either killing their children or themselves at the insanity of raising all those kids, Julian going into their private bathroom and putting on his pajamas then sits in his wing-backed chair in the corner, his reading nook with his newspapers and history books and magazines, scratching at his beard briefly as if fingering arpeggios, though tonight he's not interested in reading, he's thinking back over the events of the day, thinking about finding Stratton's cabin and the Polaroids of Cory, convinced all the more that he has to find Cory and get her away from Stratton before Kim finds out or finds her with the guy, afraid all the more of what Kim will do to Stratton if he finds out what Cory has been up to, remembering his conversation with Kim that morning at the Kwik Dog when Kim talked about loyalty among friends, what a friend would do for a friend, Julian convinced now that Kim was telling him in other words of his involvement with Dickie's death, and that it was Julian's responsibility now to do what he could to protect his friend from killing again, as across the room Marta uses the remote to turn off the television and says, "Are you coming to bed?" and Julian says, "Hmm," and Marta pulls back the cover in his direction and says their code words, "No, I mean are you coming to bed?" and Julian catches her meaning and turns off the floor lamp beside his chair and heads across the room thinking as he climbs into bed and into Marta's naked arms that it galls him more than words can say that for all his silliness and stupid questions the indications are that Bryce is right about someone else involved in Dickie Sutcliff's death . . . and in Drumlins, after he's had his dinner and spent what he considers an appropriate enough time listening to Rachel relate the happenings of her day at the hospital, Bryce sits in his armchair in the room at the top of the bell tower of his church, in the reflected parti-colored glow of the window from the spotlights trained upon it, the room sur-prisingly comfortable because of the heat of the lights—in sum-mertime when the room gets too hot, he climbs the wood ladder attached to the stone wall to the belfry above, the open bell cham-ber where the bells are, sitting on the ledge of one of the open windows looking out at the commercial district surrounding him to catch a summer breeze—he has a dream to someday restore the racks of bells into working order again, envisioning himself leading a team of bell ringers tugging on the ropes dangling down to the bell ringer's room below, the bells pealing out the Good News over the crass commercial world below, but so far it's only a dream, cleaning the rose window was one thing, that basically required only determination and a desire to be off on his own away from everybody else for a while, but to repair the wood framing supporting the bells would require more work and exper-tise than he can muster—choosing for his soundtrack tonight after his particularly stressful day Art Blakey's* A Night at Birdland, *listening to "Now's the Time" as he thinks back to what he learned today and what he didn't learn about the death of the Dickie-Bird, his run-in with Police Chief Perry Sykes being particularly dis-turbing, his talk with J. Howard Griffith leaving him with more questions than answers, but it is one other incident that sticks out in his mind, thinks as Clifford Brown takes his solo over the jungle-like drumming of Blakey, Far out, Lord, Jennifer called me a fool, she said it right to my face, You're a fool. Wow, a lot of people undoubtedly think that but she's the only one who's ever had enough cojones to come right out and say it. I guess you have to admire that, no matter how hard it is to hear, no matter that it's probably true. A fool. Help me, Lord, I'm no better than Julian. . . .*

PART THREE

19

Maybe over the doorway in the dining room, thought Kim. Or somewhere in the kitchen.

Why would Lyle say that when I know it's not true? Why would he lie to me? Now I know about Lyle too.

Kim walked through the downstairs of his house, a carved antique eagle in his hand, holding it up against the wall of the dining room above the bureau, over the doorway to the hall, then carried it on into the kitchen. He'd found the eagle in one of the antiques stores that recently opened along the main street, Things of Yesteryear taking over the space that once belonged to Lionel Miller Fine Clothes. Kim had only stopped by the shop to be neighborly, to say hello to the new store owner in town, one merchant to another, but on a shelf at the back, along with a Kewpie doll and an insect-like cherry pitter, two Coke bottles and a rusted toy motorboat, he spotted the eagle and thought it would be a good addition to his house, would fit in well with his early American decor, the way he had decorated the house after the insurance settlement several years ago, when he had to remodel the downstairs after the damage from the incident with his father. The question now was where to put it.

In the kitchen he held it up over the sink, above the refrigerator, over the doorframe. That would be fitting, he thought, to have it here in the kitchen. A tribute to where it all started. A memorial to what happened here. That night.

That night he came home early from the studio and found his father here in the kitchen with Cory. It was a warm spring evening, she was in short shorts and bare feet, her halter top showing her prepubescent eleven-year-old figure. Kim had told Sheryl to never leave Cory alone in the house with his father, but when he called earlier and no one answered on a night when Sheryl was supposed to be here, he left class and hurried home to check. And here they were. Tomi was sitting at the kitchen table, with Cory standing between his legs. He had his hands on her waist, on the bare skin between her top and shorts, and was in the process of turning her, admiring her.

"Stop, Pap-Pap," Cory was saying, giggling. "That tickles." They both looked surprised for different reasons when they became aware of Kim in the doorway.

"Hi, Dad. Why are you home so early? Don't you have class tonight?"

"What are you doing?" Kim said, ignoring her, looking at his father.

"Well, hello there, Kim. This is a surprise."

"Come away from there, Cory," Kim said. Trying his best to sound casual. Not to alarm her. "Leave Tomi alone."

"What?" the girl said. Still between his father's legs. "Pap-Pap was going to show me a trick."

"Yes, I was." His father still had his hands on the girl's waist. He smiled at Kim. His slow, sleepy, knowing smile.

"I said come away from him. Do as I say. Now." Kim crossed the room and took his daughter's hand, to guide her away but she resisted and he ended up pulling her. "Go on upstairs now. Tomi and me have something to talk about."

"What's the matter?" Cory said. Trying to pull her hand out of Kim's grasp but he wouldn't let her go. "I was talking to Pap-Pap."

"See, Kim?" Tomi said. "She likes her Pap-Pap. She wants him."

"Leave her alone."

"He didn't do anything," Cory said, still trying to pull away from Kim. Slapped at him.

"You want your Pap-Pap, don't you, Cory?" Tomi grinned at her. Grinned at Kim. "They all want it, Kim. Young girls. Young boys too. Huh, Kim?"

Cory slapped at Kim again to try to release her hand and he almost hit her, cocked his arm across his chest to release a back-fist, but caught himself. Tomi laughed. Kim towed Cory out of the room and through the dining room to the foot of the stairs to the second floor. "Get upstairs now!"

Cory was surprised; the force of his pulling her sent her up the first couple of steps. Tomi had followed them into the dining room and stood near the table.

"Just stay away from her," Kim said to him through the doorway. "Don't ever put your hands on her again."

"Why not?" Tomi grinned. "Break her in right. You need to do that with kids, don't you Kim?"

It was then that Kim saw his father was holding a kitchen knife, a butcher knife. Kim became very quiet, very calm. His years of training and experience taking over now, instinctive. Turning slightly toward his father. His hands flowing into position. One a tiger's claw. The other a fist. Balanced and centered. Thinking, Is it now? Waiting.

Kim carried the eagle back into the dining room, trying it again above the bureau. If he hung it there, he should move the pictures that were already there to give the area the proper balance, the framed reproductions on wood that he also found in an antiques store, Edward Hicks's *Peaceable Kingdom*, a primitive painting of a Holstein cow standing in a farmyard. No, there's got to be a better place for it, he thought. Besides, I like the paintings where they are.

He thought his father must be bluffing. Being dramatic. Surely he couldn't be serious. A knife? But Kim wasn't going to take the chance. He could tell now that his father had been drinking, there was a slight sway as he stood beside the dining room table, the knife down at his side. He had seen his father this way before, many times, over the years when Kim was taking classes himself at the studio, his father the teacher, the sensei, Sifu Tomi, the alcohol never impairing his father's strength or reflexes, only bringing out more of his innate meanness.

He was larger than Kim, taller by several inches, a block of a man, Kim more like his mother's side of the family, slight and wiry, though his father's earlier muscle tone had deteriorated some with age, with too much drinking, the bones of Tomi's face collapsed in upon themselves on one side, the result of a kick to the head during a fight as a young man in Jakarta before he mastered his art. Tomi had learned that art in the narrow back streets and alleyways of Jakarta and Jambi, a mixture of martial arts styles that coalesced into his own fighting system, becoming well-known in the Indonesian martial arts communities, so well-known that the Dutch government enlisted him to spy for them, to keep them abreast of troublemakers or efforts at independence; later he became a double agent for the Sukarno forces, a double cross that gave him an ample nest egg and a Chinese wife but eventually resulted in his having to flee the country with his family and seek refuge in the United States, taking his wife's surname for good measure, hiding in this little mill town from the men on both sides who were sent to track him down.

"Tomi, put the knife down," Kim said.

"He has a knife?" Cory said. She ran on up the stairs, screaming, "Pap-Pap, what's going on?"

"Get in your room and stay there!" Kim called after her, not looking her direction. Keeping his eyes on his father, on his crushed and broken face, the face of the man in the quarter moon as he thought of him while growing up, the features tucked into the sickle of what remained of the bone structure. Tomi started toward him, slowly, Kim walking backward matching him step for step, trying for time, hoping to still talk some sense into his father, or at least maneuver him to an area where there was more space, deeper into the front hall, where there was more room if he was going to have to fight him. His father continued to smile at him, the man in the sickle moon grinning through the haze of alcohol, as his eyes came to rest on the *dan dao*, the wide curved Chinese broadsword sitting on a display rack in the hallway.

He held the eagle up against the wall in the front hallway, above where the ceremonial *dan dao* used to sit on a long and narrow black lacquered table, the display Sheryl had put there to introduce visitors to their home, back when they were still married and in love, back when she was proud of Kim's involvement with the martial arts. Back when she was proud of Kim. But he wasn't going to think about that now. Perhaps if he hung the eagle here it would have the same effect for visitors to the home now. Show what was important to the household now. The eagle was originally part of a wood pediment, a decorative finial on top of a wardrobe or bureau mirror, the bird stylized, even a bit whimsical, its expression one of surprise as if it spotted something startling over its left shoulder, flanked on either side by two carved wooden knobs like the domes of a Turkish mosque. The carving was probably a bit silly, he had to admit, but it was authentic and he liked it; he thought it added something to the overall tenor of the house, what he had tried to do to the place when he remodeled it after what happened here, the symbol of the eagle important to him, a reminder that he was an American and proud of it, of his time in the marines, the gold eagles on top of the flags as they paraded at Pendleton, the eagles on top of the flags at the hospital where they flew him after he was wounded at Hue where they cleared the streets of the Citadel house by house, a kind of fighting they were not trained for but Kim unknowingly was, which he discovered when he and one of the replacements, a guy named Jake he barely knew at all, Smitherall or Southerland or something like that, burst into a house and surprised a trio of NVA and Kim's rifle jammed and the first shots took a chunk out of Kim's hip and Jake stepped forward to cover him and took out two of the NVA before he went down and the third NVA charged Kim with his bayonet and even wounded Kim disarmed him the way his father taught him and they fought hand to hand, the NVA with a knife until Kim also as his father taught him jammed his fingers into the other man's eyes and pulled off half his face into his hand but he wasn't going to think about that now either.

In the Kwik Dog yesterday Lyle said he hadn't heard anything about Stratton, Kim remembered. No, not a word. I'll let you know as soon as I do. Why would he say that when it wasn't true? I don't have to call Sheetz to know Don gave him Stratton's address in Indian Camp. I thought I could trust Lyle. I guess I can't. Sad.

His father threw the knife aside and grabbed the sword and started to pull it from the rack. Kim grabbed his wrist and said, "Tomi. Wait—" but the backfist to Kim's temple stopped him cold, it was only through instinct that he was able to deflect the blow at all, otherwise it would have knocked him unconscious or possibly killed him, and he staggered backward. His father had the sword in hand and out of its sheath now; Kim's head was still ringing, he couldn't believe this was happening, then had to believe it, fast: his father swung the sword two-handed at his head: Kim dropped to the floor—the blade missing him by inches—and scissored his father's legs between his own as he rolled to the left, knocking his father off-balance and sending him headfirst into the front door. As his father righted himself, pulled himself up by the door handle, it occurred to Kim for the briefest second that it was his father who had taught him that scissors sweep years ago, knowing it was absurd even as he thought it, that there was a part of him that wanted this man who just missed taking off his head to be proud of how well little Kimmie performed the maneuver, but there was no room in the hallway to finish the takedown as he should have and needed to, to roll the man onto the floor and in the continuation of the motion finish him with an elbow strike to the head or a flathand blow to the Adam's apple, the ground-fighting techniques, the grappling of the tiger, that his father had taught him too, the hall was too narrow, the door where Tomi hit his head, stunning him, also breaking his fall, his father on his feet again now, shaking his head to clear it, the sword still in his hand, down at his side.

"Dad, what are we doing? Why?" Kim was on his feet.

"My life is shit. Let them kill me, I'm taking you and your fucking pretty wife and that fucking pretty little girl of yours with me."

His father lunged at him, screaming, the blade swirling in front of him but either from age or the alcohol or his collision with the door without his usual speed and coordination; Kim backtracked into the living room and kicked the glass-topped coffee table into his father's shins and tripped him and knocked him off-balance again except this time his father caught himself and wheeled around and, bellowing like an animal, hurled the sword at Kim, Kim spinning out of the way—the sword zipped by close enough that he felt the breeze before it twanged into the wall—as the man with the face of the quarter moon charged him; with the coffee table out of the way, Kim threw a reverse kick that caught his father full on the side of the face and as he stood dazed Kim caught him with a number of blows to the body and an elbow strike to the head that sent him careening sideways into the tall glass-and-steel set of shelves, which toppled over onto him amid a shower of broken glassware and vases and his wife's Norman Rockwell collector plates and a couple of dying Boston ferns and the few books they used for decoration, the blood already appearing around the edge of the man's mouth as he struggled to get up and then collapsed, his eyes rolling back in his head.

"Dad, what's going on!" came Cory's voice from the hallway. She was in the doorway to the living room, crying. "I'm scared. Did you kill Pap-Pap?"

"It's okay, Cory, it's okay." He hurried across the room to her, tried to hug her but she moved away from him, wide-eyed, not knowing which way to turn. He reached for her again when he heard the stirrings behind him and his father's cackle and turned around to see his father pulling himself up out of the debris on the other side of the room, blood from his mouth and nose and the side of his face more collapsed than ever, the cheekbone and the bones around his eye broken, but still smiling, laughing maniacally, staggering across the room to take a set of butterfly swords off the wall and start toward Kim again, a sword in each hand. Kim pushed Cory back up the stairs—the girl screaming, running for her room—and took up a position in the doorway to the living room, knowing now what he had to do.

He took the eagle into the living room and tried it on the walls in various places. The room since he had remodeled it looked like an illustration from *Colonial Homes* magazine—which in fact had been its inspiration, Kim coming across a copy of the magazine one day on the magazine rack at Mikey's All-Niter and using it as a guide. The walls were pale Adam green—in his research he read that white walls were favored in Colonial America but that some pale shades were acceptable to be authentic—with white woodwork, around the fireplace and doorframes and the built-in bookcase and the crown molding. The furniture was all Duncan Phyfe—an uncomfortable straight-backed sofa with awning-striped cushions; spindly-legged straight chairs and a tallboy desk; a leather-topped round table that already bore a circle from Cory setting a glass down without a coaster. He thought the eagle would fit in well with the other decorations; over the fireplace was a painting of a severe-looking man with sickle-like whiskers and stiff white collar; an American primitive painting of a barrel-shaped little girl in a ruffled dress holding her barrel-shaped cat; and a collection of old ladles and hand tools. He was pleased the way the room had turned out but he rarely sat in it, preferring to sit at the counter in the kitchen even to watch television. The truth was he was rarely home, spending most of his time at his school; he thought he'd be home more, use the room more, once he had custody of Cory. It was unthinkable to him that she wouldn't be with him.

I guess it's understandable, he thought, that Lyle's loyalty would lie with the guys he grew up with on Orchard Hill. That he would trust them more than he trusts me. Admirable in a way. That he'd stay loyal to them no matter how badly they treat him, act toward him. Shit on him, really. The way that reverend, Bryce, talks down to him. The way Dickie Sutcliff took advantage of him. Though it's easy to see why. Lyle is gullible. Likes to think he knows how the world works and knows nothing. Nothing of the evil of the everyday. Maybe that's why he latched on to me after the trial. Thought I could show him the mean underbelly of the world. Kim the interesting legal case, something to enter into the law books, a persuasive precedent. Sheetz is right, I know that. Lyle was always slumming in a way being around me. Lyle thinks too much. About the wrong things. The world isn't about thinking, it's about acting. Doing whatever needs to be done, whenever it needs done. Acting quickly and decisively. Knowing when to pull a punch and when to follow through. When to strike to hurt. To kill. And not look back. Step over the bodies. Those are things Lyle will never know. Will never learn practicing in a mirror. I wanted him to trust me. But I know why he can't.

Knew that he not only had to kill this man but that he wanted to, that he had wanted to kill him for nearly as long as he could remember, for the never-ending bullying, for the abuse—Little boys too, huh Kim?—as his father came at him again, stumbling through the rubble of the living room, cackling to himself, trying to swing the two butterfly knives in the patterns he taught at the school but too weak now to pull it off, the man with the face of the quarter moon bleeding badly now, blood coming from a deep cut on the side of his face as well as from the corners of his mouth, drunker now than when the fight started or so it seemed, the alcohol in his system apparently clouding his brain more as time went on, his father pretending to cover his wooziness by trying to act out some of the motions of the drunken mantis form, arms akimbo, staggering a bit sideways as he still came on, though it was obvious that his real problem was that he was badly injured—or was he? The success of the drunken mantis depended on the deceptions of the fighter, and his father was a master— unrelenting, keeping both blades loosely now at his sides, unable to relent, and Kim was full of his own power, his own mind clear now and at one with himself and his abilities, he began to hit him, dispassionate, deadly serious, methodical, running through a series of blows, backfist, knife hand, straight fist, beating his father around the head and on his body at the liver, kidneys, heart, his father standing like a practice dummy, juked back and forth with the force of Kim's blows and yet remaining on his feet, Kim never once letting down his guard, not trusting the man even now not to somehow rally, never discounting the possibility that his father might be waiting for the slightest opening to strike, or unable to believe that this was actually happening to him from his son, then Kim stopped, looked at this figure swaying back and forth in front of him, the two butterfly knives useless at his sides, shoulders rolled as if hung by them from the ceiling of the room, his father gazing at him through half-closed eyes, almost sleepily, the evil grin spreading again over his battered and bleeding lips as he mouthed the word Pussy and Kim whirled and ended it with another reverse kick to his father's head that lifted the man off his feet and spun him around and sent him crashing face-first onto the glass and twisted metal on the floor.

No, the eagle was too much here in the living room. Kim carried it back to the hall, held it up once again on the wall across from the steps, above the narrow Parsons table, then went to the kitchen and down to the basement to get a hammer and a couple nails.

Thinking, That's why Lyle said that at his office the other day. That reminds me, I tried to call you Friday night, about ten o'clock. I guess you weren't home. I tried over at the studio too. . . . He didn't trust me. He's thought from the beginning that I might have had something to do with Dickie Sutcliff's death. That's why he brought up his talk with his friend Bryce at the Kwik Dog, Bryce thinks it's suspicious that Dickie would fall in his office that way. He was feeling me out to see how I'd react, if I would say anything to play into his suspicions of me. Poor Lyle. Sad that he wouldn't trust me more than that. That he'd think I'd just go kill somebody, one of his friends, just like that. I would have, of course, if he asked me to, if it was necessary, no other way. If he had asked me to at one time. But not now. Now that it's over. Now that the friendship is dead. There would be other reasons now.

Tomi's crumpled body, or what was left of it, lay in a heap amid the debris. Kim hunched over, resting his hands on his knees, exhausted, panting for breath, afraid he might be sick. His father was motionless. The damn fool. He kept coming. Didn't he know I could kill him? Didn't he know I wanted to? Or maybe that's why. Maybe he wanted me to. Behind him, from upstairs, he could hear Cory crying.

"It's okay, Cory," he croaked to her, barely able to speak. "It's all okay now, sweetheart. It's over now. Daddy'll be right there."

Still hunched over, unable to quite stand up straight, he went over to his father. "Dad? You okay?" Knowing it was a stupid thing to say even as he said it.

If the man was still alive, though there didn't seem much chance he could be, Kim had to get help for him. He reached down and rolled him on his back. His father's eyes were closed, Kim couldn't tell if he was breathing or not. Knelt down and bent over to listen for a heartbeat when his father's eyes snapped open and the man reached up and grabbed Kim's throat, laughing at him, barely able to mutter, "Fuck you. I fucked you . . ." as blood and spit slobbered out of his damaged mouth, a grasp that even as the fingers locked around Kim's neck was not strong enough to squeeze hard enough to kill him but barely hold on as Kim straightened up again, and they both knew it, his father's last futile effort not from any desire to keep fighting or even to hurt his son at this point even if he could but simply because it wasn't in the man to stop, and they both knew that too, though Kim reacted as if the threat to his life was real, reacted totally and without compunction, brought his arms together as his father had taught him and broke the choke hold easily then with his father staring up at him from the floor and with a dozen possible moves open to him—a flathand strike to the Adam's apple to crush his larynx, an upward palm strike at the pressure point below the nose, a tiger-claw strike with his knuckles between the eyes or to the eyes themselves—he gripped his father's throat with his two hands and squeezed, thinking, Just till he's unconscious, Just till he's unconscious, but continued to squeeze as he watched the life go out of the man's eyes once and for all, the face of the man in the quarter moon turning gray as the quarter moon and still did not let go, continued to hold on until his fingers ached and hands began to cramp and he became aware of Cory crying upstairs and the everyday world of his living room around him and the feel of his father's skin in his grasp and slowly, gradually, he released his hold, still half expecting the man under him to stir, for the eyes to open again, for the man to try something else, one last thing, perhaps even wanting him to, hoping he would, not because he wanted to hurt him anymore but because he wanted to know he could if he had to. That it wasn't over.

Kim took the level and made two marks on the wall with a carpenter's pencil, then drove the nails into the wall halfway and hung the eagle in place in the front hall. There. Done. He stood back and thought it looked appropriate. Land of the free. Home of the brave.

Because Lyle sees me only as a killer, that's all. Always has, always will. And it wasn't even that when he defended me at the trial, it was only a lawyer thing, able to argue either side, in this case to defend me, in another case to prosecute me, as much as he cared. Lyle never stopped to think: why would I hurt Sutcliff, why would I kill him? I didn't have anything against the guy, in fact I sort of liked him, and unlike Lyle I thought Sutcliff was actually helping him, taking Lyle's financial burden on himself. But when it came down to it, I wasn't to be trusted, I wasn't meant to be given the benefit of the doubt. Unlike someone he did trust. Someone like Bryce. Someone from Orchard Hill. His kind of people.

Kim carried the level and the pencil and the hammer back down to the basement, placed them in their appointed spots on the pegboard above his workbench, then turned off the light and went back upstairs, admiring the placement of the eagle on the wall one more time. Satisfied, he went back to the kitchen and, checking to make sure that it was after nine o'clock so he would be there, lifted the receiver of the phone from its cradle, dialed the number for the welding shop and when his friend answered, said, "Don, it's Kim. Now I need that address for Stratton."

20

The car radio was playing nothing but hopelessly cheerful Christmas music—"I Saw Mommy Kissing Santa Claus," "Grandma Got Run Over by a Reindeer"—so Julian turned it off and rode in silence—he needed the time to think anyway—as he left his house in Furnass Heights and headed down the valley's wall to Furnass, taking the back way this morning, down steep Bridge Street Hill, the older windy road hugging the bluffs of the hillside, a tight squeeze if two cars met—it was said his great-grandfather once drove a buggy off the side of the narrow road when a copperhead spooked the horse, the dense foliage of the hillside catching them in midair slowing their fall so that horse, buggy, and his great-grandfather landed right side up at the bottom and drove on home—because the road dumped him off in the Lower End of town with a straight shot toward the river. After finding the receipts at Stratton's place yesterday, he thought he'd swing by the hotel this morning before going to his office, on the chance the guy was there.

He'd barely slept last night—even after making love with Marta, which usually put him right out, but there was simply too much on his mind—torn between finding Stratton and not finding him, finding Cory and not finding her, his legalistic mind kicking into gear, thinking about his involvement with recent events in terms of unintended consequences. He realized after the fact that by doing everything he could to forestall a deeper investigation into Dickie's death, particularly in helping to convince Tinker not to have an autopsy in case Kim had something to do with it, he had hindered discovering if anyone else was involved. He didn't want to be at fault for doing something similar when it came to finding Cory. If Stratton was at the hotel—and if Cory was with him, or if he knew where she was—Julian might get her back home safely before Kim grew impatient and went on the hunt himself and that would be that. If she wasn't there—or Stratton either, for that matter—he could report to Kim with a clear conscience and do what needed to be done, what should have been done before this. They had to turn the matter over to the police and start an official search for the girl. Sheryl might think it was a legal maneuver to make her look bad for the custody hearing—which it undoubtedly would; another unintended consequence—but he couldn't take the chance in regard to the girl's safety.

The hotel sat on the corner of Third Avenue and Eleventh Street, across from where the principal train station in town used to be, when passenger trains still stopped in town, the first building that turn-of-the-twentieth-century travelers saw as they stepped out of the station, the vendors and drummers and executives who came to town primarily for business at the mill, the hotel an introduction to what was hopefully perceived as the genteel aspects of the town, such as they were—it was a large building of native stone, five stories tall, with upper-level towers bulging out over the sidewalk and stone arches over the windows and front door and Gothic dormers along the high-pitched roof—though it was anything but grand these days, a residence hotel for pensioners and welfare recipients and by-the-week contract workers who didn't want to walk too far after drinking themselves silly at night in the country-and-western strip bar next door.

The once grand lobby was now a large empty space, lit by a few bare bulbs and the light straining in the windows, the supporting pillars standing like stone columns in an underground mine; in one corner was a collection of old sofas, overstuffed chairs, and rockers placed in rows before a television set; a few additional overstuffed chairs sat facing the large front windows, where two older men sat smoking, watching the occasional car pass in the street, the demolition going on across the street at the site of the old mill. The leather soles of Julian's Wellington boots ticked on the black-and-white tiles as he approached the two men.

"Hi, excuse me. Is the manager around?" Julian said, looking about as if he might have missed the office.

"I don't know, Cyrus," one man said to the other, not looking at Julian. "Do we even have a manager these days?"

"Well, somebody goes into that office in the back now and then. And somebody must collect the checks we squeeze through the mail slot. And nobody's come to throw us out just yet. So yes, there must be a manager somewhere."

"I'll bet that's what that Mrs. Greenaway does."

"I'll bet you're right."

The two men continued to look out the window in front of them, addressing each other, not bothering to look at Julian. He moved around the side of the chairs, closer to the window so they could see him at an oblique angle, if they chose to. They chose to glance at him but that was about all.

"Mrs. Greenaway," Julian said, with a little laugh. "Well, do you happen to know where I could find her?"

"'Happen to know.' Curious phrase, don't you think Cyrus, if you stop to think about it? I mean, if we *happened to know* where Mrs. Greenaway is, we would have said so when he asked in the first place. And it wouldn't be because we *happened to know*, it would be because we did know."

"Now, don't give the boy a bad time, Anthony. He's just trying to get some information from us. No need to get into one of your difficult turn of minds."

"Well, if he wants information, he should just come out and ask for it. And don't call me Anthony."

"Actually," Julian said, "I'm looking for Jim Stratton."

"There you are, Cyrus. He's not even looking for Mrs. Greenaway, whether we *happen to know* where she is or not. He's looking for some other person completely."

"Who are you looking for?" Cyrus said, looking at Julian now, leaning forward to hear better.

"Jim Stratton. He works as a welder . . . sort of a big guy, lots of hair and a beard. . . . I know he stays here on occasion and I was wondering if he is here now. And if he is, where I'd find him."

"Well, offhand," the one who didn't want to be called Anthony put in, "I'd say if he *happened to be* here, you'd *happen to* find him in his room."

Cyrus shook his head at his companion, rolled his eyes in sympathy to Julian. "I think I know the guy you mean. Try Room 428."

"Is that the guy with all the young chippies going in and out? Oh yes, he's someone I'd surely like to see."

"Is it all right," Julian addressed Cyrus, "for me just to go on up?"

"Well," the one who didn't want to be called Anthony put in, "I think it would be pretty hard to bring the room down here to you." This time both of the older men couldn't help but laugh.

"There's an elevator at the back," Cyrus said, still chuckling at his companion. Julian started to leave but the man said, "Your name's Lyle, isn't it?"

"Yes. Julian Lyle."

"I thought so," Cyrus said. He turned to the one who didn't want to be called Anthony. "Mal Lyle's boy."

"I'm not surprised," he nodded. To Julian he said, "Your daddy is the one who killed my daddy."

Julian laughed a little, uncomfortably.

"Don't mind him," Cyrus said. "He gets funny ideas."

"It's not a funny idea," the one who didn't want to be called Anthony said. "And don't make apologies for me. His daddy frittered away the Steam Works with his bad investments."

"You mean the investments the company made in their steam passenger vehicle?" Julian said. "Actually, that was my father's father—"

"I don't mean that Lylemobile thing, that was sure dumb enough, but that particular fiasco was long gone when your daddy took down the company. I mean when he come into the company, young Mr. Know-It-All, and he was going to show his daddy and everybody else how things are done. So what did he do? Him and his investments undid the company until there wasn't enough left to undo. And what did he do then? He took off and left the entire mess sitting there until the creditors came and picked over it like a bunch of turkey vultures. Your daddy didn't dare show his face in town again until there was nothing left of the Keystone Steam Works to come back to. That was your daddy who did that, and my daddy never recovered losing his job that way, broke him in half it did, he was never the same after that. Don't try to tell me that wasn't your daddy who did that, I know who your daddy is and what he done."

Cyrus looked apologetic. "He gets worked up at certain things. Maybe you should . . . you know. . . ." He nodded toward the rear and the elevator. Julian nodded and left them sitting there, the two friends with their heads together, Cyrus trying to calm the one who didn't want to be called Anthony.

Julian took the elevator to the fourth floor and stepped off into the dingy hallway. The place smelled of dust and mold, old urine and damp plaster, the only light coming from a window at the far end of the narrow hall. Midway down the corridor a door was standing open, rock music coming from inside. Julian peered in around the frame. Stratton was sitting on the bed, rolling a series of joints, lining them up in front of him on the tattered blanket like small white party favors. When he noticed Julian he grinned as if he wasn't surprised to have a visitor.

"You want me to roll you one of these?" Stratton said.

Julian stepped into the room, shaking his head. "Hello Jim."

"Probably just as well. Wouldn't do for an officer of the court to be seen in such a compromising situation, now would it?"

"No. Can't say that it would." Julian looked around the room and was both relieved and troubled that there was no sign of Cory.

Stratton was a large man, in a sleeveless black T-shirt, jeans, and engineer boots, his hair and beard a brown tangle around his head. He and Julian knew of each other rather than knew each other directly, the kind of relationship that happens in a small town, neither one able to say if he had ever spoken directly to the other but recognized the other as if he had; Julian was aware of him as someone to avoid if possible but couldn't say he ever heard anything specific against him. Stratton licked another cigarette, watching Julian with a pretend lewd grin, sucked the cigarette into his mouth and out again, and added it to the others.

"So, what is an officer of the court doing at the Grand Hotel at this hour of the morning? You looking for me?"

"Matter of fact, I am," Julian said, stepping into the room a little farther, his hands in his sport coat pockets. "I'm looking for a young girl."

"Come to the right place for that. Lots of little pussies seem to find their way in here. What flavor you looking for? White? Black? Brown, maybe? I'm actually glad to hear you're in the market. I've sometimes wondered about you, thought you might have leanings in another direction."

"Cute," Julian said. "But that's not what I mean and you know it. I'm looking for a young girl named Cory."

"Ah. Cory."

"I heard she was with you."

"Well, I guess you heard wrong. Look around, you see anything that looks like a girl named Cory in here?"

"Not at the moment, I'll admit. But I've seen some photos that showed her in a room just like this, on a bed just like the one you're sitting on. Photos that could get whoever took them into a whole lot of trouble if they got into certain hands."

Stratton wasn't smiling now. He swung his engineer boots off the bed and sat on the edge, turned off the radio with a swat. "And how did you happen to see photos like that?"

Julian shrugged. "Let's just say I did."

"And let's just say that to see photos like that, somebody would have to be somewhere they're not supposed to be. Like in somebody's place, going through somebody's private things. That to me is called trespassing, and trespassers can end up shot, among other things."

Julian took his hands from his pockets and held them up to show they were empty. "I didn't say I had such photos, I only said I saw them. I guess your concern would be who else saw them. Such as the girl's father."

"Your friend. Killer Kim. The Yellow Peril." Stratton looked down between his legs. Then he pulled up his pants leg and took a small automatic from an ankle holster inside his boot. Fondled it as he looked back at Julian. "That karate, kung fu crap will only take you so far. Never heard of one of those guys yet that could beat a speeding bullet. So, did Leong or somebody else send you here with a message or what?"

"No, I came on my own. And I'm trying to keep Kim out of this if I can, so he knows nothing about it. I want to find Cory on my own and get her back home before something happens, for whatever reason or whoever might initiate it. I'm actually your best friend at this point."

Stratton blew air through his nose. "I don't have friends, best or otherwise. And you can see how scared I am of your martial arts buddy." He twirled the automatic once and put it back in its holster. But his attitude seemed to change. "Yeah, she was here. For a couple of days. I let her hole up here for a while, she seemed to have a lot on her mind, about one thing or another. Nice kid but kinda mixed-up. I even took her with me when I made a run out to the cabin for some stuff. But she's not here now. Left last night."

"Where did she go?"

"Don't know. Don't care." He thought a moment. "And yeah, we did some photos. She was pretending she was a bad girl. But it was pretty evident she didn't know what she was getting herself into. And believe it or not I left her alone once I figured that out. It ain't no fun if they don't know what they're doing, not even if you get 'em stoned and incapacitated. Never was into the rape thing, or doing it with dead-like girls. There's enough young stuff out there. Young stuff that knows what to do with it when they get it."

"She just took off?"

Stratton shrugged. "We was having a party here last night with a couple people but she didn't have the taste for it and ended up sitting there in the corner messing herself up with some shit. I didn't actually see what happened to her or when she left, I had my face buried in a sweet little muff."

"And you don't know where she went."

"Not a clue. And good riddance. If I'm going to have jailbait hanging around I want to get something for my trouble, you know?"

As Julian rode back down in the elevator he felt slightly sick at his stomach, thinking, I know I can't trust the guy, but I wonder if I can believe him. If he really didn't touch Cory, it's a relief to know she was with him, at least up till last night. Weird, to think she would be safer with him than out on her own, Stratton as good guy, even if he chose not to take advantage of her for the wrong reasons. But then where did she wander off to? And what condition was she in? Where did she end up? Where is she now?

When he got back to the lobby, Cyrus and not-Anthony were gone, their overstuffed chairs sitting empty in the pale light coming through the large front window. Damn, I wanted to ask him about that story of the end of the Steam Works, that's not the way I ever heard it. . . .

21

"How's Mrs. Harrington?" Rachel said.

"About as you'd expect for an eighty-three-year-old woman with a hip replacement," Bryce said. "They've got her sitting up but she's still out of it with the drugs. She thinks she's on a Mediterranean cruise and that I am the purser."

He thought he might have trouble tracking down Rachel as she made her rounds in the hospital, but he happened on her at the nurses' station at the end of the corridor, looking through a stack of charts as she stood at the counter. She pointed out one entry to the nurse sitting at a computer; the nurse shrugged and made a face and started typing. Rachel closed the metal folder with a practiced flick of her wrist and added it to a second stack.

"I didn't know you were coming into the hospital today," she said, looking around, obviously thinking of something else.

"I didn't know I was either. But after you left Fred called and said Ena fell and was here, so I thought I should stop by. Comfort the sick and all that."

Rachel smiled absently. Then she turned back to him. "I was afraid you were still obsessing about Dickie."

Bryce shook his head. "I gave up. Seems to me it's fairly likely that somebody else had something to do with the Dickie-Bird's death. But the only thing I got for my trouble was a lot of blank looks and some outright hostility. The police even started trailing me. Have you seen Perry Sykes lately? He was always big, but now he's *big*."

"He comes in once in a while. Yes, he's a big guy. Did you ask him how Judy is doing?"

"You mean his wife Judy?"

"Who else?"

Sykes said So you really don't know that Judy DiBona and I are married. That that's my wife you're talking about having sex with Dickie in the back of his father's car. "Yes," Bryce said, "her name came up. Sykes said she's doing okay."

A nurse, her shoes squeaking on the polished floor, came up to Rachel and said something quietly to her; the woman at the computer raised her head to listen in. As Rachel and the other nurse conferred for a moment, Bryce wandered a discrete distance away. He was always proud of Rachel when he saw her here at the hospital, taking care of business, totally in control of things, so obviously in her element. He also thought she looked great in her nurse's uniform, all starched and trim and white, thought she looked better, sexier—in the words he would have used with a parishioner, *they hadn't had conjugal relations*, or in the way he thought of it himself, *they hadn't fucked*, in more than fifteen years, not since William, one of their twins, Mary's brother, was struck and killed by a speeding car while playing in the alley behind Bryce's church at the time in Sharpsburg, dragged under the car for more than a hundred feet, the little boy's face nearly torn off; the fact that William died, and particularly died in that way, became Bryce's fault in Rachel's mind, or at least that was the way Bryce interpreted the change that came over her afterward, though he was never quite sure how or why she would blame him, maybe because at the time he hadn't risen high enough or fast enough in the church hierarchy to have a better parish, to only have a church in a rough neighborhood where bad people could speed heedlessly down alleys, or maybe because she thought such things shouldn't happen to the child of a Man of God, and if such things did happen maybe it meant he wasn't that much of a Man of God after all (that was certainly his own interpretation of William's death; and if he hadn't been much of a Man of God before William died Bryce certainly wasn't much of one afterward, the beginning of the end of his faith), but Bryce still dreamt of her, her soft stocky body, dreamt that despite everything else that had happened between them, including the onset of menopause, they still might someday . . .—than when she got all dressed up to go out somewhere, but he'd learned about that too, learned never to say anything one way or the other about how she looked for fear of getting The Look. When the other nurse squeaked off down the hall again, Bryce wandered back to the nurses' station where Rachel had already picked up another chart.

"I guess I better get going," he said.

Rachel finished reading something, then said, "Oh. Okay." Then stopped reading and looked at him. "Wait a minute."

"What?" Thinking, What did I do?

"While you're here . . . this will be perfect."

"I like to think I am."

"Silly man," she said and patted his upper arm. "Come with me."

"Yay," Bryce said quietly to the woman at the computer terminal and raised his eyebrows. The woman smiled but didn't look up as she kept on typing. Rachel took his arm not from affection but to guide him and keep him from getting away.

"Here's the thing. A girl in pretty bad shape turned up in the ER a little while ago. She's obviously coming down from taking something but she had the good sense to get herself here and we admitted her until we can find out more about her. We're also running tests to see if she was a rape victim, or anything else. Before we call the police, you could talk to her. She hasn't had a whole lot to say so far, maybe she'd respond favorably to a member of the clergy."

"So, you want me to find a member of the clergy for you, is that it?"

She pushed him through the double swinging doors to the emergency room and guided him to a curtained-off bed at the back. She mouthed Go and gave him a push to the opening of the curtains.

Bryce peeked around the curtains cautiously. The teenage girl was propped up in the bed, an IV in one arm, a connection to a monitor in the other. She had her eyes closed when Bryce stepped into the enclosure, but she opened them when she heard someone.

"Hi," Bryce said and toodled his fingers. *Oh Christ, did I just toodle my fingers?* "I'm Reverend Orr. . . ."

"Or what?" the girl said and blinked slowly.

"Heh heh," Bryce said. "No, that's my name. Orr. With two *r*'s. But you can call me Bryce."

"Why would I want to?" She kept her eyes closed.

"Why would you want to call me Bryce? Well. . . ." *This isn't going to be as easy as it looked. Is it the drugs talking or is she always this way?* "There are people here who are concerned about you, and they thought maybe you'd like someone to talk to for a little bit. And if you're going to talk to someone it's always easier if you know their name."

"Like who?"

"Like who, what?"

"Like, who are these people here who are so concerned about me?"

"Well, my wife, for one person."

She opened her eyes. "Your wife? Who's your wife?"

"She's one of the nurses. In fact, you might say she's the Big Nurse—she's a supervisor. Maybe she was in here earlier. Her name's Rachel."

"There were a lot of people in here, one time or another. But I was pretty much out of it, until a little bit ago. So I'm not sure if she was here or not."

"You mean, this is you when you're not out of it?" He cocked his head to look at her and grinned.

She grinned a little in spite of herself. "Could you hand me that water?"

Bryce got the glass of water from the stand and helped her with the straw. When she was done, he wheeled the tray closer and placed it so it was over her body, the glass of water in front of her.

"And you're a minister?" she said.

"That's me."

"I'm not fond of ministers."

"I'm not either," Bryce said. He moved the chair from beside the bed stand and placed it at an angle near her feet it so she could see him when he sat down. "You tell me your reasons and I'll tell you mine."

"I don't think they tell the truth," she said. "They try to make you believe all this stuff that nobody can prove and they don't act like they believe it themselves."

"Yep," Bryce nodded. "That's about it. We're a pretty sad crew, if you ask me."

"So, if you think that, why are you still a minister?"

"Because I was never going to make it as a shortstop."

She smiled a little again. "You're funny."

"Funny, strange? Or funny, ha-ha?"

"Little of both."

Bryce nodded. "I'll buy that. Okay, you mind if I ask you your name? They're sort of curious around here who wandered in off the street and is drinking all their water."

She thought a minute. "Cory."

"Names usually come in twos."

"Cory. Leong."

Oh good Lord. "Kim Leong's daughter?"

"You know my dad?"

"I know *of* him."

"Everybody in town knows *of* him," Cory said, closing her eyes and turning her head away.

"I said that wrong," Bryce said hurriedly. "I meant, I've met him a couple of times, but I don't know him that well personally. He's a good friend of Julian Lyle."

"That's too bad."

"You're not fond of him?"

"Are you?"

"I grew up next door to him. I'm sort of stuck with him."

"Like I said." Cory took a sip of water. "No, I guess Julian is okay. He's kind of dorky, if you know what I mean."

"I do indeed. I always thought he looked sort of like Ichabod Crane."

"That's cold. True, but cold." Cory's eyes closed slowly and opened again.

"You're tired, you should get some rest."

"You going to tell my dad I'm here?"

"Not if you don't want me to. But somebody needs to tell him. How long have you been gone?"

"What day is today?"

"Thursday."

"Four days. No, five."

Bryce grimaced. "That's quite a while. It might be easier if I told him. Pretty soon they tell me the police are going to show up to ask you a bunch of questions. Your dad might like to hear where you are from someone else rather than them."

"The police would probably like it better. I think they're scared of my dad."

"Why would they be scared . . . oh. Well. . . ."

"Yeah. Oh well."

He didn't know why he thought of it, and once he had, he didn't know if he should say it. But he said it anyway. "Are you scared of your dad?"

She looked at him, then thought a minute. "I used to think I was. I even told my mom that I was, she thinks that's why I didn't want to be around him for a while. After all, I was in the house when he killed my grandpap. But the more I think about it, and the older I get, and the more I see what guys are like, a lot of guys, I can see why my dad did what he did. My grandpap, Tomi, wasn't a good guy. I'm pretty sure he was going to try something with me that night. And my dad knew it. There are a lot of guys who aren't good guys in this world." She yawned.

"That's true. Look, you're exhausted, I'm going to go—"

"Would you stay for a little while longer?" she said with her eyes closed, already drifting off.

Bryce sat back down. "Okay. Sure. I can stay for a while."

"Will you tell me a story?" As she drifted further into drowsiness, she seemed like a little girl. "You must know lots of stories. . . ."

"Well, yeah. I guess." Bryce warmed to the idea. "How about if I tell you the story I'm going to use this Sunday—"

Her eyes snapped open. "No sermons."

"No sermons. But it's a pretty good story. It's about this angel."

"Okay." She closed her eyes again. "I can get into angels."

"Well, this angel had a problem. He was supposed to come down to earth and spread the word about this . . . well, let's call it a Big Event. Now, we're not sure who the angel was though we're pretty sure it was an archangel, you wouldn't give the job of announcing a Big Event like this to any old angel. Some say it was the archangel Gabriel, but he already delivered an earlier message about the Big Event, and I tend to think the Great Dispatcher in the Sky would spread the deliveries around. It might have been the archangel Michael, but he was known more as a fighter among the heavenly orders, and this delivery was supposed to inspire joy and celebration, peace on earth, not scare everybody half to death. No, to my way of thinking the job was given to the other archangel whose name we know, the archangel Raphael, or Ralph as we'd know him today.

"So, Ralph had this problem, because he knew right from the start that people were going to have a hard time believing what he was supposed to tell them, first of all because they were seeing and hearing it from an angel, and second of all because he was telling them about this Big Event that people were going to have trouble believing no matter who told them. I mean, think about it, let's say you're an accountant—no, let's make it like Julian, say you're a lawyer—are you going to believe it when an angel pops up in your office out of nowhere and tries to deliver a message? Not hardly. Nope, you're going to try to find a reasonable explanation for it, you're going to think maybe you're seeing and hearing things or maybe it's something you ate, or maybe smoked, because things like angels making a guest appearance just don't happen in this world, it's beyond your experience and therefore is not to be believed, because as we all know, the Julians of the world know everything there is to know about everything."

Cory, her eyes closed, her breath deep and regular as if she were asleep, smiled.

"And the same would be true for store owners or politicians or anybody else in the everyday world. So the archangel Ralph knew he had his work cut out for him. And then it occurs to him: he needed somebody who was outside the mainstream, on the fringes of society, somebody who was a little crazy to start with— because if you weren't crazy before, seeing angels was probably enough to send you over the edge. So his first thought was street people, beggars and panhandlers and bums, guys who sleep in doorways and under bridges, but Ralph realized they're too far out of it: they might believe his message all right but nobody's going to believe them when they try to talk about it, they've got street cred among the other street people but not with society at large. And then he had it: shepherds. They're sitting out there all alone on the hillsides so he's not going to disturb anybody else with all the celestial pyrotechnics, and shepherds stay up all hours of the night—I mean he didn't want to make the trip all the way down here and deliver the message to someone who is going to sleep right through it, think it was just some crazy dream—and shepherds are used to seeing weird things in the darkness as they tend their flocks. So down comes Ralph, his wings ablazing, all white and gossamer and trailing angel dust. . . ."

Rachel's face appeared around the side of the curtain, a look on her face as if to say, What are you doing?

Bryce put a finger to his lips and waved her away. Mouthed to her A couple more minutes, and went back to his story: "So here comes the archangel Ralph in the middle of the night, and the shepherds look up and say, Okay, like we see a lot of things out here in the dark, so this time it's an angel and a band called the Heavenly Host, and what's this he's saying, some babe in a manger, Son of God, the Messiah, savior of the world, sure thing, why not, far out, groovy. . . ."

When he was certain the smile wasn't going to leave the girl as she slept, he tiptoed out of the enclosures to where Rachel was waiting for him a few feet away.

"What were you telling her in there?" she asked.

"Nothing. Just a story."

22

Julian left his aging Cherokee, the engine knocking a full thirty seconds after he turned off the ignition, on the side of the gravel road—it might have been gravel at one time, maybe even black-top or at least oiled, but now it was mainly frozen mud—and walked up into the field on the hillside. He guessed this was where his family's house must have been; on either side of the open field there was second- and third-growth brush, and with a little imagination he thought he could see where there might have been an entrance drive. Farther down the road a quarter of a mile or so were the burnt-out remains of shacks and lean-tos, overgrown with decades of brush but still recognizable, the shantytown that grew up here during World War II, before some vigilantes burned it down, sending the blacks who squatted there while they worked in the mills to the subsidized projects built for that purpose in the Lower End of town by Harry Sutcliff, Dickie's father. Hmm, never thought of that before, maybe they weren't vigilantes at all, maybe Harry Sutcliff paid them. Wouldn't put it past him, what I know of Dickie's father, or what I've heard. No wonder Dickie carried a lot of baggage in town, he had a family reputation before he even flipped the OPEN sign on his door. At least I never had to fight something like that, at least I don't think I did. Did I? He turned and looked back down the hill, beyond the railroad tracks at the base of the valley to the blocks of narrow, high-peaked frame houses phalanxed on down the slope of the town, plumes of smoke from hundreds of chimneys trailing skyward into the chill gray winter's sky, to the remains of the mill along the river, the project known as Furnass Landing that Dickie Sutcliff started and that Julian hoped he would soon be instrumental in finishing. He continued up deeper into the field.

You're Mal Lyle's boy, the old man who didn't want to called Anthony said at the Grand Hotel. Mr. Know-It-All, him and his investments ruined the company, and then what did he do, he took off and just left the remains for the creditors to pick over what was left like a bunch of turkey vultures. Your daddy didn't dare show his face in town, he ran away till there was nothing left of the Keystone Steam Works. That was your daddy did that, and my daddy never recovered losing his job that way, broke him in half, killed him. Don't tell me that wasn't your daddy who did that, I know who your daddy is and what he did. He must have been talking about when Pappy went down to live in Hickory, at

Aunt Mary Lydia and Uncle Claire's farm, I always heard he went down there for a couple of years, that's where he met Mother, she lived on a neighboring farm, but I never heard why he went there, I guess I always supposed it was for the same reason Suzie and I went there when we were kids, because we loved the place. We went there every summer for four or five years, the first time I must have been six and Suzie was close to eleven. Mother came too, sometimes to visit her family but Father would never come, he said he didn't like the farm, said he didn't trust breathing air he couldn't see, but that wasn't it at all, was it? I heard why but I didn't pay attention, I didn't let it sink in, what it meant. . . .

One day I was down at the springhouse, it was at the bottom of the side yard, in a deep ravine where you couldn't see the main house and the only way anyone could see you there was to stand at very edge of the bank. I liked to play there when Suzie was up at the house talking to Aunt Mary Lydia, that's probably where Suzie got all her ideas about being a feminist and not being like everybody else, not wearing clothes meant for girls and all that, she really loved Aunt Mary Lydia and spent a lot of time with her. And it gave me a chance to play by myself at the springhouse, it was always cool down in the ravine and quiet with the murmur of the spring coming down from the hill, I liked to collect crawdads and watch the dragonflies flitting back and forth, and all the little guppies in the shallows, at least I thought they were guppies. That day I heard voices above in the yard and I squatted down beside the stone wall of the springhouse to listen to Uncle Claire talking to another man: "They're Mal and Helen Lyle's kids. You remember Mary Lydia's nephew Mal, don't you?"

"He's the one who hid out here a couple of years, wasn't he? Guess you have to call it hiding out, can't be no other name for it."

"'Fraid not. Hiding out it was. I guess there were folks up in Furnass mad enough to want to kill him. At least he thought there were. I always wondered, but I couldn't say anything, Mary Lydia and all."

"As I recall the guy was pretty useless."

"The whole time he was here, never did a stick of work. Not a stick. Wandered around here with his head in the clouds, said he was working on ideas to get the company back. But nothing never came of it. He finally just snuck on back home."

"Shame. Kids seem nice enough, though."

"Yes, they're good kids. Turned out better than one could ever 'spect. Course, Mal met his wife here, Helen Niblock? You remember the Niblocks? Good people. Probably made up for all the other stuff those kids inherited from their daddy. . . ."

There was snow in the field like an underlayer among the clumps of grass. It was rough walking; he stepped in a hole, his foot twisted, he almost fell. Damn it. Good thing I wear these Wellingtons, gives support up the leg beyond the ankles. Never understood Bryce and those low zipper boots he likes, makes him look like a Spanish dancer or a fruit or something. Farther up the slope there were a number of old sycamore trees, their trunks strangled in dead vines. He had heard his family talk of the sycamores around the old house, shading the backyard. He tried to envision the spacing of the trees among the outbuildings, where the big house would have sat among them, walking back and forth across the rough earth, kicking at the clods, digging with the toe of his boot, looking for some sign of a foundation, burnt timbers or flat stones of a walk. But there was nothing here. Maybe this wasn't even the right location, just another field. He looked around at the bare trees, the black branches reaching against the gray sky. What was he doing here, looking for who knew what? Did he seriously think he was going to try to rebuild his family's house? Even if he did start to have more money now, handling Dickie Sutcliff's affairs through his estate. Rebuild the Lyles' past glories? A fool's errand, at best. He was getting cold, the air damp, he could see his breath. Wait—was there something moving in the brush farther up the hill along the treeline? Somebody there? Maybe a bear, wolves. You're losing it, Julian old son, seeing things everywhere you go. He pulled up the collar of his sport coat around his neck, closed the lapels across his chest, started back down the slope.

Those summers on the farm taught me about the world underneath the sidewalks and backyards of Orchard Hill, the natural world of fields like this, I knew more about the real world than Bryce or Dickie or any of the other guys ever did, maybe not Needle-Prick Brown the Insect Fucker but Brownie was older, he had been in the marines, he was half-crazy to start with. I used to go with Uncle Claire up to the barn twice a day when he did the milking, later on he used to let me help herd the cows out of the barn after milking, feed the pigs though you had to be careful they didn't knock you over. I would sit on the plow, Uncle Claire said it helped weigh it down, behind the team, Big Bob and Tom, as he plowed, though maybe Uncle Claire just said that to make me feel like I had a real job to do; I'd watch the blade under me as it turned over the dark earth, sometimes right through a rabbit's nest, but Uncle Claire said we couldn't go back to help the survivors, that that was just the way things were, a lesson he said I had to learn.

There was the time Uncle Claire took the team into town to the smithy to have them shod, he let me ride on the back of Big Bob because he was the gentlest, my legs sticking out on either side across his wide back as if I'd split down the middle. I rode that way up to the top of the lane and along the shoulder beside the highway, Tom plodding along behind us, till we got to the gas station at the wye where Aunt Mary Lydia met us in the truck to take me back home, knowing I'd be wore-out. Aunt Mary

Lydia always dressed like a man, often in clothes she got from army-navy stores, olive-green jodhpurs and a flat-brimmed, tall-crowned army service hat, tall leather boots up to her knees like they wore in the cavalry. People thought she was crazy as a loon, but we didn't mind, we thought it only showed how special the Lyles were, showed we were true eccentrics in the best upper-class tradition. Crazy or not, I loved her, she was always kind to me, like you wanted your mother to be though Mother never seemed to have time, but I could always talk to Aunt Mary Lydia, ask her things that bothered me. That day as she drove me back to the house in their old flatbed truck, the cab without doors open to the wind, I asked her, shouting to be heard against the clatter of the engine and the whine of the gears and the road rushing by, "Why doesn't my dad ever visit the farm? He lived here for a while, didn't he?"

Aunt Mary Lydia smiled to herself, a crooked one-sided smile that always looked like it might slide off her face if she wasn't careful. "I guess he doesn't love us anymore. No, I shouldn't say that. It's probably because he doesn't need to be here now. When he was here wasn't his best time."

"Because of the trouble with the company back home?"

"Oh, you know about that? We wondered if you knew, how much you heard about it."

"I only heard a little."

She thought a moment as she braked and downshifted to enter the lane to the farm, start down the long hill to the house in the little valley. She had to speak even louder against the new complaint of the transmission, the squeal of the brakes, the crunch of the macadam road under the tires. "I guess you're old enough to know. It's something you should know, seeing it's your family and you have to live with it. Your father got too big for his britches, he thought he could save the company by making a bunch of investments but ended up losing the whole kit and caboodle when the market crashed. He came here because he didn't have anyplace else to go, they more or less ran him out of town, he was scared to go back. The damn fool. He never appreciated that Claire let him stay here either. Your father never recognized that he took the rest of us down with him as well, I lost any legacy I might have had coming from the company. He took a lot of people down with him."

As we bumped down the narrow lane, the branches of the brush along the side whipped at me through the missing door, the opening where the door should be. "I only heard that he came here, nobody ever said why. I guess I thought, I don't know . . ."

"That he came here for an extended vacation?" Mary Lydia laughed. The brush knocked her army hat cattywampus on her head; she reset it, steering one-handed out of one of the ruts in the road. "Oh it was a vacation for Mal all right. He never did a thing to help out while he was here. Just sort of thought he was entitled to our hospitality. No, he didn't come for a vacation, he came with his tail between his legs, we weren't supposed to tell anybody even in Hickory that he was here. But word got around eventually. I always felt bad for your mom, she didn't know what she was getting into when she met him."

Mary Lydia drove past the house and left the truck near the cow barn. I hurried to walk beside her as we headed toward the kitchen door. "What was wrong with my mom?"

"Oh, there was nothing wrong with your mom. She just thought she was getting hooked up with some big industrialist or something, the way Mal talked about himself. Your dad told her all about the Keystone Steam Works, world-famous well drillers and all, he just didn't bother telling her that the company was belly-up, and that the man she was talking to was more or less responsible for its demise. I always gave your mom credit, when she found out what she got herself into, she would have been more than within her rights to turn around and come back to

Hickory. But she stayed with it, mainly I'm sure for you kids. Claire and I respect that, and I guess we probably feel a little responsible that she met Mal here, for not warning her. That's why we're glad to help her out, having you and your sister down here every summer, give the woman a little rest. . . ."

That was the last summer I ever went down there, I guess Suzie went down again but I never went back, I never told anybody why, I just said I didn't want to go, that I had other things I wanted to do, but I couldn't stand to go back after I heard that, heard it and then quickly forgot it, stored it away in a back closet never to be opened again. I knew about it all this time, and I never—

As he walked he heard something behind him. He stopped and looked over his shoulder. Out of the line of trees above the house a pack of dogs was slowly emerging from the brush, eight or ten of them, big dogs, shepherd and Doberman mixes and hounds, not running, more like slinking, keeping close to the ground, ears back, fixed on him, making steady progress toward him. Julian kept walking, a little quicker now, though smart enough to know not to run, not until he was within twenty yards of his car, then he took off, running as fast as he could, certain that the dogs were closing behind him, afraid to look back, concentrating all his energy to get to the car and not trip on the uneven ground, hoping he hadn't locked the door, no, it was unlocked, he got the door open and jumped inside, locking it behind him, looked then to see that the dogs had stopped at where he thought the house must have been among the sycamores, pulled up in a rough line, looking at him, tongues hanging out, as if laughing at him, Whatcha running for? We weren't going to hurt you, we were just going to say hello. . . . Julian got the keys from his pocket and started the engine and did a three-point turn there on the dirt road, driving back down the hill toward the town.

When he got to the Alhambra he was still shaky. He parked behind the building and took the fire escape up to his office. Donna Bruno was sitting at her desk waiting for him, a manila envelope dangling from her upturned hand like a semaphore.

"Heard you coming," she said. Batting her eyes at him.

"You always do."

"That's one thing about this place. No one can ever sneak up on us. Not with the creaking hinges and squeaky floor and all."

"Yes, we've talked about that."

"Can't imagine what it would have been like if the Shoppers Bizarre had ever caught on, the racket out there would have been deafening."

"Shoppers Ba-zaar," Julian corrected her. "Yes, we've talked about that."

"Not that it ever would have caught on," Donna Bruno said, waving the manila envelope back and forth. "What a crazy idea that was."

Donna Bruno's dark brown hair streaked with gray reminded Julian of a skunk; the dark circles under her eyes gave the impression that she was peering at him through an opening. Why do I keep this woman? Well, I know why—the only reason I hired her in the first place was because Dickie made me, a Sutcliff family sexual castoff. And I knew at the time I was hiring his spy. You'd think now that Dickie is gone she'd be a little more careful, a little less disrespectful, but I guess that would be too much to ask. . . . "What's this?"

Donna Bruno flipped the envelope into his outstretched hand. "A messenger brought it a little while ago. I thought you'd want to see it, it's from one of the law firms we contacted in Pittsburgh that we knew Dickie used once in a while." When Julian looked questioning, she added with a shake of her head as if talking to a dumb person, "About the will?"

"Oh," Julian said.

"Yes, oh."

"Did you open it?"

"Well, of course. I am your secretary."

"So you know what it says."

"Yes I do," said Donna Bruno, giving an affirmative nod. Obviously pleased to be one up.

Yes, too much to ask. Julian opened the already opened envelope, glanced over the transmittal note explaining how they were in possession of the last will and testament of Richard Bruce Sutcliff and their instructions to forward it to Julian A. Lyle, Esq., in case of etcetera, etcetera, etcetera, then, still standing in front of Donna Bruno's desk, quickly scanned the first page of the attached document. "Oh."

"Yes, oh," Donna Bruno said. Looking up at him, batting her eyes. "I guess you'll be on your way again to see Tinker."

Julian's knees felt slightly gimpy. A pit suddenly in his bowels. He stood for a moment where he was, his thoughts whirling.

Donna Bruno picked up a yellow slip from her desk and offered it to him. "And your friend Kim called. He sounded upset."

"That'll have to wait," Julian said, in a fog, not taking the slip.

"Well, that's a first," Donna Bruno said. Raising her eyebrows and giving a little sideways nod as she placed the slip back on her desk. "I thought we always dropped everything whenever Kim called."

He put the papers back in the envelope and turned to leave—and then thought, I don't have to put up with this. "And you should start cleaning up your things . . . cleaning out your desk . . . and all."

Donna Bruno looked at him. "And I would be doing that, why?"

Julian swallowed hard. "Because, well, I won't be needing your . . . services . . . anymore."

"Julian, if you're firing me, you should just say so."

Here goes. "You're right. Donna, you're fired."

"Don't be ridiculous," Donna Bruno said and straightened a stack of papers on her desk.

Julian blinked. I started this, I can finish it. "I'm afraid I have no choice. I have to let you go."

"Well, I'm not going," Donna Bruno said, not looking at him. "And that's all there is to it."

This is a nightmare. "I don't have a choice. You know that Dickie was, let's say, subsidizing your salary here. Now that Dickie's gone, I can't afford to keep you on my own."

"That's all been taken care of in the will, as you'll see when you get around to reading it through. Dickie put me on the Sutcliff Realty payroll, to keep me here as long as I want to stay here. And though I don't particularly want to stay here, what else am I going to do?" She looked at Julian, shrugged, and pulled a face.

"You read the will?"

"I figured someone should. Before you went tearing out of here to go talk to Tinker." She pushed her face out at him, as if to say, What? "Besides, you need me, whether you recognize it or not. Now, you better go see Tinker. Leave the will here. I'll make copies to distribute and get it filed at the courthouse."

Julian looked at the envelope as if it had just materialized in his hand. When he continued to stand there—I don't believe this. I fired her and she's not going. I'll have to deal with her later, and she's right, I have to talk to Tinker—Donna reached up and took the envelope out of his hand, then shooed him. "Go! Go!"

Julian turned and hurried out the door as he was told, his footsteps thudding down the false floor of the corridor past the abandoned Shoppers Bazaar.

23

The entryway to Kim Leong's Five Animals Kung Fu Studio was set back from the sidewalk, the door at the end of a short serpentine of display windows, the art deco design a holdover from when the shop held Gelston Jewelers, the windows in matching S-curves as if cut with a monster jigsaw and pulled apart; in the windows, on the faded velveteen pedestals that once held watches and engagement rings and jeweled necklaces, were the trophies that Kim and his students had won at martial arts tournaments, photographs of the competitions and the fighters in action, studio portraits of students in various fighting styles, Shaolin Tiger, Eagle Claw, Dragon. The black-and-white tile was gritty underfoot; wind had blown leaves, crushed take-out cups, old newspapers into the recesses of the storefront. Bryce peered in the door but couldn't see anything, couldn't tell if anyone was inside or not. He tried the door and was surprised when it opened. He stepped into a dark entryway—If this is designed to make you nervous, he thought, it's working—and continued on, arms outstretched, half expecting to bump into something, toward a strip of light between the flaps of a curtain and into the brightly lit studio.

It was a large empty space, a row of metal folding chairs against one wall, a few mats laid out toward the middle. At the far end was a young man dressed all in white in his bare feet, practicing fighting forms in front of a floor-to-ceiling mirror. Like a ballet dancer, Bryce thought, doing pas de deux or whatever they're called, except these were meant to do damage, smash someone in the face. Fascinating rhythm. When the young man noticed Bryce behind him in the mirror, he bowed to himself and came over.

"Hello. Can I help you?"

"I was looking for Kim."

"He's not here right now. Is there something I can help you with?"

"No, no," Bryce said, embarrassed and not sure why. Sticking his hands in the pockets of his too-short raincoat. "I just thought I'd stop by. . . ."

"I'd be happy to show you around and explain what we do here."

"Yes, I was watching you there for a little bit. It's . . . very interesting."

The young man smiled; then his face turned suddenly blank and he did several of the moves in front of Bryce, his hands moving as gracefully as figures in an aerial ballet, at first slow to show him the movements, then at triple the speed, faster than Bryce could keep track of. When the young man returned to a rest position, Bryce laughed nervously.

"Heh heh. Well, then. That's something. Far out."

"Those are just a few of the basic moves we teach here," the young man said, smiling again. "Was there anything particular. . . ."

"No, no. Nothing in particular."

"Well, did you want to sign up for a class, then? We have beginners classes two nights a week. . . ."

"Who, me?" Bryce said. Taking a step backward.

"You don't need to be embarrassed. We have a lot of people in . . . your age-group. And there's no pressure, you can progress at your own speed. . . ."

"Er, no," Bryce said. For a brief second flattered the young man would think such a thing, picturing himself in an all-white outfit going through some fighting motions, until reality set in again. "I really just wanted to talk to Kim. There's something I wanted to ask him. . . ."

"What did you want to ask him?" the young man said, cocking his head, becoming suspicious. "Are you a reporter or something?

Because Sifu has had enough of people coming around and bothering him about all that. What happened was a long time ago. . . ."

See Phoo? "No, no, it's about his daughter—"

"Cory? What about Cory?" Now the young man looked ready to strike.

Bryce tried to laugh. "I'm not explaining this very well. No, I'm not a reporter, nothing at all like that. I sort of know Kim, through Julian Lyle, he's—"

"I know Julian. He's a good friend of Sifu Kim. And he was a student here."

"Good. Julian can vouch for me. I come in peace." I come in peace? Bryce thought. I sound like I'm talking to Sitting Bull. Bryce sighed. "Look, I've got some information that I think Kim should know about. I was talking to his daughter at the hospital."

"She's at the hospital? Sifu has been very worried about her."

Sea Phew? "Well, I thought so. I hoped so. I was hoping he could go see her and—"

"He's not here—"

"Which is what you said."

"—but I'll be sure to try to locate him and let him know."

"That would be great. That's actually all I wanted." Bryce looked around uneasily then turned to leave. And then it hit him. "You said Julian was a student here?"

"Yes. He studied with Sifu for a while. Maybe a year or so. Shortly after the trial . . . you know about the trial?"

"Yes, of course." Who doesn't, he almost said, and was glad he didn't.

"Julian said he wanted to learn more about the martial arts. After he represented Sifu, so he could defend himself in case of trouble."

C-Few? "Was he any good? I mean is he a brown belt or black belt or however you judge these things?"

The young man laughed tolerantly. "No, he never earned anything like that. I'm afraid he wasn't very good at it. He tried okay, but he gave it up after a while. . . ."

"But he did learn some of the basics."

"Yes. Of course."

"Enough to hurt somebody if he wanted to."

"I'm not sure I know what you mean. . . ."

"He knows enough to, say, for instance, hit somebody on the side of the head—"

Before Bryce had finished, the young man's hands crossed rapidly in front of him, his left backhand fist coming to a stop against Bryce's temple.

"Whoa!" Bryce yelped and jumped backward.

"Julian wouldn't be as quick," the young man grinned. "And I wouldn't trust him to be able to stop in time like I did, if he didn't want to follow through and strike his opponent. But yes, such blows were part of Julian's training. A backhand thrown like that, the way the wrist snaps like a whip, can do a lot of damage."

Bryce brushed his hands across the front of his raincoat as if dusting himself off. "Okay, then. Okay. Well, thanks for the, er, demonstration. And you'll tell Kim when you see him about Cory. I know she'd like to see him."

"Yes, I'll tell him." The young man seemed to be looking at Bryce as if, having once almost hit him, he'd like to do it again, this time not holding back. Bryce bowed inadvertently, more like a little juke, and turned and hurried back through the curtains and the passageway and out the front door. They're killers in there, he thought, not slowing down until he was half a block down the street. A den of them. Killers.

24

"The whole thing?" Tinker said.

"The whole thing," Julian said.

"Not just Furnass Landing, or your Towers or some other projects. The entire company."

"The entire company."

"To Jennifer?"

"To Jennifer," Julian said and shrugged.

Tinker threw the flowers she was trimming down on the metal-topped table, slamming her clippers beside them. "Let me see it."

"See what?"

"The will, of course. The will."

"I didn't bring it with me," Julian said. What he didn't say was, Because I thought you might try to tear it up. "I'm having copies made and we'll distribute them as soon as the will is registered. Besides, given the situation, I think the first person who should see it is Jennifer. Don't you?" he added, trying to somehow appease her.

Tinker glowered at him. The back room of the flower shop always made him think of a shop floor, a machine shop for plant life. Cement floor strewn with colorful cuttings, tin-covered worktables, trash barrels sitting around, the hum of compressors and other machines. Except the smell was cloying, he missed the bite of metal being cut and ground and sparks flying. . . . In a moment she was up off her stool and pacing back and forth.

"That son-of-a-bitch. That rotten son-of-a-bitch. He screwed me every way he could while he was alive, and now he's still doing it while he's dead."

Julian was afraid to say anything. Afraid of how she'd react to anything he might say. He was still puzzled by his phone conversation with her the day before, it was almost as if she was dismissing him—I'm moving forward, Julian, I'm getting on with my life, I'll let you know if we have any business to discuss, nice talking to you—he wanted to know how things stood with them, needed to know that she hadn't changed her mind about their working arrangement, that when she learned Dickie planned to leave her for Pamela DiCello, she enlisted him to help her gain control of the company as part of a divorce settlement, and help her run the company or her share of it afterward. He was hoping now that she'd take action against the will, contest it—he could help her with that too—but was concerned that if he said the wrong thing it could set her off in another direction. His hopes and dreams were on the line here, his future.

They were interrupted by one of the women who worked for her coming through the strips of heavy plastic that curtained off the back room, holding a Christmas arrangement. "Tinker, Mrs. Scarlatti would like to know if we can put this bouquet in a white vase rather than this red vase."

"Of course Mrs. Scarlatti wouldn't want the red vase. The only way she'd want the red vase is if the arrangement came in a white vase." She stopped her pacing to light a cigarette, slamming the pack and lighter back on the table. "You can tell Mrs. Scarlatti she either takes it as it is or she can go somewhere else. Now, don't bother me again."

The woman blinked twice and carried the arrangement back through the translucent curtain, her voice lilting as she spoke to the unseen Mrs. Scarlatti.

Tinker resumed her pacing. "Jennifer doesn't know the first thing about running a company. She doesn't know the first thing about real estate."

Neither do you, Julian thought. That's why you asked me to help you.

"What was Dickie thinking?" Tinker stopped and looked at him. Taking a puff on the cigarette strong enough to make the ash glow. "No, I know what he was thinking, all right. Well, we'll see about this."

Julian decided to take the chance. "We can always contest the will."

"You're damn right I'll contest the will. Daughter or no daughter, I'm not going to simply roll over and let that young woman get everything I've worked so hard to get. That son-of-a-bitch."

Julian breathed a sigh of relief. Thinking, Hope that wasn't out loud. "I'll start the paperwork right away."

Tinker stopped pacing and looked at him. She tapped the ash off her cigarette with one pointed finger. Tap. Tap. Tap.

"No, Julian. I'm going to contest the will, all right. But with somebody else. Another attorney."

"Who?"

"I don't know yet. But I know it won't be you."

"But why?"

"Are you really going to make me say it?"

"You certainly thought I was good enough to help you get the company away from Dickie while he was still alive."

"That was before I found out what your business relationship with Dickie actually was. I thought you were Dickie's attorney, I thought you knew what went on in Sutcliff Realty and would be able to help me get my share of it. Well, the problem of the divorce has been taken care of, obviously."

"You're going to need me more than ever if you contest that will. And more than ever if you get control of the company from Jennifer. You're going to need somebody who—"

"Julian," Tinker said, stubbing out the half-smoked cigarette. "You know less about Sutcliff Realty than I do. I know what your relationship to my husband's business was. I know he was in effect paying your bills, keeping you afloat. I know the only reason he gave you any work was from some kind of misguided loyalty to somebody he grew up with. The good old Orchard Hill kids. Well, you better hope that I don't win contesting the will, because if I do that kind of charity is going to stop— What?!"

The woman was standing among the plastic curtain in the door, afraid to come any closer. "The phone—"

"Answer it, damn it. That's what I pay you for."

"It's for Julian."

Julian and Tinker both looked at the phone on her worktable, one button flashing red.

"Go on, take it," Tinker said.

It was Donna Bruno from his office saying that Rachel Orr had called, she was trying to locate Kim Leong; Kim's daughter was at the hospital, but she was unable to locate him and wondered if Julian might know where he was. Julian hung up, the message pinballing for attention in his mind along with what Tinker had been saying about their relationship. He felt dazed, unable to think clearly.

"I should be going. . . ."

Tinker nodded him toward the door. "Sure, go on, we're done here. I've got things to do."

25

Bryce sat in the *God Runner* in the municipal parking lot behind the main street, going over in his mind his discussion with the young man at Kim's studio, keeping an eye out to make sure the guy didn't come after him, scuffling across the lot in his bare feet and loose white outfit, oblivious to the cold and the wind and traces of snow left on the concrete, coming after Bryce to . . . to . . . well, he wasn't quite sure why the guy would want to come after him, but the feeling seemed real enough—Whatever happened to my friendly little hometown? Somehow it got to be a scary place with drug dealers and bully cops and kung fu killers on every corner. And that doesn't even include the fact that there's somebody wandering around the streets who did in the Dickie-Bird, except I think I know now who was responsible for that travesty of injustice too. Fascinating rhythm—watching the occasional car on the side street or passing in the alley, ready to duck down not to be seen. Even paranoids have enemies, he thought, but this isn't funny.

So ol' Julian studied at Kim's studio, he could do all that kung fu stuff, he has to be the one who dealt the death blow to the Dickie-Bird, hit him upside the head, which if it didn't kill him outright sent him into the corner of the desk that did. Ol' Julian. Who'd'a thunk it? But I should have guessed, Julian always had a violent streak to him, a lot of pent-up rage, why else would he pal around with a killer like Kim, it's called *transference*, Herr Doktor, and he always hated Dickie and Harry Todd, jealous of them I'm sure, thought the Sutcliffs had the prominence in town that belonged to the Lyles. Yep, I should have known it was him all along. But what brought it to a head? I wonder. What set Julian off, what made him trip out, what was the trigger—the motive, Herr Doktor, what was the motive? Probably something financial, to cause such an extreme reaction, or extreme action as the case may be, Julian was always getting himself into one bad deal or another, what a fool, what a fool, could never admit he didn't know his ass from a hot rock, always had to act like he knew everything about everything. Jennifer said there was some kind of deal between Julian and Tinker, wonder if that had something to do with it. Wonder who would know about something like that . . .

He was getting cold, sitting in the car, his breath steaming up the windshield. Forgetting his earlier paranoia, nightmare visions of Perry Sykes in a fire-breathing (or at least a red-light-flashing) patrol car and white-suited kung fu fighters chasing him through the back streets of Furnass, he left his car in the parking lot and, his hands tucked deep in the pockets of his shorty raincoat to hold it tight against the chill, crossed the alley and skipped sideways down the narrow passageway between the building that once held the Reid Brothers Bank and Julian Lyle's Alhambra

Theater, humming, "Here comes Santa Claus, Here comes Santa Claus," as he popped out on the main street and scuffed down the sidewalk to First City Bank.

It was a large granite building on the corner of Eleventh Street, the intersection generally considered to be the center if not the heart of the town (and maybe that too), with Doric columns flanking the entryway and the sculptured head of a woman jutting from the cornerstone of the central arch, the face stained with runoff below the eyes as if she were crying (the local wits said it was because she had a loan with the bank and was distressed at the interest rates but that was just mean). The inside of the structure matched the theme of a temple of commerce with polished marble floors and wainscoting, an arched ceiling with gold inlaid tiles (long since dulled from the soot in the air of the mill town), and milk glass and brass chandeliers shaped like ornate wedding cakes. At the rear of the lobby was the walk-in vault, the glimmering stainless-steel door standing open as if to reveal the untold riches within. The line of tellers was on one side, the platform with the bank officers and assistants was on the other under tall narrow windows. Still humming to himself, Bryce brushed in the front door, took his hands from his raincoat pockets and toodled his fingers at the guard to show he was unarmed, and bustled across the lobby and through the thigh-high gate that marked off the service platform. The woman at the first desk, in the midst of explaining a sheaf of forms to an older African American couple, looked up startled as he passed.

"Can I help you? Sir? Sir?"

Bryce paused and said, "Thanks anyway, I'm just here to see ol' Harv." Pointing to the man in a suit coat sitting at his desk in the glassed-in office.

"Do you have an appointment? Sir!"

Bryce kept moving, past the other bank officers and assistants at their desks, some with customers, each one raising his or her head as he shuffled past, through the glass door to the manager's office. He scooted into the chair beside the desk, slouching down and crossing his legs as if he'd been sitting there for some time. Harvey McMillan looked up at him with a wary look on his face.

"Hi, Harv."

"Hello, Bryce. Or should I say Reverend?"

"No, it's Bryce today. This is a friendly call, not the Lord's work. Though of course everything in the world is the Lord's work in some way, so I guess you could call me Reverend if it makes you feel more comfortable, but as far as I'm concerned Bryce will be fine."

"Oh boy," Harvey McMillan said. He adjusted his open suit coat around him. Both of them looked up as the guard appeared at the door.

"Everything okay, Mr. McMillan?"

"Yes, George. Everything is fine."

The guard gave Bryce a once-over—Bryce's stomach, even though the man was a rent-a-cop, went *Ker-Chunk!*—and headed back to his post near the door.

"Don't like cops," Bryce said.

"George apparently didn't like you either."

"They make me nervous."

"Shouldn't. Unless you have something to hide."

"Ah. Well, we all have something to hide, don't we?" Bryce picked up a pen from the blotter and started to beat a rhythm on the edge of Harvey McMillan's desk. Harvey McMillan reached over and took the pen from him.

"I thought maybe you were here because of the church furnace."

"The church furnace," Bryce said. "I forgot about that. As a matter of fact, we could use an additional contribution for the church furnace. Thanks for bringing it up."

"The bank is paying for most of it as it is. And the church isn't even in town, it's ten miles in the hills."

"You make it sound like we're on the western frontier or something."

"Still, I'm afraid the board could question the bank's involvement. If the board members ever wake up long enough to know what's going on about anything."

"So maybe you could spring for a little extra, huh?" On the front of Harvey McMillan's desk was a square glass container shaped like the Fort Pitt Blockhouse. Bryce picked it up, almost spilled the lid on the floor, and saw there were gold paper clips inside; he took several and started daisy-chaining them together.

Harvey McMillan watched him for a moment, then shook his head and took the container and the daisy chain of paper clips from him, placing them on the other side of his desk. "Seeing as how you asked so nicely, I'll see what I can do."

"Much appreciated, Harv. Much appreciated. You'll be glad when you and Margaret and the boys are nice and toasty next winter at Sunday service. When you make it to Sunday service. Then we'll have to talk remedial steps to make sure you and the family aren't rained on, what with our leaky roof and all. And I still want to get those bells in the tower working again. How is Margaret these days?"

"You're married, you tell me."

"Partly cloudy with lowering temperatures and the threat of freezing drizzle overnight."

"Exactly."

"This evening I have to go to Rachel's Christmas party. A bunch of doctors and nurses and administrators all standing around who are only interested in talking about who they want to get into bed, patients or otherwise."

Harvey McMillan looked at the papers in the folder in front of him for a moment, then turned back to Bryce. "So why did you stop by, Bryce? I can't remember you ever coming here to the bank."

Bryce picked up the stapler from the desk and started to open and close it, open and close it. "Dickie Sutcliff."

Harvey McMillan leaned back in his high-backed leather chair. "Ah. Tragic. Tragic."

"And Julian Lyle."

"I'm not sure I understand the connection."

"I don't either. I was hoping you could enlighten me."

"Why would you want to know about the connection between Dickie Sutcliff and Julian Lyle?"

"I'm also interested if there was a connection between Julian and Tinker, Dickie's wife."

"You mean, a romantic connection?"

"Good Lord, I hope not. That's an image I don't want bouncing around in my head." Bryce gave a little shiver. "Br-r-r-r."

"I'm not aware of any business connection between the two, if that's what you mean. Frankly, I find that equally hard to imagine." Harvey McMillan gave a corresponding shiver. "Again, why would you want to know?"

"I'm working on a theory." Bryce opened and closed the stapler. Open and close. Open and close. Then he worked the jaw like a mechanical alligator, chomping through the air.

Harvey McMillan leaned forward and took the stapler from Bryce and put it back on his desk. "You're always working on a theory. You've been working on one theory or another since the ninth grade."

"Actually, earlier than that. But you Furnass Heights kids didn't come down off the mountain until junior high."

"I'm sorry we did then, if you want to know the truth. Thank heaven my parents sent me to a private school after a couple of years. That was more than enough of your world for me."

"Funny, we felt the same about you. Funnier still, here you are twenty-five years later sitting right in the middle of it all. What goes around, etcetera. But I digress. If you're unaware of anything between Julian and Tinker, then what about Julian and Dickie? That's the real question anyway."

Harvey McMillan shook his head. "Julian was really out of his league when he tried to match deals with Dickie. Now, I have to say, I'm not one of the ones in this town who are down on Julian. . . ."

"You're one of the few, then."

"That may be. But I have to give him credit. He tried to do something good for this town, the Furnass Towers and all."

"All for selfish reasons, I'm sure." Bryce picked up the stapler again and thumped it, producing a staple bent in the shape of a tiny pair of eyeglasses. He hit the stapler again a couple of times until he noticed Harvey McMillan looking at him. Bryce shrugged and swept the tiny metal glasses onto the floor.

"If that's the way you talk about your friends," Harvey McMillan said, looking at the bent staples on his floor, "I'm glad I'm not listed as one of them."

"You're part of my flock," Bryce smiled. "You should hear what I say about you to the Good Shepherd."

"I'm afraid to think. Regardless," Harvey McMillan said, leaning back again and forming a tent of fingers in front of him. "Julian got himself in trouble by overextending himself to finance the Towers. And then he was hit by a stream of bad luck, with Sycamore Savings & Loan going under. Like a great number of savings and loans in the country, Sycamore's fiscal practices were leading them to bankruptcy anyway. They were out of their league, trying to get into banking areas that they frankly didn't know anything about and weren't prepared to handle. As for Julian, I wish he had had enough good sense to come see us when he was looking for financing in the first place. And then once he got in trouble I wish he had just cut his losses and stopped there. But he got it in his head that he was going to find a way to save his project and ace Dickie in the process. And nobody could ace Dickie when it came to deals."

"So what happened?"

Harvey McMillan sat up again, warming to the subject. "It was pretty interesting, when you came right down to it. Dickie was a master, that's for sure. I'm not going to go into all the details, that wouldn't be in my best interests or the interests of the bank. But I will say that Dickie worked it out so that he both obtained the funds for his Furnass Landing project as well as owning the title for Julian's Furnass Towers, all in one fell swoop. Dickie certainly did know how to work the system. It was particularly unfortunate, for the bank and ultimately I suspect for the town, that he died when he did, he didn't have the chance to finish off his plans for the Towers. He told me that he planned to let the bank take over the unfinished building, default on the loan or sell it to us for a dollar, something of the sort. He didn't want the project and thought maybe we could do something with it. There was a side to Dickie that most people didn't see."

Bryce was working at the stapler, pulling at the top, poking at the sides, trying to open it to see the staples inside. "And Julian?"

"In the process, Julian more or less became totally beholden to Dickie. The only way Julian was able to do anything—keep his house, his office in the Alhambra, his secretary—was through Dickie's good graces."

"I would think Julian would resent Dickie quite a lot for that," Bryce said. "More than just resent it, hate it. Nobody likes to feel they're that beholden to somebody else. Particularly not to somebody like Dickie Sutcliff."

"Maybe so. But I have to say that Dickie was a benevolent overlord. He even gave Julian enough legal work to pay his bills, keep his practice afloat. Why, I'm not sure. But we handled the transactions so I know what they were."

"All the more reason for Julian to have a grudge against Dickie. Though I'm sure Julian could use the help."

"Not sure I follow you."

Bryce reached over and took a couple sheets of paper from Harvey McMillan's desk and stapled them together. He looked around for something else to staple but Harvey McMillan reached over and took the stapler from him again.

"I wouldn't think that Julian is considered one of the better legal minds in Furnass."

"I know that's the way he's generally thought of in town, though I'm not sure why."

"What about if it walks like a duck, quacks like a duck, practices law like a duck. . . ."

Harvey McMillan looked at the pages Bryce had stapled and reached in his drawer for the staple remover. When he saw the way Bryce was looking at it, he put the staple remover back in his desk drawer when he was done.

"I've always found that Julian was more than competent," Harvey McMillan said. "For the range of legal matters that he was called on to perform. I don't believe he set out to be F. Lee Bailey or someone of that ilk. On the other hand, when that unfortunate business with Kim Leong came along, Julian defended the man successfully and got him acquitted."

"Do you think he should have? I mean the guy did kill someone. His father."

"Judge not, etcetera," Harvey McMillan said. And smiled.

"God love ya, Harv," Bryce said. "Somebody should."

"What does that mean?" Harvey McMillan said.

Bryce reached across Harvey McMillan's desk and swung the end ball of the executive-model Newton's cradle against the other four, the end balls clicking back and forth against the line. As

All Fall Down

Bryce headed out the door, Harvey McMillan was trying to stop the swinging balls.

. . . the day has turned sunny bright in the middle of the after-noon, though it is still cold, will chill you to the bone as the saying goes, the downtown of the little mill town divided by the low sun of early December into extremes of light and dark, the patches of intense color intersected by angles of deep shadow, as Bryce ditty-bops along the sidewalk, for reasons he couldn't explain staying close to the storefronts, acting silly for his own amusement after leaving First City Bank, then funning himself again as he comes to the walkway between what used to be the Reid Brothers Bank and the Alhambra Theater, now more than ever wanting to avoid running into Julian after his disparaging conversation about him with Harvey McMillan, pretends to be sucked into the opening, leaps sideways into the narrow passageway wondering if anyone saw his little performance, his bit of street theater, and shuffles down the brick-lined corridor, the four-foot-wide walkway recog-nized as enough of a thoroughfare to have been paved at some point, Bryce humming tunelessly to himself again, convinced more than ever that Julian was responsible for or at least involved in Dickie Sutcliff's death, and equally convinced more than ever that there is nothing to do or be done with the information anyway—not that he ever intended to do anything with it in the first place, even if he could prove it beyond a shadow of a doubt, that was never his intention, he wouldn't think of turning Julian in, the knowing was enough, thinking I am the Diogenes of Fur-nass looking for an honest man, and incidentally, Lord, I just want to go on record that I'm not having a whole lot of luck in that regard, thought I should mention it—looking up at the crack of sky several stories above him when he hears something behind him, like a small rock and pebbles falling from overhead, a chunk

of brick or maybe a piece of the ledge along the roofline and he looks behind him but doesn't see anything on the walk and thinks Far out, fascinating rhythm, and looks ahead again as he's halfway through the passageway and sees a figure standing in the entrance to the walkway though with the brightness of the day behind the figure Bryce can't make out the man's face or features, he's only a silhouette or shadow, a very large silhouette or shadow, standing with his arms at his sides apparently watching or waiting for Bryce and Bryce yells to him, "Hold on, I'm almost out," and happens to glance over his shoulder to see if anyone else is coming along behind him and sees at the entrance to the main street what appears like another figure though when he sees Bryce looking he ducks back out of sight and Bryce turns around again and the figure in front of him is gone too, and Bryce thinks Heh heh, what's going on here, and feels for the first time ever, in all the hundreds of times he's been through this passageway, first as a kid and then in high school on his way to get a root beer float at the counter of the drugstore in the Colonel Berry Hotel, claustrophobic, a sensation that the buildings could close together and squash him like a bug between bookends and he's shuffling faster now, what you could call a run, down the passage though he's wary who or what might be waiting for him once he's outside and pops out between the buildings into the alleyway looking for the big guy he saw earlier and in the process almost gets himself run over by a Schwan's ice cream truck that blasts its horn and sends him jumping back into the passageway until it's passed and then hurries across the alley and into the parking lot to the God Runner and unlocks it and gets in and locks the door behind him, realizing now that he's soaked with sweat and laughs a little at himself, thinking You messin' with my head, Lord? . . . while on the main street Julian leaves the Five Animals Kung Fu Studio, where he went after talking to Tinker at her flower shop, after getting the message that the hospital was trying to locate

Kim to tell him Cory was there, but Curtis, one of the instructors, said he didn't know where Kim was . . .

"I haven't seen or heard from him all day," Curtis said. "Which is really weird, because Sifu always checks in."

"Okay, thanks," Julian said and started to leave.

"A friend of yours was in here earlier. He also was looking for Sifu."

Julian stopped and turned around. "A friend of mine?"

"Said he was. He left before I got his name."

"Let me guess. Sort of a pug-faced guy with wispy hair. In a too-short raincoat."

"That's him. I thought at first he might be a reporter but he said you'd vouch for him."

"Yeah," Julian said. "I'll vouch for him. Matter of fact he's a minister."

"No shit," Curtis said and thought about that. "Well, I guess that sort of explains it."

"Explains what?"

"He said he wanted to let Sifu know that his daughter was at the hospital."

"How did he know that?"

"He didn't say. But I guess he was talking to Cory and she said she wanted to see her dad. And this guy wanted to let Sifu know. . . ."

. . . thinking *How did Bryce find out Cory was at the hospital?* as he cuts across the street and continues up the sidewalk toward his office in the Alhambra—if he continues a few more paces and looks down the narrow walkway between the theater and the old Reid Brothers Bank he would see Bryce making his way down the passageway, though instead of recognizing his friend he would probably see only a figure, a shadow, a lump—*he must have learned about Cory through Rachel but how did Bryce get involved? though it would be like him, sticking his nose in where it didn't belong, and now it's even worse, if Kim finds out that Bryce was poking around and gets the idea that Bryce was somehow involved in Cory's disappearance, Kim could end up going after him too, he already said he didn't like Bryce, didn't like the way he treated me, Somebody should do something about people who use other people, but Julian stands before the doors of the old theater and simply can't go in, the truth being he can't stand the thought of facing Donna Bruno again, especially not after his talk with Tinker—when Donna called him at Tinker's flower shop to tell him that Rachel had called about Cory, the last thing she said to him was, "You see, what did I tell you? You need me," and retraces his steps to the corner and turns up the hill on Twelfth Street and waits at the entrance to the alley while a Schwan's ice cream truck trundles past then walks down the alley to the back of the Benson Building where his car is parked and sits for a while, going over in his mind the conversation with Tinker, and decides he didn't hear her correctly, he must have misunderstood what she said, she didn't outright say that her arrangement with him to help her manage Sutcliff Realty was over, or if that was what she said she didn't necessarily mean it, she was still distraught over Dickie's death, and then the shock of the will, of everything going to Jennifer, there was no reason for her to say such things to him, no reason at all, he must have misheard, misunderstood, he must have, and starting the car, backs out of the space and heads down the alley, thinking I should go talk to Cory, maybe somebody contacted Kim and he'll turn up there . . . while in Indian Camp, at Stratton's cabin beside the Little Berry Creek, Kim closes the back door of the cabin and starts back around the side of the place, listening to the running of the creek behind him, his footsteps, as light as ever in the black canvas shoes, still crackling through the dry leaves, the fallen twigs, in the pocket of his satin jacket the Polaroid pictures of Cory posing naked on what appears to be the bed in a cheap hotel*

*room, along with the receipt for the Grand Hotel, the crows talk-
ing in the trees, gets in his car and heads back toward Furnass,
not hurrying, keeping within the legal speed limits, breathing
calmly, centered, at peace with himself, with what he knows he's
going to do. . . .*

26

Julian waited at the light on Twelfth Street, waited while a supersized woman pushing a baby in a stroller and herding three
others under four years old made their way across the pedestrian
walk, then drove up the main street through the little town,
through the angled shadows along the narrow street, the diago-
nals of light to dark, dark to light, his vision going from squint
to pop-eyed and back again. In the intense December sunlight
the strings of Christmas decorations over the street each became
an arc of glitters, before the intense December shadows made
them once again sagging imitation garlands. There were few people on the sidewalks, and most of those were the handicapped
and mentally ill, the patients farmed out to halfway houses and
community homes after the state closed the institutions, spending
their days looking for someplace to go. Above it all, between the
roof lines the sky was a blue ribbon, crystalline. Sad, Julian
thought, you'd never see a sky that blue before the mills shut
down, it took economic devastation to bring a touch of beauty
back to the town.

At the cross streets he caught glimpses of Furnass Landing
down along the river, the brownfields and demolished buildings.
Tomorrow, when he had copies of Dickie's will, he'd have to go
down there to talk to Jennifer. Let her know that everything was
hers now, Furnass Landing, Sutcliff Realty, even the abandoned
construction site of his own Furnass Towers. The keys to the
kingdom, as it were, in the hands of a babe. A red-haired babe,

to be sure, but a child, really. Julian wondered how she'd take the news, if it would surprise her. Somehow he didn't think it would, she seemed an old soul in some ways, mature beyond her years, she'd probably take it all in stride. Pick up where her dad left off, never skip a beat. Any idea of trying to get the better of her as unfeasible as trying to get the better of Dickie. Business as usual for the Sutcliff clan. He had the idea at one time of taking a camera and trying to get some pictures of the old Keystone Steam Works buildings that had been absorbed by Buchanan Steel, but he didn't get it done and it was too late now, the old brick buildings were rubble now. Nothing left now. Only the stories.

What was he supposed to think about his family? Believe about his family? About himself? He had always felt he had been chosen in some way, that he and his family were somehow special—he knew it was silly and misguided but the feeling persisted, was there nonetheless: that they were destined for special things by God or Fate or the Great Whatever. That he was, if not among the Chosen, at least Favored. If he took a lesser position in the world, if he was only a small-time attorney in a small-time town, it was his choice to remain lesser, that those Greater Powers were aware of his situation and blessed him that he knowingly kept his light under a bushel, that because he had elected to take a lesser station in life than was his due he was no less fit for and even worthy of greater things. But suppose . . . just suppose . . . he wasn't meant for greater things at all, whether he took them or not . . . suppose he was meant to be lesser, that it was ordained that he was one of those who would always be lesser in the world . . . and more, worse, suppose there wasn't Anyone or   Anything keeping track of the Greaters and the Lessers . . . suppose he was simply lesser . . . or say it: A Loser . . . suppose he was only who he was . . . and all things considered it certainly didn't seem to amount to much. . . .

Keep thinking like that, he told himself, and you'll deserve everything you get. Or don't get, as the case may be. . . .

When he got to the hospital he stopped at the information desk to ask to speak to Rachel Orr and gave his name. In a few minutes Rachel came through a pair of double doors, a stack of metal clipboards cradled in one arm. When she saw Julian she became all smiles.

"You didn't have to bother coming here," she said, embracing him with her free arm and kissing his cheek. Then she leaned back as if to get a good look him, a friendly appraisal rather than a nurse's evaluation. Sad, he thought, I'm always more comfortable with Rachel than with Bryce.

"It's no bother," Julian said. Probably because I never feel she judges me. "I was hoping Kim would turn up here by this time."

"Not that I know of," Rachel said. "I called your office when I couldn't get hold of him because I know you two are friends. I also spoke with the girl's mother. . . ."

"Sheryl."

"Yes, Sheryl. She sounded greatly relieved, but she's at work, she can't get away for another couple of hours. It was good of you to come. I think Cory would appreciate another friendly face, know that there are people who care about her. She did something quite remarkable for a girl her age, getting herself here to the hospital when she knew she was in trouble with drugs."

"She's a remarkable girl," Julian said.

Rachel smiled at him and took his arm, guiding him to the elevators and into an empty car. "I'll take you to her. She was in the ER but I had her admitted to a room for observation."

"Bryce spoke to her already?"

"Yes, how did you know?"

"One of Kim's students. Apparently Bryce stopped by the studio looking for Kim."

Rachel looked at the closed elevator doors in front of her face. At her reflection in the polished stainless steel. "He was here to see somebody from the congregation and I thought maybe Cory would respond well to a minister. It turned out she hates ministers but loved Bryce. You know Bryce."

"Go figure," Julian said as the doors parted and they stepped out onto the floor. "Maybe she felt comfortable talking to someone in her own age-group." As soon as he said it he wished he hadn't. *Am I always going to say the wrong thing?* He looked at Rachel as she guided him down a corridor to see how she took it but she was grinning.

"You could be right. Bryce has a, shall we say, youthful exuberance about him."

"I shouldn't have said that," Julian said.

"Of course you should have," Rachel said, stopping and looking at him. "It's true, you and I both know it. We both know it's part of his charm and can be absolutely infuriating at times." She reached out and touched his upper arm with the flat of her hand, rubbing it up and down a couple times, scanning his face. "You know, someday you two are going to have to admit you're friends and that you care about each other. Cory's room is over there."

She nodded to a door and gave him one last flat-hand tap before swinging back down the corridor, white shoes squeaking. Julian watched her go, as if watching the last chance for a reprieve walk away. He realized he was feeling apprehensive about talking to Cory, inadequate as to know what to say to her. He hoped maybe she was asleep; he poked his head in around the door . . . and found the girl sitting up in bed watching a soap opera on television. When she noticed him, she clicked the TV quiet and settled herself for a visitor.

"Hi, Cory. Mind if I come in?"

"Sure, it's a free country. What are you doing here?" Something occurred to her. "Did my dad send you?"

"No, I haven't seen your dad. Matter of fact, that's why I came, I thought maybe he was here."

She nodded. He realized it sounded wrong. Yes, I'll always say the wrong thing.

"I mean, I came to see you too. . . ."

"It's okay, Mr. Lyle. You don't have to. I haven't seen my dad."

"I'm sure he'll be here as soon as he finds out where you are. That's why I was looking for him, to tell him. . . . I mean, I guess if I found him here, he'd know where you are, wouldn't he?" He tried to laugh but caught himself, realized it wasn't a joking matter.

"Like I said, you don't have to explain. I know you wouldn't come here just to see me, and that's okay. Not unless my dad sent you, of course. I think it's nice Dad has a friend. You're probably his only one. Even though you were his lawyer when he killed my grandfather."

"I was his attorney for his trial but I like to think we became good friends after all that business was over."

"You are, don't worry" she grinned a little. "I think my dad always had trouble trusting people. After what his father did to him and all."

"Did to him? You mean the fight. . . ?"

"No, a long time before that. . . ." Something dawned on her; she cocked her head at him. "You don't know about that, do you? I would have thought he would have told you. But I guess not."

"Tell me what?"

She thought a moment. "His father molested him while he was a kid. I guess 'molested' isn't the word for it. Grandpap raped my dad for several years. I guess he was screwing dad's older brother, Tom, too—excuse my French—but Tom wasn't strong enough to fight him back. I guess that's why Dad decided to get so good at martial arts, he got good enough so he could defend himself and Tom, so Grandpap was afraid to do anything."

"How do you know all this. . . ?"

"My mom told me, after Dad killed Grandpap. She thinks that's why Dad killed his father, that he just wanted to get back at him for all the things Tomi did to him as a kid."

"Is that what she told you?"

"I was afraid of Dad after that. I saw what he could do to people. . . ."

"I didn't know anything about that story. But I can tell you without equivocation that your father loves you very very much. And the reason he had that fight with your grandfather that night was because he was afraid he was going to . . . molest you. He told me that the first time I interviewed him. Now that I know more of the background, I'm more sure of that than ever. He would do anything for you."

She looked at her hands folded on the bedsheet. She looked like she was about to cry.

"I saw him Friday night."

"Your dad? Kim? Where?"

"I saw him going into Mr. Sutcliff's office. By the back door. The night Mr. Sutcliff died."

Julian couldn't think of what to say. Cory raised her head to look at him.

"I was in a car in the alley. With a guy I know, he was bringing me back to my dad's place. We had been . . . foolin' around, you know, and we were parked in the next block from Dad's studio when we saw Dad coming down the alley, we were afraid he had seen us and was coming for us but he walked on past, he must not have noticed we were there. He went on down the block and up the back stairs to Mr. Sutcliff's office and jimmied the back door and went in. Then a little while later he came back out again, and I saw him wipe the door handle with a handkerchief and then he came back down the alley, I guess he went back to the studio. It seemed peculiar but I didn't think that much about it, I was just glad he didn't catch me with Jim. Then a little while later we heard sirens and there were police cars around and we took off out of there fast."

"Jim Stratton."

Cory blinked, surprised. "How did you know?"

"And that's why you disappeared?"

"I didn't know what to think. And Jim didn't want any part of the cops, we took off and he took me out to his cabin in Indian Camp and stayed there for a couple of days. I heard on the television that Mr. Sutcliff died in his office and I was afraid Dad had something to do with it and I got scared of him all over again. So I stayed with Jim for a couple of days, until I couldn't take it anymore."

"You did the right thing, to get away from that scene. I'm . . . Your dad would be very proud of you."

"Did my dad do it?"

"I don't know. That's why I'm looking for him. Officially, Dickie, Mr. Sutcliff died from hitting his head on the corner of his desk, but there are some questions that I'd like to clear up."

"You won't tell my dad that I saw him going into Mr. Sutcliff's office, will you? And that I was in the alley with Jim."

"I promise, Cory. You have my word on it. Look, I think I should be going. You need your rest, and I need to find your dad for a couple of reasons. Are you going to be okay?"

"Yeah. There's a nurse named Mrs. Orr that's been sort of looking after me."

"She's good at that, she's had lots of practice. I'll check with her later to make sure everything's okay. If you need anything just let her know or have Mrs. Orr contact me, I'll make sure it's taken care of. And most of all, don't worry. Your father loves you more than anything."

"If you see him, could you tell him I love him too? And that I'm sorry."

"Sorry for what?"

She started to say something then shook her head and wasn't going to say any more.

27

When Julian left the hospital it was late afternoon, the crystalline blue sky had become crystalline blue-black, a streak of cream above the ragged hills, the bare trees along the ridgeline like fringe, as if a last peek at the day before the lid was finally closed. He drove along the back streets of Orchard Hill, then down steep and curvy Tool & Die Hill Road to the road along Walnut Bottom Run and up Downie Hill Road to Furnass Heights, feeling good, good about himself, as if he had accomplished something talking to Cory, the same feeling of accomplishment he got when he represented a client well in court, in this case representing himself well with the girl, his friend's daughter—and represented Kim well to his daughter too, he thought, felt he was able to reassure her how much her father loved her. Though thoughts of Kim sobered him again. Julian hadn't known that Kim had been molested by his father. Was that a motive for Kim to kill Tomi? Was it self-defense, as Julian had argued at Kim's trial, or did he kill his father on purpose? Waited until the right time, the auspicious occasion? The convenient excuse. There were no other witnesses to what happened that night, there was only Kim's testimony. Kim's word. Julian hadn't questioned it at the time, during the trial, but the questions started to come as time went on, as he got to know Kim better, and he found himself despite himself questioning it now. At the time, if he was honest with himself, he had been too taken with talking to a killer, amazed to find himself sitting in a jail cell with such a person, someone who had a history of violence, who knew worlds and ways of thought that Julian had only read about. Not only confidant of a killer; best friend. It had been flattering in some respect to be Kim's friend, a way Julian himself would never, could never be, in Julian's mind a kind of deadly put-on to the world. Had he played the joke too far? Had he been blind to what the man really was?

Now there was what Cory said about seeing Kim entering Dickie Sutcliff's office the night Dickie died. In the beginning Julian only felt a general uneasiness, an unfounded suspicion that Kim might be involved, but now it seemed a certainty. What at first was an intellectual possibility, now was a genuine horror. And if Kim was involved, then Julian was too, if only by implication. Kim must have killed Dickie to try to help Julian, eliminate the source of Julian's problems. Kim's warped sense of loyalty. Julian never should have complained to Kim about Dickie and his whole financial mess, he should have known better than to wave such a red flag in front of someone like Kim. It sickened him to think he didn't have better judgment.

To say nothing of the old man at the Grand Hotel talking about his father's failings, the idea that Pappy was not only solely responsible for ruining the Keystone Steam Works, but then ran away from the responsibility. Or that Dickie's will gave everything to Jennifer, which effectively ended any chance that he and Tinker could get control of Sutcliff Realty and Julian might still have the chance to complete Furnass Towers. Irrespective of the fact that Tinker already told him to take a flying leap. By the time Julian reached home, he was no longer sobered, he was outright depressed.

He left his Cherokee in the driveway to the garage, off the side street behind the house—he hadn't been able to park inside the garage for decades, it had always been more of a storage shed than a garage—and walked across the backyard, attended by Reggie the basset hound doing his best to dance around his master though it came out more like an intense waddle, and in the back door into the kitchen. Marta was at the sink and had been watching him approach. Julian went over, kissed her on the cheek, and followed Reggie's wriggling rear end into the dining room.

The downstairs of the house had the feel of a hunting camp—not a hunting lodge, a step down from that, more like a cabin—not from a conscious decorative motif, more from its helter-skelter clutter, Marta not the tidiest housekeeper and Julian with his family's penchant for collecting things—or rather, reluctance to throw anything away, whether it be furniture or magazines or old blankets and throws or books or mail or knickknacks, either those they appropriated themselves or inherited from one side of the family or the other. Julian unwound his wool scarf from around his neck, took off his tweed sport coat and draped both over the back of his slouch-backed leather chair and went to the mantel above the stone fireplace. Marta had followed him in, wiping her hands on her apron.

"The mail is there at the end," she said.

"Any Christmas cards?" Julian asked, shuffling through the small stack. Bill, bill, bill, bill. . . .

"Just Dan Standish, the insurance man. And Mrs. Ridley."

"Who's that?"

"Remember? She was that bank teller you once represented for something or other. She's always one of the first with birthday and holiday cards."

Julian looked at the card—the Wise Men following a star—and Frisbee'd it and the insurance man's card into the cold fireplace. "I guess nobody loves us anymore," he said, half-joking.

"We stopped sending cards, remember?" Marta said, bending down and reaching past him to retrieve Mrs. Ridley's card. "Funny, how that works. . . ."

"Yeah, I guess," Julian said absently. He looked around as if looking for something, but knew whatever it was wasn't here. "I'm going upstairs and change clothes. I want to do some chopping before dinner. . . ."

He went up to their bedroom on the third floor, changed into his old jeans and work boots and green-and-black buffalo shirt, and went back through the house and out the kitchen door. He worked at his woodpile for close to an hour, concentrating all his energy on splitting the wood, focused on dropping the heavy maul axe at arm's length on the upturned log, refusing to think of anything else, until Marta called him in for dinner. She had fixed a pot roast, Julian's favorite, and after they joined hands, his left to her right, and he said the blessing—"Thank you, O Lord, for these thy gifts. In Jesus' name, amen"—they ate talking about their plans for the coming holiday, which of their five children would make it home this year, either with spouses or significant others, for those with children what their grandparents would give them, where everyone would sleep, a full house to be sure just the way Julian and Marta liked it for a few days at least, Julian continuing to keep his mind from drifting to those subjects that were standing just beyond the fringe of consciousness, mumbling and grumbling among themselves in the shadows, waiting until his guard was down and they could wander into the foreground of his thoughts again. He did okay later as they sat in the living room—Julian in his slouch-backed leather chair, Marta on the couch with Reggie tucked in beside her—to watch their TV shows, the local and network news, the local magazine and *Wheel of Fortune*, but *Miami Vice* and the sight of a body found in an alleyway, the victim of a brutal beating, proved to be his downfall; rather than Don Johnson pursuing bad guys through the glamorous shadows of Miami, Julian saw in his mind's eye Kim in his black satin outfit slipping through the back alleys of Furnass—and Jim Stratton sitting unsuspecting in a car. He had been wrong to block the investigation into Dickie Sutcliff's death, he knew that with certainty now, knew there was no way to undo that now. It would be equally wrong not to do everything he could to stop Kim from killing again—he tried to tell himself that it was an act of friendship to try to stop Kim from hurting anyone else, to protect him from himself as it were, but even he did not quite believe it, knew it wasn't the full reason he felt the over-powering need now to do what he could to stop Kim, that it had to do as much or more with his with his own feeling of responsi-bility or lack of it, his foolishness and self-delusion and failure to see what was plain as day in front of him, his all-too-apparent shortcomings as a person—knew that if he couldn't locate Kim, the least he could do was to warn a potential victim, a man Kim would undoubtedly be after once he found out whom Cory had been with the last several days.

"I have to go out," he said to Marta, getting up suddenly and taking his sport coat hanging off the back of his chair, putting on the coat and scarf over his buffalo shirt, the shirttails hanging down below the coat. When Marta looked quizzically at him, he said, "I forgot something at the office," gave her a kiss on the forehead and headed out the back door.

He drove again down windy Bridge Street Hill, his headlights sweeping alternately the face of the sandstone bluffs and the tops of the black trees down the steep slope, and into the Lower End, along Third Avenue, though he could already tell that something was wrong—No, it can't be—something was going on at the Grand Hotel, the street at the corner of Eleventh Street was clogged with police cars and emergency vehicles, the red and blue lights pulsing against the stone facade. No, I should have known. He parked half a block away and ran to the hotel. Perry Sykes was standing beside his police car pulled up to the curb near the front door. When he saw Julian he held up his finger to wait a moment. No, I did know. I should have said. Sykes signed off the call and reached in the car to return the microphone, then walked over to Julian.

"And what are you doing here, Counselor? Doing a bit of ambulance chasing?"

"I came to see Jim Stratton," Julian said, then saw the look the policeman gave him. "Don't tell me it's him."

"Afraid you're a little late, if you want to talk to him."

"Is he dead?" I should have said something to somebody.

"Gives new meaning to the term *beaten to a pulp*," Sykes said. "No sign that whoever did it used a bat or anything, looks more like somebody's bare fists." He studied Julian for a moment. "Curious you'd show up here, just at this time. I don't suppose you know where your best-known client is this evening, do you?"

"I was afraid of something like this. I came to let Stratton know that Kim . . . might be looking for him." He told Sykes the story that Cory had spent time with Stratton for several days, and his concern what Kim might do if he found out about it. He left out that Cory and Stratton had seen Kim entering Dickie Sutcliff's office the night he died, he didn't want to get into that now, it seemed a different issue, one he didn't have the strength for right now, he felt weak in his legs, he thought he might throw up. I could have prevented this I could have stopped this from happening.

"Well, I don't want to jump to any conclusions," Sykes said. "But it certainly looks like I need to have a conversation with Kim Leong about his whereabouts this evening. I'm guessing you don't know where I could find him."

"I've been looking for him all day but it's like he's been keeping out of sight."

"Sounds to me like I better have that conversation with Kim as soon as possible. Anyone else you can think of that Kim might have anything against?"

"Not really," Julian said. "If Kim did this, I'm sure it had to do with Cory." Of course he did this I could have stopped him should have stopped him. He thought of Bryce, that Kim might have something against Bryce because of the way Bryce treated Julian, talked down to him, took him for granted, but that all seemed trivial now—Bryce's running around asking questions, his moral superiority, sticking his nose where it wasn't wanted—compared to what had happened here. They were interrupted by the medics bringing a body bag out the front door of the hotel, the bag sagging between them almost touching the steps. They lifted it onto a gurney and wheeled it to one of the waiting ambulances. The flickering lights were getting to Julian, the glare of spotlights; he felt dizzy, he leaned against the fender of the police car.

"You feeling okay, Counselor?" Sykes said. "You're looking a little peaked there, you better come inside and sit a spell."

Sykes took him by the elbow and guided him up the steps and into the empty lobby, directing him to one of the empty armchairs in front of the front windows. "I'll let you know if I find anything else," the police chief said.

"Thanks, Perry."

Sykes gave him a wry look. "I have a feeling we're going to be dealing a lot with each other in the coming months. Again," he said and headed for the elevator.

Julian sat in the chair looking out the windows as the street gradually cleared of ambulances and emergency vehicles, the police cars turned off their lights and settled in for the investigation, technicians coming and going. When the dizziness had passed, he thought about going upstairs to take a look at the crime scene—he knew he should, it could be advantageous to see the room for himself rather than rely on the official police photos—but he realized it might call attention to the fact that he was there at all, a heads-up prosecutor could say his being on the scene was an indication of his client's guilt. When he saw a TV news crew from KDKA in Pittsburgh pull up, he knew he should get out of there. While the cameraman was setting up his light and the reporter started asking questions to whomever she could collar, Julian went through the lobby to the side door and back up the street to his car. Thinking, How do I live with this? Knowing I didn't do what I could? How does anyone go on after something like this? He turned into the maze of angled streets till he got to Seventh Avenue and followed it up through the town, through the business district, past the old Alhambra Theater with his office and in the next block the remains of Furnass Towers, the main part of town totally deserted at nine o'clock, the stoplights flashing warnings only to themselves, on past the traffic islands and up Orchid Hill Avenue and past the college, finding himself in front of his family's house. He sat for a moment, trying to slow the whirr of his thoughts, then gave up, got out and went to the front door, expecting to have to use his key, but it opened without it.

The heat in the house was stifling, it had to be close to ninety degrees. He unwound the scarf from around his neck as he followed the pathway between the stacks of paper and cardboard boxes—his father's chair was empty under the floor lamp, his writing board and charts and papers scattered in a semicircle in front of it—on through the clutter of the dining room—the table covered with books and magazines and papers—and into the kitchen. His father was bent over getting something from the refrigerator. He looked over his shoulder at Julian as if his son's presence didn't surprise him in the least.

"Pappy, the front door was unlocked again. Somebody could just walk in."

"Looks to me like somebody did."

"I've told you, you really have to keep that door locked. The town's not as safe as it used to be. There's drug dealers and all kinds of things going on nowadays." Like killings in hotel rooms, he thought. Killings in offices late at night.

His father took a cup of brownish liquid with a spoon sticking out of it from the refrigerator. He looked at his son as he took a few sips from the spoon.

"You want some coffee?" he offered it toward Julian.

"No thanks. How long has that been in there?"

"This particular cup?" Pappy said, looking down at it. "Oh, it's down about halfway, I'd say probably three days. I don't take too much at a time, only my sippies. This one's about due for a recharge though," he nodded to the aluminum percolator sitting on the stove.

Julian held up the coffeepot and shook it, then looked inside. "How long has this coffee been in here?"

"Couple of weeks, I guess. It can't spoil, you know. It only gets cranky if I leave a cup out too long once I've added the cream and sugar. I can usually get a good two or three weeks out of a pot. As long as I remember to put the top on, otherwise it tends to get dusty."

Julian shook his head. "You really need to keep that door locked."

"Yes, yes, yes," Pappy said, brushing past him and heading back through the downstairs of the house, along a pathway through the boxes and stacks of papers, under the bare light bulbs in the ceiling fixtures, toward the living room. "I've heard it all before. Like the proverbial broken record. You'd think a college-educated attorney like yourself could think of something more original to hound me about. Though I guess that could be my fault, not being able to send you someplace better than Covenant next door and then Penn State."

"I'm just afraid—"

"That's the thing, I'm not." He stopped and looked back at Julian to see how that registered, and went on. "If somebody comes in here, they'd take one look at this mess and turn around and run for it, afraid if they start to wade in here they'll lose their footing and all this stuff will suck them under and they'll never be heard from again."

"And suppose he doesn't run. Suppose he attacks you and hits you. Beats you to a pulp." Great, he thought, of all the words I could use. Perry Sykes said Gives new meaning to the term beaten to a pulp. What am I really talking about here?

His father made it back to his chair in the living room and sat down, pulling his writing board with its scattered papers across his lap. "If that happens, it happens. I'll go down swinging, just to make sure he finishes the job while he's at it, because inside I'll be thinking It's better than a home, better than a home. . . ."

He sipped a couple spoonfuls of his coffee and pursed his lips at his son. "But you didn't come here to lecture me about the front door or my coffee, now did you? What's on your mind?"

What was on his mind? Why did he come here? He didn't really know, it was like his mind was on autopilot and this is where he ended up. But he knew that wasn't true either. "I was talking to a couple old-timers. Down at the Grand Hotel—"

"Ah, the Grand Hotel. Now there's a misnomer if I ever heard one. It was run-down when I was still able to get out and about. I can't imagine what shape it's in these days. What were you doing down there, another one of your rehabilitation projects?"

Julian checked himself from saying something he might regret and went on. "There was a guy there who said his father used to work for the Keystone Steam Works, back in the day."

"I 'spect you could find a number of those around, if you were so inclined. You could probably also find a few still alive who actually worked at the Works, though they'd probably be in the same shape as me. Your guy must have had some tales to tell."

"He did, as a matter of fact." Was he really going to do this? Bring this up to his father? "He said the reason why the company went under wasn't because of the Lylemobile—"

"Well, of course it wasn't. The Lylemobile had its heyday a few years after World War I, if you can say it ever had a heyday. It was pretty much dead by 1923, nobody was going to go for a vehicle like that, to say nothing of the fact that steam engines for vehicles of any sort were obsolete by that time, everything was geared for the internal combustion engine, for better or for worse. It was nothing but a crazy idea in the mind of a crazy man who, sadly enough, happened to be my father."

"I always heard stories about the Lylemobile growing up, and stories about the company going under. I always thought they were connected."

"I guess the college education didn't help you to learn to count either," his father said, spooning something off the top of his coffee and flicking it onto the floor beside his chair. Then he looked at his son. "The company going under had nothing to do with the Lylemobile. Oh, I guess you could say it did, in a roundabout way. If my father hadn't sunk so much of the company's resources into that damn fool idea, he might have been able to pull things together once reality set in. He might have been able to keep the company up with the times, realized that the days of the steam engine as we made them were numbered and adapted our machines for internal combustion engines. Become a heavy equipment manufacturer like Caterpillar or John Deere or somebody, rather than insisting to hold on to a worn-out technology. Lyles seem to have a history of not adapting well, I'm afraid. We try to be proud of our stubbornness and intransigence, but we're just damn foolish, is all."

"The old man at the Grand Hotel said it was investments that brought down the company." Yes, I guess I am going to say this to my father. It's time I knew what my heritage actually is, not just what I wanted it to be. "He said they were the bad investments you made."

His father sighed. Took a couple of spoonfuls of coffee. Made a wry face. "When I came into the company—or let's say when my father had pretty much lost his marbles and what was left of the company was dumped in my lap—it was pretty obvious that we weren't going to recover by any of the traditional ways of selling more products or introducing new ones, we weren't geared up for either of those options, we were way beyond that point. We were going to need a heavy infusion of cash to stay alive, and need it real quick. The thing was, in those days there was no problem getting a loan, folks were more or less throwing money at you, so I took out a number of loans, but it still wasn't going to be enough to get us out of the hole the Lylemobile drove us into. Then it occurred to me that I could invest on margin, so I started to do that with the loan money, in high-risk but high-yield stocks. And I did okay too, if I say so myself, I made enough that I was already thinking how we were going to upgrade the product line and introduce a gas-powered well driller. But then the bubble burst, the bottom fell out, and it all came tumbling down. People think the stock market crash caused the Great Depression. Fact is there were a number of reasons, all clustered together, the stock market crash was more a symptom of the problem than anything else, if you ask me, and I know you didn't. The real problem as I see it was easy money, there was easy money to be had just for the asking, and I bought into it, I thought it was going to be our savior. It wasn't the investments that did us in, it was the loans."

"So we share something after all," Julian said. Thinking of his own ill-advised loans with Sycamore Savings & Loan, the easy money to remodel the Alhambra Theater, to build Furnass Towers. The euphoria of riding that wave of easy money that seemed destined to carry you to success, then the devastation when

Sycamore failed with the other S & Ls across the country, the sinking feeling as you drowned in debt.

"Probably more than you'd like to admit," his father said, idly stirring his coffee, then sucked the spoon dry. "I never said anything at the time you were going through your kafuffle. I figured you had enough pain in your life, without me bringing up the similarities. If you haven't discovered it already, there are times when the last thing you need to be reminded of is a family connection. Particularly when it involves some damn foolishness."

"I'm learning," Julian said, thinking a moment. "Is that when you went to live on the farm in Hickory?"

"A sad chapter of my life," his father said, patting one particular stack of papers on his writing board, "but it was what it was. After all that had happened, there was nothing left of the Steam Works, the only thing to do was to walk away. But I was reluctant to do that, I was still young and headstrong, there was only me—this was before I met your mother—I kept thinking there must be something I could do to make it right. But there was a lot of anger in town, Buchanan wasn't doing much better than the Steam Works, they let everybody go except the maintenance crews. So there was a lot of men hanging around the streets with nothing to do except think about how unfair the world is. And there was my daddy sitting in plain view in his big house up there on the side of the hill, and people starting to get ideas about getting even. So I had a reporter I knew put a story in the paper about how it was actually the bad investments that did in the Steam Works. That gave people something else to think about, and then I made a big production of leaving town. Worked pretty good too, I couldn't show my face in town for a couple years there."

"When you came back you moved in here. . . ." Julian looked around at the clutter, the rooms where he grew up. The house had always been full of stuff, but now it was as if the stuff had won in its bid to take over.

"By that time my daddy had burned the big house down around his ears. And this place was low-key, we owned it since the time the Steam Works started, a company house for a supervisor or somebody. I thought we could just settle in here without a fuss. Your poor mother, I think she was expecting something a little grander, but we made do."

"And you got the job at Buchanan."

Pappy smiled, looking around at the papers on the writing board in front of him. "Ironic, huh? Well, they knew I was a good engineer, even if I wasn't a good businessman. It was sort of a relief, if you want to know the truth, not to have to run anything, to just work nine to five reviewing drawings, and then come home in the evenings."

"I remember Suzie and me going down to Uncle Claire and Aunt Mary Lydia's when we were kids. But you and Mother never talked about them, like they were a forbidden topic."

"Not forbidden, just sad. Mary Lydia had it in her head that once the Steam Works affairs were settled—things were tied up in the courts for years—she and Claire would come into some significant money. When she finally realized there wasn't going to be money from any settlement, she went crazier than she was to start with, blaming me for losing her birthright and all kinds of things. Claire and I decided that it was better for everyone concerned if I didn't go down there again, though your mother went to see her family."

"I didn't know."

"And no reason why you should. Your mother and I tried to keep the past in the past, no sense in dredging up old hurts. And the people around us here were great, treated us just like normal people. Pearl and Eddie next door. Turned out he had worked at the Steam Works before the closing, he lost his job with everybody else, but he never said a thing about it when we moved in, I always appreciated that. A really good friend. I miss him terribly since he's gone. Pearl too, she was a pistol. Used to run around over there stark naked, liked to clean the house that way, I spent a lot of time avoiding the windows on that side of the house whenever spring or fall cleaning came along. Always wondered if that had a hand in making Brycey as dicey as he is."

"Bryce seems to have made me into a congregation of one for his ministry, to purge me of all my sins and faults."

"If he's chewing on you, he's undoubtedly chewing on some things he can't quite swallow about himself. I always got a kick out of Brycey-Dicey, he always was a peck of compensations, making up for one thing or another. He sure did come into the world unprepared, the wrong set of tools for whatever job he was undertaking. I'm sure it's easy now, for both of you, to forget how close you were as kids, for years you two were inseparable. You were good for each other though, like two poles of an engine hoist I always thought."

"I guess we were pretty close there. . . ."

"Close? You remember that time you were laid up with scarlet fever for six months or so, I guess you were eight or nine or so, Bryce brought your homework every night and the two of you would work at it up there in your bedroom so that when you went back you could advance with the rest of the class? . . . Now where are you off to in such a hurry?"

"There's something I've got to do," Julian called over his shoulder as he threaded his way back to the front door.

His father called after him. "Hey, don't forget to lock that on your way out."

. . . and Julian gets in his car and makes a U-turn and drives back through the dark streets of Orchard Hill, thinking So Pappy

was a hero after all, but not in any way you'd notice, shifted the blame for the demise of the Steam Works away from his own father so the town would leave him alone, took the blame himself, then spent the rest of his life under that blanket of public scrutiny, no wonder he wants to write the family history now, set the record straight for anyone who cares to know what really happened, and all this time I thought . . . I don't know what I thought, but none of it applies now, drives past the lights of the college, the tower of Old Main glowing in the spotlights beyond the bare branches of the trees in the chill dark early December evening, wondering for a moment about a comment Pappy made, wondering if his life would have been different if his family had had the money to send him to another school instead of here to Covenant College, a better school, because the school's strict Christian focus wasn't good for much besides teaching a strict Christian focus, it certainly didn't prepare you for what you'd encounter in the broader world, but thinks again I guess all things considered it wouldn't have made much difference, even when they were force-fed the basic message of those good Christian principles didn't get through, especially that one about loving your neighbor even when he happens to be your neighbor, thinking I don't even remember now what I thought Bryce did was so terrible, I only know that I complained about him to Kim and now I've got to get to him before Kim the Avenger does, I don't want another Stratton on my conscience . . . as earlier in the evening, across the river from Furnass at the Riverview Inn, the restaurant that sits at the top of the long grade across the granite and sandstone bluffs that face the little mill town on the other side of the Allehela, at a Christmas party in the special events room being held for the doctors and nurses and staff of Onagona Memorial Hospital, the Reverend Bryce Orr stands holding a cup of eggnog, his third of the evening, by the large stone fireplace, eggnog that he is certain is spiked with something though he is unschooled in the tastes or uses of alcohol so he doesn't recognize the dark rum, he only knows he really really likes the taste of it and that it is doing wonders in making him more sociable to these people to whom he usually has nothing to say, is actually enjoying himself talking to his wife's boss, Dr. Ingram, the hospital's chief medical officer, thoroughly enjoying this swell party with all these swell people in this swell restaurant and can't for the life of him think why he didn't want to come here tonight . . . while across the room, Rachel Orr, in the midst of talking to young Dr. Malory who is ten years at least her junior and who is definitely suggesting that they get together sometime to get to know each other better—no, not suggesting it, coming right out and propositioning her—offering to take her to a conference coming up in February in San Francisco and that they should have dinner next week to discuss it, and though she is flattered and even a little grateful for the attention she is finding it difficult not to laugh in the younger man's face, sees Bryce talking animatedly to Dr. Ingram, and thinks if she's going to get screwed by anyone this evening it'll be Bryce with his alcohol-inflamed cheeks talking to her boss and it certainly won't involve a form of intercourse that requires a condom . . . while in Furnass Heights, Julian Lyle's wife, Marta, sits on the sofa in their living room—some might call the room rustic, the entire house for that matter, being kind; some might call it shabby, which is more the case; Marta knows and has come to accept that the house is a reflection of her husband's trying to get closer to the earth, back to the basics, his search for what he refers to as authenticity—cradling Reggie their basset hound on her lap, watching Dynasty *on television and wondering why Julian left in such a hurry earlier, thinks that the one thing she knows that it isn't is another woman, and smiles to herself, thinks about their life together, the man she married, whom she obviously loves though has nothing to compare her feelings to, having never been with any other man, she and Julian meeting at*

All Fall Down

Covenant College where she came from Kansas because the college's Covenanter focus was as strict as her family's, their quick and sex-filled courtship a liberation for her, the expression of her repressed individuality that soon enough became subjugated to her new role as a wife and mother in that same strict reformed Christian context—a value system implied if not overt, theirs a Christian household in general principle if not in actual practice such as bothering to attend services—Julian's interpretation of traditional values, Christian or otherwise, when it comes to marriage best summarized as keeping a wife barefoot and pregnant, though when she thought about it after they were married, after her initial disappointment that this was what the world held for her, she decided the role suited her well enough; thinks about Julian's traditional values in regard to other people, his genuine and secular concern for those he considers his friends though she fails to see how those so-called friends return his concern, thinks about his concern for doing things for the town when she knows the town thinks he's a fool and knows in some regards they're probably right, and wonders how he keeps going, cradles Reggie in her arms and offers a silent prayer for her husband, Forgive him, Lord, he knows not what he's doing . . . while in the big house on the edge of Orchard Hill overlooking the dark town, the town more sensed than anything else by the streetlights marking the grid of streets as they climb the slope from the black space marking the river, though each night toward Christmas more of the small frame houses become distinct in the night, more of the houses outlined with lights or spotlighted to display their holiday decorations, the nights previously defined by black and white now taking on patches of red and green, Harry Todd turns away from the tower windows in the second-floor room that was once his parents' bedroom and then just his mother's, in the light of the bare bulbs of the floor lamps he's carried in to continue work at night, the room completely empty now of any trace of anyone who ever lived here, having carried down the last armful of his mother's clothes to burn in the fire pit at the side of the house, and thinks of what his niece, Jennifer, told him a short time ago, that she just heard from her mother that the attorneys found her father's missing will and that Jennifer is the sole inheritor of her father's firm, that Dickie left Furnass Realty to Jennifer alone, so that's that, there's no question now of his taking over the company or even a piece of it, it's all in her hands, that in fact she is now his boss in regard to the know-nothing, do-nothing job with the company that Dickie set up for him, Harry Todd's return to Furnass a complete bust, there's nothing for him here and no reason why he should continue to stay, nothing more can come of his being here, he might as well load up his car and head back to California, back to where the weather suits his clothes as the song says, starts running through in his mind the things he'll need to take care of for such a trip—I need to get that front tire looked at and make sure there's air in the spare, I wonder if there's snow in the passes yet, guess I better check with Triple-A, and I'll call Emily to see if I can stay at her place or if I've worn out my welcome, I wonder if it's too late to get my job back at Denny's or if I'll have to try one of the other chains—realizing as he does so that there's nothing back in California for him now either, wondering where exactly he can go, recognizes that if he thought he was out of options before returning here he is truly out of options now, a recognition that he knows should fill him with desperation and despair, but doesn't, the desperation and despair surfacing only when he thinks about leaving here, getting back in his car and driving away, turns and looks one more time at the figure standing between the two shadeless floor lamps in the blackened windows, the repeated images of the stocky, fifty-plus blond-haired man in an old T-shirt, a man for all that who looks like he totally belongs here in Western Pennsylvania, is at home here, thinks I really don't want to go anyplace else, I'm happy here, pulls himself up short as he thinks Who would have ever thought it, I'm a happy guy, I'm as happy as I'm ever going to be, this is what I wanted . . . while in her apartment a block above the main street, Jennifer sits at her kitchen table after returning from the Big House to tell her uncle in person the news about her father's will, to give him that courtesy because she knows he was anxious to know what the will said, and, if she's truthful with herself, to establish in the gentlest yet most forceful way possible that she's the boss now, she's not going to put up with any more of his foolishness about making a play for the company now that she's in charge, then deciding it was probably best that she didn't stay there at the Big House tonight as she has been doing, sensing that rather than needing to know someone was around in the house with him Harry Todd will need time to digest the ramifications of this turn of events—it's certainly true for herself: she needs to be alone tonight to think over what all has happened over the past week and her next steps—going over in her mind the phone call this evening from her mother telling her that she had inherited Sutcliff Realty and Development Company, "You got it all, Jenn, you won, you got what you set out to do, I hope you're happy now," wondering if her mother was right in some way, that she did in fact set out to take over the company, looks out her rear window as she sits at the kitchen table, looking through the black framework of the unfinished building across the alley, the abandoned Furnass Towers—her building now, one of many, smiles to herself at the thought—the lights of the main street glowing up from between the rows of buildings like the glow of a split in the earth, and thinks she certainly didn't anticipate that her father would die at such an early age, but has to admit to herself that yes, this was her goal, she was indeed that ambitious, that driven to succeed, being her father's daughter, "I'll make you proud, Dad, you just wait and see," what she is now the same as what she has always been, in the best sense of the term, his equal,

Daddy's girl . . . while in the other house in the area known as the Sutcliff House, this one in the expensive borough of Highland Hills, Tinker Sutcliff meanders through the Mediterranean villa-like mansion, the showcase rooms decorated like sets for a photo shoot—rooms like you might see in Architectural Digest *or* Town & Country, *something a step up from* House Beautiful *or* Better Homes and Gardens—*and feels surprisingly relieved and happy, realizing that whether he meant to or not—and knowing Dickie as she did, since they first got to know each other in junior high school, he undoubtedly meant to—Dickie has set her free, by not leaving Sutcliff Realty to her he's made her free of the struggle, free of the worries and the hassles and the daily wars in which she would have been involved if she had tried to run a company and a business that was beyond her, for which she had no experience or talent or training—or even inclination, when you came right down to it, realizing that the only reason she thought she wanted it in the first place was to cause trouble, to get back at Dickie for reasons she couldn't name now, probably didn't know in the first place, an accumulation of the nameless, obscure, un-identified disappointments and recriminations and frustrations of so many years together; if she were honest with herself perhaps she only wanted it to get him to notice her if only as a source of grief—he has left her the house and the funds to maintain her lifestyle for the rest of her life, to be comfortable till the end of her days, thinking again that Dickie undoubtedly meant to set her up this way because Dickie never made a false move in his life, he has given her the greatest gift of love that he could give, he denied her what she didn't want in the first place, thinking That son-of-a-bitch, that miserable rotten son-of-a-bitch, thank you, Dickie, wherever you are . . . while in another suburb to the north of Furnass though this one, Seneca, is more to the east and younger, newer, growing, in Seneca Towne Centre, in another house that Dickie Sutcliff built though in this case Dickie not only built the townhouse—or rather, as the developer, determined how it would be built, how the money would be spent to build it—but also the entire townhouse complex as well as the nearby shopping plaza that includes a Home Depot, a Giant Eagle, and a Target, Pamela DiCello lies on the carpeted floor, stretched out on her yoga mat after finishing her nightly hour-long routine, feeling once again open and centered and calm, and allows herself to think again of Dickie—the truth being that she thinks of little else these days, he is always somewhere in her thoughts, though she knows that's not much different than when he was alive, only now the thoughts are always tinged with a sense of loss, so that she has learned that she needs to consciously limit the amount of time she can allow herself to think of him, so she can go on—but for once, for the first time since he died, or as she suspects, was murdered, she doesn't think of what might have been, how their life together might have been after his divorce and they could be open with their love, but what Dickie would want her to do now, the way things are now, if he were somehow able to see her now— though she has no illusions that he can, she has been a nurse for too long, seen too many broken and devastated bodies, witnessed too many deaths both violent and simply slipping away, to harbor any notions of an afterlife with rewards or punishment for deeds done on earth; she believes there is only this moment and reminds herself that Dickie would be the first one to say she should make the most of it—and gets up from the floor, stretches like a cat, rolls up her yoga mat and takes it into the bedroom, stashes it in the bottom of her closet, then thinks of something, opens the sliding closet door further and kneels down and digs beyond the line of shoes, white nurse's shoes and trainers and her dress-up high-heel ankle-strap sandals and takes out a shoe box kept at the back, opens it as she kneels there and takes out a small framed picture, the photograph of a construction worker, construction superintendent to be exact, taken on the project across the alley from her old apartment in downtown Furnass—the photo taken from the waist up though behind him you can see her apartment build- ing, her windows where she first saw him and he saw her—a man in his early forties, overweight, pudgy, his face like that of a tough Broderick Crawford though there is a twinkle in his eye, his hard hat cocked at a jaunty angle, Jack, the love of her life, also dead now, and she returns the shoe box to its corner in the closet and gets up and slides the door closed again and takes the small framed picture into the living room and places it on the mantel, sliding the picture of Dickie Sutcliff over a few inches to make room for it, so the two pictures, the two men in her life, can sit side by side—aware that if Jack hadn't taught her how to appre- ciate every moment, "You make your own party, honey britches, don't you forget it. Isn't that wonderful?" she never would have appreciated what was special about Dickie, his impatience with the world, his hunger to have everything the world had to offer— knowing that each would approve of them being there together, because besides being her lovers they were also her friends, the best friends she ever expects to have, giving them a chance to appreciate her as she appreciates them, then pads off back through the townhouse to take a shower . . . while in Holy Innocents Church in Furnass long after the church is closed and locked for the night though Father Mulroy and the other priests know that she knows how to let herself out, Donna Bruno kneels in the empty church before a side altar with a manger scene overlooked by her favorite statue of the Virgin Mary, looks at the doll lying in a bed of straw that represents the Baby Jesus and thinks of the child she and Harry Todd conceived before his father sent Harry Todd away to school in California and paid to have her sent to a home in Ohio to have the baby, thinks of their child though she knows it's no longer a child, she's found out through her connec- tions working in an attorney's office that he's a young man named Alex, that he's graduated from Ohio State and is married now, probably having children of his own, and she offers a prayer to the Virgin and the Baby Jesus to keep her child safe throughout his life, can see him in her mind's eye all grown up, tall and thin and blond, can see him and his beautiful young wife, also tall and thin and blond, and their own baby boy coming to visit her and Harry Todd in the Big House, because she knows in her heart that it is only a matter of time before Harry Todd discovers her again, discovers his feelings about her again, and they are reunited again, as she has always known they would be, known it from the day his father drove them apart, known it from the last time they were together in the back seat of his father's car parked by the little creek beyond a picnic shelter in Berry's Run Park, the last time they made love before he drove her back to her parents' home on Seventh Street and dropped her off and she didn't see him again until he returned to Furnass this past year, and she blesses herself and gets up and goes over to the bank of votive candles and lights a candle for Harry Todd as she does every evening and then lights a second candle this evening for the spirit of Dickie Sutcliff, offers a special prayer for Dickie for his help over the years, for making sure she had a job at Sutcliff Realty and then with Julian Lyle, a job now that will last for the rest of her life, a provision of Dickie's will subsidizing her salary with Julian to make sure she's provided for, a gift she knows that is as much to Julian as it is to her, Dickie's way of taking care of an old Orchard Hill friend, but also Dickie's way of acknowledging her love for Harry Todd, that it is only a matter of time until she and Harry Todd are together again, that she is part of the Sutcliff family and always will be, world without end, amen . . . while at the Grand Hotel, Chief of Police Perry Sykes takes one last look around the room where Jim Stratton was beaten to death earlier this evening, then closes the door and locks it, stretches tape across the door that reads CRIME SCENE DO NOT CROSS, and heads back down the dark narrow corridor, takes the rickety elevator back down to the lobby and returns to his car, the last of the emergency vehicles on the street and thinks it's his job to clean up other people's messes and he's getting sick and tired of it, knows in his heart that Kim Leong did this and that it's too bad, he genuinely likes Kim though the guy has to be stopped now, Kim has gone too far though the police chief in Perry Sykes is secretly glad to have a lowlife like Stratton out of the mix, thinks for a small-town police chief he certainly gets a lot of violent deaths on his plate, the good thing is that as soon as he gets Kim into custody his workload, particularly these late nights, is going to lighten considerably . . . while in her room at Onagona Memorial Hospital, in the daze of the sedative they've given her to help her sleep, Cory Leong remembers waking or remembers dreaming of waking to find her father sitting in the dark corner of the room, keeping watch over her, but before she could say anything she drifted off again, or continued to dream, she can't really say, remembers waking later, or dreamt she woke later, to her father leaning over her, the sweet smell of the incense he burns at the studio like a blessing flowing over her, felt his lips on her forehead and his voice soft, a whisper, not to disturb her, "I love you, Cory, always remember your daddy loved you," and wonders in her waking or dreaming state why he said "loved" instead of "loves" and why the last thing he said to her was "Good-bye" . . . and in the township of Drumlins, Kim Leong turns off Berry Highway—it's actually Colonel Berry Highway, named for an important Native American chief during the French and Indian War and Pontiac's Rebellion though few know why or what he did nowadays and the locals have shortened the name for so long now it even appears that way on maps—with its car dealerships and strip malls, franchise restaurants and drive-ins, low-rise medical and dental buildings, modern office buildings set back on what are at this time of night empty parking lots, onto the quiet tree-lined side street called Graystone Drive, a short street only a block or so long that's a reminder of when this was a sleepy residential area before urban sprawl took it over, past a few incongruous older frame houses, the homes of the few older residents who refuse to give over to the changes in their community, past the back lot of Wild Bill Januzzi's Cycle World on one side of the street and Pets Aplenty Veterinary Clinic & Hospital on the other, to Graystone Church sitting at the end of the street, literally at the end of the street so that if Kim were to keep going he would bounce up the dozen or so granite steps and into the large medieval-style oak front doors, the large rose window at the top of the church's tower glowing against the night sky like a vision, pulls into the empty parking lot between the veterinary clinic and the trim Christmas-card-looking house beside the church, built of the same gray stone as the church so that Kim is confident it is the parsonage, parks not beside the house but drives on toward the rear of the lot, into the shadows under the bare branches of a weeping willow tree along the row of tall rather unkempt shrubs that separates the backyard of the house from the parking lot, turns off his headlights and the engine and sits in the darkness and the quiet for a few moments, letting the dark and the stillness settle around him, until he is certain that no one is about, that no one has seen him pull in here, then gets out, careful not to let the car door give more than the slightest click, a black figure among the shadows, and moves along the row of shrubs until he comes to a space between the bushes and slips through into the backyard and approaches the house where a few lights burn though they appear to be the kind of lights left on when no one is at home, not as if they are somewhere else in the house watching television or reading or upstairs asleep, looks cautiously in the windows of the kitchen—there is only the small light in the hood shining down over the stove, there is no one here—then moves around the side of the house, checking in the windows of the dining room and living room as he goes—there are only occasional lamps turned on low, there is no one here—to the front door, but then on a hunch moves on to the door with a sign marked CHURCH OFFICE, tries the handle and finds it unlocked, thinks Silly Christians and smiles to himself and slips inside the dark anteroom, waits a moment to be sure, then moves on in his soft canvas shoes into what must be Bryce's study, on down the corridor and into the downstairs of the house, finding no one, then quietly, swiftly up the stairs two at a time to the second floor, his footsteps on the carpeted treads making only a whisper, checking each of the bedrooms in turn before returning again to the downstairs, satisfied there is no one here, the house is empty except for a black-and-white cat curled asleep on the cushion of a chair in the dining room, the cat suddenly awake as if it sensed rather than heard him, for a moment the cat staring at him, directly in the eyes as if the cat recognizes him, knows him from some time long ago, Kim reaching out and touching the cat, rubbing its head between the ears, the cat opening its mouth as if to speak or bite him but does neither, only watches the man's hand as Kim turns and leaves the room, returns through the house the way he came, slipping back outside and moving in the shadows between the house and the church and goes back and gets in his car, to wait . . . and the river flows, the Allehela, out of the Allegheny old-growth forests to the north, a gathering of small trickles and runoffs until it gains the status of a creek and then joins with other creeks to form a stream and then joins other streams to form a river, the river following the valleys cut by glaciers during the Ice Age some twenty thousand years earlier, a time when wooly mammoths and saber-toothed cats, giant sloths and camels, three-toed horses and beavers, yes beavers, roamed these hills when these hills were covered only with tundra vegetation, some grasses, a few spruce trees, low shrubs, the river in its own valley now wending its way past where Kim sits in the darkness in his car on one side of the river and Dickie lies in the darkness of his casket on the other, where Bryce and Rachel leave the Riverview Inn and head home not speaking to each other on one side of the valley and Julian is talking to his father on the other when something dawns on him . . . and time flows—or does it? Certainly in the popular idea of time it flows like the river but perhaps not, perhaps time is only a construct of the conscious mind, of consciousness as it constructs the world around each of us, each in his or her own center of the universe, his or her own world, a construct of a world within worlds and layers of reality beyond comprehension, the only question being then in whose consciousness our story now is taking place. . . .*

28

As they pulled out of the parking lot of the Riverview Inn, Rachel sent a spray of gravel up against the pan of the front-wheel-drive car, causing Bryce beside her in the passenger seat to jump, followed by a squeal of tires as they set off down the highway, back toward Drumlins and home.

"Yee-haw!" Bryce said, trying to get into the spirit of it. "Ride 'em, cowgirl!"

Rachel didn't say anything, keeping her eyes on the road, her mouth set.

It's not looking good, Lord, Bryce thought. I'm not only getting The Big Silence, I'm getting The Look on top of it, when she'll look at me at all. What did I do? I'm not sure it even matters, at this point I couldn't do anything right, according to Rachel's Ten Commandments. A major transgression, obviously. Punishable by Freezing Out till death do us part. Too bad, really. I had a good time. That eggnog was something.

They rode on through the night several miles, neither one speaking, Rachel driving too fast and with no signs of slowing down, until Bryce couldn't stand it any longer.

"You might as well tell me what's bothering you."

"You seriously don't know?"

"If I knew, I wouldn't ask you, would I?"

Wrong. They fell silent again. This is an argument, Lord, measured in miles not in transgressions. I should just shut up and let her stew in her own juices, I should just let it go, let it pass, time heals all wounds, or wounds all heels, whatever. But I can't do that, can I, Lord? I'm supposed to be a Man of God, bringing peace on earth. I should at least be able to make peace with my own wife. Probably can't but can't resist trying either.

"Okay, lay it on me."

"You told Dr. Ingram that you look forward to your prostate exams because they're the only sex you get these days?"

Oh, that. "Well, yes. . . ."

"How could you do that?"

"Actually, it was pretty easy," Bryce said, trying for humor. "I just opened my mouth and out it came. Seemed funny at the time. . . ."

"Funny?"

"Well, you know. He is a doctor and all. A little proctological humor."

"He's somebody I work with! He's my boss, for Christ's sake!"

"You shouldn't swear, dear. A minister's wife—"

"To hell with what everybody thinks a minister's wife should or shouldn't do! I'm tired of it!"

"I've never heard you talk like this before," Bryce said. Then waggled his head. "It's kind of sexy. . . ."

"You more or less told my boss that we don't have sex."

"Well, we don't."

"But I don't want the whole world to know that. That's none of their business."

"If it's the truth, I don't see why I should try to hide it and lie about it."

"You really don't see the position you put me in when you say things like that, do you? You're really are that thick, aren't you?"

"I also asked him how he liked working around assholes every day. That I had enough of them in my congregation to sympathize with him—"

Rachel veered into the empty parking lot of the Colonel Berry Mall and screeched to a halt.

"Out!"

"Out? As in get out?"

"Out! Right now! You can walk!"

"But we're almost home. . . ."

"The walk will do you good. Maybe it'll walk some sense into that fuzzy brain of yours. If nothing else it will keep me from strangling you with my bare hands or running us into a telephone pole. Oooooh, I'm so mad at you!"

"That's pretty obvious. Don't you think it would be better to just go home and—"

Her finger pointing to the door on his side of the car almost stabbed him in the nose. Bryce chuckled to himself and slowly climbed out. Then he leaned back in. "You know, this is going to make a great story for me to use in next Sunday's sermon. Judge not, less ye be judged, or something of the sort—"

Rachel floored it and the car leaped forward, the car door slamming shut with the acceleration and Bryce almost falling facedown on the asphalt. He watched as the car swung out onto Berry Highway and barreled into traffic.

"Or maybe, the truth shall set you free," he said out loud. Then thought, Or at least it will get you a walk home in the crisp night air. Far out. Fascinating rhythm.

Bryce, still chuckling to himself at the turn of events—there was a part of him that couldn't help feeling proud of Rachel, that was the kind of no-nonsense response he would have expected of her, that attracted him to her in the first place; a lot of women might want to throw their husbands out of the car, but Rachel was the only he knew who would actually do it, you had to love a woman like that—walked across the parking lot to the sidewalk and started toward home. It was only a half mile or so, he was grateful they hadn't started talking several miles sooner. He wrapped his too-short raincoat about himself, the collar up. Next time he went to a party where there was a chance he'd drink too much, he told himself, he'd be wise to wear hiking boots.

The sidewalk in most places, when there was any sidewalk at all in front of the strip malls and franchise restaurants, was little more than a path in the grass parallel to the highway, few people having the occasion to walk here. Bryce chugged along, traffic whizzing by him, trying to think of what he'd say to Rachel when he got to the house—I guess I should apologize, but I still think it was funny; okay, I have to admit Dr. Ingram didn't smile when I said it—hoping maybe she'd be in bed asleep by the time he got there. The traffic came in waves, the cluster of cars timed by the few stoplights. When traffic was clear, he crossed the momentarily empty highway to the other side as he neared the corner of Graystone Drive; across the empty parking lot of Wild Bill Januzzi's Cycle World, the church sat at the end of the street, glowing in the spotlights against the dark night like a vision. Funny old church, looks more like a lost section of a medieval battlement than a place of worship, but I love the place. Ahead in the darkness a figure was coming toward him along the narrow path. Bryce couldn't see his face. The Christian thing to do, he moved over into the ankle-high grass—Damn, Wild Bill needs to keep his place trimmed—but he couldn't resist the Bryce thing to do either. As the other got nearer, Bryce said, "You might as well go back. I was just there and it was closed."

The figure, a man in a dark topcoat whom Bryce didn't recognize, continued past without looking at him. "You just don't get it, do you?"

Bryce stopped and looked after him. "Get what?" The figure continued on, not looking back. Bryce tried to laugh. "What did you mean by that?" The figure kept walking, in and out of the shadows, then seemed to disappear completely in the lights of another wave of cars coming down the highway. Bryce squinted, shaded his eyes to try to see him, but couldn't locate him. He laughed again, but a shiver ran down him. Far out. Fascinating rhythm. Maybe he wasn't there at all. That eggnog. He hunched his shoulders in his raincoat and cut across the end of the parking lot toward home.

Her car was in the garage beside Bryce's *God Runner*; Rachel had made it home okay. The lights in the downstairs were the way they left them; upstairs there was a light on in their bedroom, she must be waiting for him. He knew he should go in and face her, confront her and apologize . . . but he decided to keep her waiting, make her wonder a bit what happened to him. If she got worried enough, she'd figure it out that he'd gone to his hideaway in the church tower; he shouldn't make it too easy for her, after all she did throw him out of the car on a cold winter's night. He noticed a car parked in the shadows at the back of the Pets Aplenty parking lot but didn't think anything of it, he supposed one of the docs or a technician was working late, or maybe it was a car that wouldn't start after a visit to the clinic, bummer. He went on past the house to the side door of the church and let himself in the basement.

He made his way through the dark Sunday school rooms, upstairs through the nave, the arcs of the rows of empty pews ghostly in the dull light from the church windows—Like a schematic of planets in orbit around a sun, Bryce thought, maybe I can use that in a sermon, no, that would imply that I was the sun and I don't want people to start confusing me with the Son, heh heh, or maybe they're like the rings in water after you drop in a pebble, but then somebody could say my sermon sank like a stone, I'll have to work on it—through the double doors at the back and across the foyer to the base of the tower, unlocked the door and climbed the spiral stone stairway into the parti-colored glow coming from the bell ringer's loft.

He felt better as soon as he was in the room, the spotlights trained on the circular window reflecting back in the room, filling it with color. The eggnog was staring to wear off, leaving him thirsty and feeling heavy. Maybe a little blue too. He was about to put on some music, maybe some Coltrane, he could do with some *Love Supreme* at this point, when he thought he heard something. A door closing downstairs? A thump? He waited, listened. Maybe it was Rachel. She got worried and came over to see if he was back yet. In her nightgown. Maybe they could have sex in the sanctuary—well, that would be a bit much, he had to admit, even though he considered making love to her holy. But maybe out in the congregation. Stretched out on a pew. Sanctify the church in a real way. Sure she would; in your dreams, mate. He listened again. He could almost swear he had heard something. But there was nothing now. Deathly quiet. The church ghost. Another angel, like the guy along the highway.

What am I going to do, Lord? You sorta got me by the short hairs here. He knew better than anyone his failings as a minister, that he wasn't made for this, the more he studied the orthodoxy he was told to believe and preach, the less he believed any of it. He believed more the things they told him he shouldn't believe. The disciples asked Jesus, What do you want us to do? Do you want us to fast? How should we pray? Should we give to charity? What diet should we observe? And Jesus said it all comes down to this: Don't lie, and don't do what you hate. Whoo-boy, tell that one to my shit-ins and blue-haired ladies and watch 'em run. So, if he no longer believed, why did he stay on in the ministry? But he knew the answer to that too. He had no place else to go. He had no other way to make a living now, he had no marketable skills; every time he made a pastoral visit to a workplace—whether to a real estate office or body shop, a clothing store or food market—it reinforced how unprepared he was to do any other line of work, and he was too old now to be hired to learn a new one. More than that, though, he literally had no place else to go: he and Rachel had never owned a home of their own, they were always dependent on the houses provided by the congregations he ministered to, and with his salary and two children to put through college they had never been able to save anything, he had to stay around now to get his pension or they would be homeless and destitute. At this stage of the game, Lord, it's hard to say whether I'm stuck with you or you're stuck with me.

He went over and stood close to the large circular window; he wondered if outside he cast a shadow on the patterns of red and blue and green trefoils and quatrefoils, a silhouette cut from colors standing over the night. Near the center of the window he noticed some of the glass was loose, he was going to have to find someone who could come and tighten up the leading, the last thing he needed was for a big wind to come along and shower his unsuspecting parishioners standing below with multicolored glass—"Holy shit!"

The figure standing in the doorway didn't move. Bryce squinted, raised his hand trying to block the glare of the racks of spotlights but he still couldn't make out who it was. A black shape. There really is someone standing there, isn't there, Lord? I'm not making this up. After a moment, the figure moved a step closer.

"Kim? What the hell?"

"I didn't mean to scare you," Kim said, taking another step into the room, looking around, his face expressionless.

"For someone who wasn't trying, you sure did a good job of it," Bryce said, his hand to his heart. Thinking, What the hell is he doing up here at this hour of the night? This is really freaky, this isn't for fun, talk about ghosts he's the one who looks haunted. "Did your guy tell you I stopped by the studio? I didn't mean for you to come all the way out here, I just wanted to let you know about Cory."

"Yes, he told me. Thank you. I really appreciate that." Kim thought a minute, studying Bryce. As if weighing something in his mind about him. "You didn't have to do that. Talk to her, I mean. Be concerned about her."

"Yeah, I kinda did," Bryce said, trying to make a joke, to lighten the situation, give himself some time to figure out what was going on here. "My wife is a nurse at the hospital, she's the one who sent me in to see Cory. If I hadn't been nice to her, Rachel would have had my head."

"Oh," Kim said. Obviously disappointed. Then he smiled slightly to himself, shrugged. "Well, thanks anyway."

Why the hell did I say that? It definitely wasn't what he wanted to hear. What the hell does he want to hear from me? Why would he come here now? "You okay, Kim?"

"It's bright up here." Kim moved cautiously around the back of the room, staying out of the beams of the spotlights, looking things over, his black satin pants and jacket making a slight whispering sound. Then he stopped, looked by Bryce. "What's so special about the window?"

"What do you mean 'special'?"

"I mean, why do you have it lit up like this? Is there some special significance to it or something? Or is it just for show?"

"That's a good way to put it. It's really just for show," Bryce chuckled. But Kim wasn't amused, nor, it was apparent, did he mean it to be amusing. Bryce coughed, cleared his throat. "Well, technically it's called a wheel window, for obvious reasons, or a rose window, because the complex designs are thought to look like the petals of a rose. I'm sort of proud of it, I cleaned it up myself, took me a couple of years, it was dingy as a dishrag when

I started. I think it's a nice touch for the church, makes us stand out among all the commercial stuff along Berry Highway. Sort of a beacon in the night, you know, calling all the wayfaring souls home."

"Wayfaring souls," Kim repeated.

"Yeah, I guess that does sound a little heavy-handed." Bryce looked around. "It's also called a Catherine window after Saint Catherine of Alexandria, I think it was, who was executed on a spiked wheel. But I don't like to think about that. The things people do to each other."

"Yes, the things people do to each other." Kim thought a moment. "You know, despite what you might have heard, I never meant to kill Dickie Sutcliff."

Bryce swallowed hard, hoping he hadn't made a noise. "I never thought you did. I mean, I never heard anything like that. I thought if anybody killed him, maybe it was his brother."

Kim wasn't listening, preoccupied with something else. "I just went to talk to him that night. Lyle said Sutcliff was pressuring him about a couple of things, and all I wanted to do was to ask him to back off. You know, from one man to another. But I guess Sutcliff wasn't used to being talked to like that. Especially by somebody he obviously didn't think was worth listening to. Maybe he didn't think I was in the right social class. Or race."

"Heh heh, yeah, the Sutcliffs always were kind of snobbish, but I can't imagine ol' Dickie would hold that against—"

"He pushed me and I told him to back off and he told me to get out of his office and he pushed me again, harder, and then again and before I really thought about it I hit him with the back of my fist on the side of his head, it was more a reflex than anything else. The blow staggered him but wasn't enough to kill him except he stumbled backward and hit his head on the side of his desk. He dropped like a stone. I knew he was dead soon as it happened."

Is that what this is about? He wants me to absolve him or something? "Kim, I don't know about . . . er, your religion or anything, but maybe there's a priest or someone who could hear a confession. . . ."

"My religion." Kim gave him a wry look. "You don't know the first thing about me, do you? You don't know if I'm Buddhist or Muslim or what, do you? You only know I'm not like you. One of those, what do they call it in the media, third world people. What the forms list as Other." Kim shook his head, looked at Bryce almost as if he pitied him. "No, I didn't come here to confess or ask for your absolution or anything like that. I'm not sorry I killed Sutcliff, he shouldn't have died but he did and that's that. As for Stratton, he deserved to die a hundred times for what he did to Cory. I'd do it again in a heartbeat."

"Stratton?"

"Ah, you didn't know. Well, now you do."

There was a voice from downstairs, somebody calling, coming closer. "Bryce! Bryce! Are you up there? Is Kim up there? His car's in the parking lot."

Kim shook his head, looking regretful. "Of course he would come here."

"What's going on?"

"Bryce! Are you okay?" Julian called.

"He undoubtedly thinks I'm here to kill you," Kim said. "Tell him to stay down there, not to come up."

"Julian, stay where you are, don't come up. Everything's fine, everything's okay."

Then it registered, what Kim said.

"He thinks you came to kill me? Why would he think that?"

"He's trying to protect one of his old Orchard Hill friends. He's afraid I'm going to kill you because you were asking too many questions about Sutcliff's death. He must have figured out I was there that night and assumed I did it. You'd think he'd have more faith in me, wouldn't you?"

"And are you? Going to kill me?"

"Tell him to stay down there. It would be like him to come up anyway."

"Julian, I mean it, stay down there. You'll only make things worse. Everything is okay. Kim and I are just having a little talk."

There was no response, but there was the sound of shoes scraping on the stone steps, getting settled.

"Why do people do that?" Kim said. "I thought Lyle was my friend but it's obvious he doesn't trust me. Not like a friend would. And he outright lied to me, about a couple of things, like where Stratton was, he tried to keep it from me. Like he was protecting Stratton or something."

"Maybe he was trying to protect you. Maybe he knew what you'd do if you found out where Stratton was, and he was trying to keep you from doing something you might regret. Or not regret, as the case may be."

"Maybe," Kim said, but it was obvious he didn't believe it.

"It seems the only way anyone can get through this world is to accept that sometime or other your friends are going to let you down, it's a given. Just like they have to accept that sometime or other you're going to let them down. Nobody means to, nobody wants it to happen, but it seems to anyway. I guess I'm guilty of that in regard to Julian, I've let him down, if I think about it. That's the thing, nobody wants to think about it."

"But he's proving to be a good friend to you. Here he is, trying to save you from Big Bad Kim."

"I'm sure he'd try to help you too. . . ."

In the distance came the wail of a siren, several sirens coming closer. "This isn't the way I wanted this to work out. I wanted to come here to thank you about Cory and ask if you'd continue to keep an eye on her, you seemed to have reached her in some way. Then I was just going to disappear. But now Lyle's here, and he must have called the police. I wish he hadn't . . . it only proves. . . ." He was sad for a moment, then shook his head, clearing the thoughts away, looked around the room as if weighing his options, looked at Bryce again. "Well, no matter now. And I'm not going to spend any more time in jail. I'm sorry about your window, you seem really proud of it."

"What's to be sorry about?" Bryce said. But before he could say anything more Kim was airborne, flying past him in a kind of kick, one leg extended one leg folded under him, through the window, the patterns of multicolored glass shattering and falling with him out of sight, only darkness where the window had been.

"Bryce! What's going on? I'm coming up!"

But Bryce was already running down the spiral staircase, meeting Julian halfway, turning him around. "Kim went out the window!"

When they got down to the foyer, Rachel was coming through the side door, hurrying, her black trench coat thrown over her nightgown, her arms wrapped about herself. "Bryce, thank God you're okay. . . ."

"Yeah, I'm okay. Hurry, call an ambulance. Maybe there's still something we can do. . . ." As Rachel headed back toward the rectory, Bryce and Julian pushed through the outer doors into the night. But it was obvious there was nothing anyone could do for Kim now. His body was lying facedown on the steps, broken over the steps, one leg bent as no leg should ever be, a pool of blood the color of motor oil seeping from his head. In the glow of the streetlight, the multicolored grains of glass glinted like broken strings of children's beads.

Julian sat down on the steps, moaning softly, cupping his hand over the top of his head. Bryce headed back inside, the shards of glass crunchy underfoot, already thinking of church business, he needed to call the janitorial service to clean things up after they removed the body, and he should probably call their attorney, there was no telling the liability for something like this— thinking, Take this man, Lord, embrace his spirit, may he rest in peace, wow, fascinating rhythm, that's not something you see every day, the way he went flying past me and right through the window—then caught himself. What the hell am I doing? He went back and sat down on the cold step beside Julian.

"I never meant for anything like this to happen," Julian said, staring at the body.

Bryce hesitated only a second. "He knew you were there to help him."

"Do you think he did?"

"I know it. It was the last thing he talked about. What a good friend you were."

The lights of the emergency vehicles were coming down Berry Highway, sirens screaming. Bryce put his hand on Julian's shoulder, patted him a couple times, gave an extra squeeze. Sat with him as the first responders turned into the street, rushing toward them.

Acknowledgments

There are four people—friends, actually; dream catchers—without whom I could never have brought these books to publication:

Barbara Clark
Kim Francis
Dave Meek
Jack Ritchie

I also thank Eileen Chetti for struggling through my quirks of style and punctuation; Linnea Duly for writing a study guide; Aimee Downing for her patience with all my questions about self-publishing; and Bob Gelston, who is always around to answer questions and take on anything else that's needed. And then, of course, there's my wife Marty. . . .

*

Richard Snodgrass lives in Pittsburgh, PA with his wife Marty and two indomitable female tuxedo cats, raised from feral kittens, named Frankie and Becca.

*

To read more about the Furnass series, the town of Furnass, and special features for *All Fall Down*—including a Reader's Study Guide, author interviews, and omitted scenes—go to www.RichardSnodgrass.com.

www.ingramcontent.com/pod-product-compliance
Lightning Source LLC
Chambersburg PA
CBHW021002120726
47905CB00009B/2810